*Murder on the
Brighton Express*

*Murder on the
Brighton Express*

EDWARD MARSTON

First published in Great Britain in 2008 by
Allison & Busby Limited
13 Charlotte Mews
London W1T 4EJ
www.allisonandbusby.com

Copyright © 2008 by EDWARD MARSTON

The moral right of the author has been asserted.

A CIP catalogue record for this book is available from
the British Library.

10 9 8 7 6 5 4 3 2 1

13-ISBN 978-0-7490-7945-1

Typeset in 11/16pt Sabon by
Terry Shannon

Printed and bound in Great Britain by
MPG Books Ltd, Bodmin, Cornwall

EDWARD MARSTON was born and brought up in South Wales. A full-time writer for over thirty years, he has worked in radio, film, television and the theatre and is a former chairman of the Crime Writers' Association. Prolific and highly successful, he is equally at home writing children's books or literary criticism, plays or biographies, and the settings for his crime novels range from the world of professional golf to the compilation of the Domesday Survey. *Murder on the Brighton Express* is the fifth book in the series featuring Inspector Robert Colbeck and Sergeant Victor Leeming, set in the 1850s.

www.edwardmarston.com

To

Peter James,

my Brighton peer

CHAPTER ONE

1854

Hands on hips, Frank Pike stood on the platform at London
Bridge station and ran an approving eye over his locomotive.
He had been a driver for almost two years now but it was the
first time he had been put in charge of the Brighton Express,
the fast train that took its passengers on a journey of over fifty
miles to the increasingly popular town on the south coast.
Because it did not stop at any of the intervening stations, it
could reach its destination in a mere seventy-five minutes. Pike
was determined that it would arrive on time.

A big, sturdy, shambling man in his thirties, he was a dutiful
and conscientious employee of the London Brighton and
South Coast Railway. His soft West Country burr and gentle
manner made him stand out from the other drivers. Pike was
a serious man who derived immense satisfaction from his
work. Arriving at the shed an hour before the train was due
to leave, he had read the notices of speed limits affecting his
shift then carefully examined all the working parts of his
locomotive, making sure they had been properly lubricated.

Everything was in order. Now, minutes before departure, he felt a quiet excitement as he stepped on to the footplate beside his fireman.

'How fast are we going to go, Frank?' asked John Heddle.

'We keep strictly to the recommended speeds,' replied Pike.

'Why not try to break the record?'

'It's not a race, John. Our job is to get the passengers there swiftly and safely. That's what I intend to do.'

'I've always wanted to push an express to the limit.'

'Then you can do so without me,' said Pike, firmly, 'because I'm not taking any chances, especially on my first run. Excessive speeds are irresponsible and dangerous. You should know that.'

'Yes,' agreed Heddle, 'but think of the excitement.'

John Heddle was a short, skinny, animated man in his twenties. He had a mobile face that featured a bulbous nose, a failed attempt at a moustache, a lantern jaw and a permanent gap-toothed grin. Having worked with the fireman before, Pike was fond of him though troubled by Heddle's impulsiveness and lust for speed. They would be glaring defects in the character of a driver. Pike had impressed that fact upon him a number of times.

After a final check of his instruments, Pike awaited the signal to leave. It was Friday evening and the train was filled with people who either lived in Brighton or wished to spend the weekend there. One of the passengers, a clergyman, suddenly materialised beside them.

'Good evening to both of you,' he said, amiably. 'Do excuse me. I've just come to bless the engine.'

'Bless it?' said Heddle with a laugh. 'It's the first time I've heard of anyone doing that, sir. What about you, Frank?'

'It's been sworn at before now,' said Pike, 'but never blessed.'

'Then you can't have driven the Brighton Express,' decided the newcomer, 'because I travel on it regularly and always bestow a blessing on the engine before departure.'

He closed his eyes and began to offer up a silent prayer. Driver and fireman exchanged a glance. Pike was mystified but Heddle was highly amused. The clergyman on the platform was a diminutive figure of middle years, jaunty, dapper and good-humoured. He had long, wavy, greying hair and a goatee beard. Even in repose he seemed to be bristling with energy. Pike was afraid that the blessing would go on too long but the clergyman knew exactly how much time he had at his disposal. Opening his eyes, he gave them a broad smile of gratitude then stepped smartly into a first class carriage near the front of the train. Thirty seconds later they were in motion.

'There you are,' said Heddle, nudging the driver. 'You've got the Church's blessing now, Frank. You can go hell for leather.'

Pike was circumspect. 'We'll maintain the speeds advised,' he said, solemnly. 'Then we can be sure to arrive in one piece.'

The Reverend Ezra Follis was comfortably ensconced in his seat. He was on nodding terms with two of the male passengers and recognised another, Giles Thornhill, a tall, spare, beak-nosed man with pursed lips and an air of supreme arrogance, as a Member of Parliament for Brighton. Having severe reservations about the man's suitability as a politician, Follis had never voted for him nor tried, on the few earlier occasions when they shared a carriage, to engage him in conversation.

Two people caught Follis's attention. One was a big, solid, red-faced fellow with mutton-chop whiskers decorating both cheeks like ivy spreading across the walls of a house. When he realised that he was being scrutinised, the man gave a loud sniff of protest before disappearing behind his newspaper. Diagonally opposite Follis was an altogether more interesting subject of study, a slim, attractive, auburn-haired young woman, impeccably dressed and well-groomed. What diverted the clergyman was the fact that some of the other men in the carriage were pretending to read or stare through the window while shooting her surreptitious glances of admiration. Smiling tolerantly, Follis opened his Bible and searched for the text on which he would base his sermon the following Sunday.

Driving an engine was a test of concentration. Since the footplate was unprotected, Frank Pike and his fireman were exposed to the elements and to the clouds of thick, black smoke bursting rhythmically out of the funnel. As well as listening for any defects in the operation of the engine, the driver had to keep a wary eye on the line ahead for any potential hazards. Even on such a clear, warm summer's evening, visibility over the engine from a juddering footplate was not ideal. There was an additional problem. Those who designed locomotives had somehow never thought to provide seating. Both men had to stand throughout the entire journey.

The route took them almost directly southward across the grain of the Weald. It was undulating landscape. When they steamed through Norwood, they had to climb a seven-mile rise towards a gap in the crest of the North Downs. There was a long cutting through the chalk before they plunged into the

Merstham Tunnel, over a mile in length. Emerging back into the light of day, the train had over seven miles of down grade, easing the strain on its engine and effortlessly gathering speed. After shooting past Horley, they began another gradual climb to a summit pierced by the Balcombe Tunnel.

Pike knew every station by heart, having stopped at them regularly when in charge of slower trains. Stationmasters and porters gave him a friendly wave as he rattled past. He felt an upsurge of pride at being on the footplate of the Brighton Express. When it was first built, almost the entire line passed through open country with only a few cottages punctuating the scene. Signs of habitation had slowly increased now as people sought a rural escape that was yet within easy reach of a railway station. Cows, sheep and crops, however, still dominated the fields on both sides of the line.

Out of the Balcombe Tunnel they hurtled and started another descent, speeding on until they crossed the thirty-seven arches of the Ouse Viaduct, one of the engineering marvels of the day. Pike was enjoying his initial run on the Brighton Express so much that he released one of his rare smiles. The thunder of the train and the fierce rush of wind precluded any conversation at normal volume. When his sharp eyes spotted something ahead of them, therefore, Pike had to shout to make himself heard. There was a note of panic in his voice.

'Can you see that, John?' he yelled, shutting off the steam and applying the brakes. 'Can you see that?'

'What?' asked Heddle, peering hard through the swirling smoke. 'All I can see is a clear line. Is there a problem?'

What the fireman could not see, he soon felt. Within a hundred yards, the wheels of the locomotive left the rails with an awesome thud and pulled the string of carriages behind it. Heddle and Pike were thrown sideways and had to hold on to the tender to steady themselves. Surging on and quite unable to check its momentum, the train miraculously stayed fairly upright as it ploughed a deep furrow in the ground and ripped up the track behind it with ridiculous ease. They had completely lost control. At that speed and on that gradient, it would take them the best part of a mile to stop. All they could do was to hang on tight.

Gibbering with fear, Heddle pointed ahead. A ballast train was puffing towards them on the adjacent line. They could both see the continuous firework display under its wheels as the brakes fought in vain to slow it down. A collision was inevitable. There was no escape. Pike's immediate thought was for the safety of his young fireman. Turning to Heddle, he grabbed him by the shoulder.

'Jump!' he bellowed. 'Jump while you can, John!'

'This bloody train was supposed to be blessed!' cried Heddle.

'Jump off!'

Taking his advice, the fireman hurled himself from the footplate and rolled over and over in the grass before hitting his head on a small boulder and being knocked unconscious. Pike stayed where he was, like the captain of a doomed ship remaining on the bridge. As the two trains converged in a shower of sparks, he braced himself for the unavoidable crash. He was writhing with guilt, convinced that the accident was somehow his fault and that he had let his passengers down. Fearing that there would be many deaths and serious injuries, he was overwhelmed by remorse. A sense of helplessness intensified his anguish.

When the engines finally met, there was a deafening clash and the Brighton Express twisted and buckled, tipping its carriages on to the other line and producing a cacophony of screams, howls of pain and groans from the passengers. Both locomotives were toppled by the sheer force of the impact. The long procession of wagons behind the other engine leapt madly off the rails and broke up like matchwood, scattering their ballast far and wide in a vicious hailstorm of stone. It was a scene of utter devastation.

Somewhere beneath the engine he had driven with such pride and pleasure was Frank Pike, crushed to a pulp and wholly unaware of the catastrophe left behind him. His first ever run on the Brighton Express had also been his last.

CHAPTER TWO

Alerted by telegraph, Detective Inspector Robert Colbeck left
his office in Scotland Yard at once and caught the first
available train on the Brighton line. His companion, Detective
Sergeant Victor Leeming, was not at all sure that they would
be needed at the site of the accident.

'We'll only be in the way, Inspector,' he said.

'Not at all, Victor,' argued Colbeck. 'It's important for us to
see the full extent of the damage and to glean some idea of
what might have caused the crash.'

'That's a job for the Railway Inspectorate. They're trained
in that sort of work. All that we're trained to do is to catch
criminals.'

'Did it never occur to you that this accident may be a
crime?'

'There's no proof of that, Inspector.'

'And no evidence to the contrary, Victor. That's why we
must keep an open mind. Unfortunately, the telegraph gave us
only the barest details but it was sent by the LB&SCR and
made a specific request for our help.'

'*Your* help,' said Leeming with a sigh of resignation. 'I'm not the Railway Detective. I hate trains. I distrust them and, from what we've heard about this latest disaster, I've every reason to do so.'

Leeming was a reluctant passenger, glancing nervously through the window as the train clattered into Reigate station and shuddered to a halt. Colbeck, on the other hand, had a deep affection for the railway system matched by a wide knowledge of its operation. As a result of his success in solving a daring train robbery and a series of related crimes, newspapers had christened him the Railway Detective and subsequent triumphs had reinforced his right to the nickname. Whenever there was a crisis on the line, the first person to whom railway companies turned was Robert Colbeck.

He knew why Leeming was so disaffected that evening. The sergeant was a married man with a wife he adored and two small children on whom he doted. Being parted from them for a night was always a trial to him and he sensed that that was about to happen. A train crash on the scale described would need careful investigation and it could not be completed in the failing light. He and Colbeck might well have to spend the night near the scene before continuing their enquiries on the following day.

After stopping at Horley station, the train set off again and soon entered the county of Sussex. More passengers alighted at Three Bridges station then they chugged on for over four miles until they reached Balcombe. Amid a hiss of steam, they came to a halt.

'Out we get, Victor,' said Colbeck, rising to his feet and reaching for his bag. 'This is the end of the line.'

'Thank heavens for that, sir!'

'No down trains can go beyond this point. No up trains from Brighton can get beyond Hayward's Heath. The timetable has been thrown into complete disarray by the accident.'

'How do we get to the scene?'

'We take a cab.'

'I like the sound of that,' said Leeming, brightening at once.

Colbeck opened the carriage door. 'I thought you might.'

'You know where you are with horses. They're sensible animals. They don't run into each other.'

'Neither do trains, for the most part.'

They stepped on to the platform and made their way towards a waiting line of cabs. Mindful of the great disruption caused by the accident, the railway company had tried to lessen its impact by arranging for a fleet of hansom cabs to be hastened to Balcombe station. Passengers destined for Burgess Hill, Hassocks Gate or Brighton itself would be driven to Hayward's Heath where a train awaited them. The detectives were going on a shorter journey.

'That's better,' said Leeming, settling gratefully into the back of a cab as it moved away. 'I feel safe now.'

'My only concern is for the safety of the passengers on the Brighton Express,' said Colbeck, worriedly. 'The train was almost full. According to the telegraph, there have been some fatalities. The chances are that others may die of their injuries in due course.'

'You know my opinion, Inspector. Railways are dangerous.'

'That's not borne out by the statistics, Victor. Millions of passengers travel by rail each year in complete safety. Of the accidents reported, the majority are relatively minor and involve no loss of life.'

'What about the engine that exploded last year, Inspector?'

'It was a regrettable but highly unusual incident.'

'The driver and his fireman were blown to pieces.'

'Yes, Victor,' admitted Colbeck. 'And so was an engine fitter.'

He remembered the tragedy only too well. A locomotive due to take an early train to Littlehampton had exploded inside the engine shed at Brighton. The building had been wrecked, paving stones had been uprooted and one wall of an adjacent omnibus station had been shaken to its foundations. The three men beside the locomotive had been blown apart. The head of the engine fitter had been discovered in the road outside and one of the driver's legs was hurled two hundred yards before smashing through a window and ending up on the breakfast table of a boarding house.

'The boiler burst,' recalled Leeming, gloomily. 'I read about it. This company has had a lot of accidents in the past.'

'It was a tank engine that exploded,' explained Colbeck, 'and it had run over 90,000 miles without a problem. When it was built, however, its boiler plates were thinner than has now become standard. Over the years, they'd been patched up. Under extreme pressure, they finally gave way.'

'What a horrible death!'

'It's a risk that railwaymen have to take, Victor. Boilers burst far more often in the early days of steam transport. There have been vast improvements since then.'

'I've never known a horse blow up,' said Leeming, pointedly.

'Perhaps not but they have been known to bolt before now and overturn cabs or carts. Also, of course,' Colbeck reminded him, 'even the largest coach can only carry a limited number of passengers. When the London to Brighton line first opened, four trains pulled a string of carriages containing 2000 people – and they arrived at their destination without any mishap.'

'What do you think happened in this case, Inspector?'

'It's too early to speculate.'

'The telegraph said that two trains had collided head-on.'

'One of them, fortunately, was carrying no passengers.'

'We're going to find the most terrible mess when we get there.'

'Yes,' said Colbeck, looking up at the sky. 'And the light is fading fast. That will hamper rescue efforts.'

'What exactly are we looking for?'

'What we always look for Victor – the truth.'

It was like the aftermath of a battle. Mangled iron and shattered wood were spread over a wide area. Bodies seemed to be littered everywhere. Some were being lifted onto stretchers while others were being examined then treated on the spot. Dozens of people were using shovels and bare hands as they tried to clear the wreckage from the parallel tracks. The listless air of the wounded was offset by the frenetic activity of the railway employees. Carts were waiting to carry more of the injured away.

By the time that Colbeck and Leeming arrived at the site, lanterns and torches had been lit to illumine the scene. A few bonfires had also been started, burning the wood from the fractured carriages and the ruined wagons. Having met in a fatal collision, the two locomotives lay on their sides like beached whales, badly distorted, deprived of all power and dignity as they waited for cranes to shift their carcases. A knot of anxious people had gathered around each iron corpse, men for whom the destruction of a locomotive was tantamount to a death in the family.

As they picked their way through the debris, the detectives presented a curious contrast. Colbeck, the unrivalled dandy of Scotland Yard, was a tall, handsome, elegant man who might have stepped out of a leading role on the stage. Leeming, however, was shorter, stockier, lumbering and decidedly ugly. While the inspector looked as if he had been born in a frock coat, cravat, well-cut trousers and a top hat, the sergeant seemed to have stolen similar clothing without quite knowing how to wear it properly.

They soon identified the man they had come to see. Captain Harvey Ridgeon was the Inspector General of Railways, a job that consisted largely of investigating accidents throughout the system. He was standing near the two locomotives, talking to one of the many railway policemen on duty. Colbeck was surprised to see how young he was for such an important role. Ridgeon's predecessor had been a Lieutenant-Colonel who, in turn, had been preceded by a Major-General, both in their fifties and at the end of their military careers.

Ridgeon, however, was still in his thirties, a fresh-faced man of middle height with an almost boyish appearance. Yet he also possessed a soldier's bearing and a quiet, natural, unforced authority. Like all inspector generals, he had come from the Corps of Royal Engineers and thus had a good understanding of how the railways were built, maintained and run. When the detectives reached him, he had just parted company with the railway policeman. Colbeck performed the introductions. Though he gave them a polite greeting, Ridgeon was less than pleased to see them.

'It's good to meet you at last, Inspector Colbeck,' he said. 'Your reputation goes before you. But I fail to see why you made the effort to get here. What we need are doctors, nurses and stretcher-bearers, not a couple of detectives, however distinguished their record.'

'We were summoned by the company itself, Captain Ridgeon.'

'Then you must feel free to look around – as long as you don't impede the railway policemen. They can be very territorial.'

'We've found that in the past, sir,' noted Leeming.

'I've had occasional difficulties with them myself.'

'I have to admire the way you got here so promptly,' observed Colbeck, weighing him up with a shrewd gaze. 'I didn't expect you to turn up before morning.'

'This was a dire emergency,' said Ridgeon, taking in the whole scene with a gesture, 'and I reacted accordingly. As luck would have it, I was staying with friends in Worthing so I was able to respond quickly when the alarm was raised. Had I still been in Carlisle, where I investigated an accident at the start of the week, then it would have been a very different matter. Before that, I was in Newcastle.'

'You're very ubiquitous, Captain Ridgeon.'

'I have to be, Inspector. Accidents occur all over the country.'

'That's my complaint,' Leeming put in. 'There are far too many of them. Step into a train and you put your life in peril.'

'Part of my job is to eliminate peril,' said Ridgeon. 'I only have powers to inspect and advise but they are important functions. Each accident teaches us something. My officers and I make sure that the respective railway companies learn their lesson.'

'Then why do accidents keep on happening?' Leeming saw two men vainly trying to lift a section of a wrecked carriage. 'Excuse me,' he said, moving away. 'Someone needs a helping hand.'

Taking off his coat, Leeming was soon lending his considerable strength to the two men. The timber was easily moved. Ridgeon and Colbeck watched as the sergeant started to clear away more debris.

'We could have done with Sergeant Leeming's assistance when the accident actually happened,' said Ridgeon. 'It was a case of all hands to the pumps then. Believe it or not, things are much better now. It was chaos when I first arrived. Those with the most serious injuries have all been taken away now.'

'There still seem to be plenty of walking wounded,' said Colbeck, looking around. 'Who is that gentleman over there, for instance?'

He pointed towards a man in clerical garb whose hands and head were heavily bandaged yet who was helping an elderly woman to her feet. Having got her upright, he went off to console a man who was sitting on the grass and weeping copiously into a handkerchief.

'That's the Reverend Ezra Follis,' explained Ridgeon. 'He's a remarkable fellow. He was injured in the crash but, as soon as he was bandaged up, he did his best to offer comfort wherever he could.'

'He obviously has great resilience.'

'He also has a strong stomach, Inspector Colbeck. When they hauled out the driver of the ballast train, he was in such a hideous condition that some people were promptly sick. That little clergyman is made of sterner stuff,' Ridgeon went on with admiration. 'He didn't turn a hair. He threw a blanket over the remains then helped to lift them on to a cart, saying a prayer for the salvation of the man's soul.'

'How many fatalities have there been so far?' asked Colbeck.

'Six.'

Colbeck was surprised. 'Is that all?'

'Yes, Inspector,' replied Ridgeon. 'Given the circumstances, it's a miracle. Mind you, some of the survivors have terrible injuries and are being treated in hospital. According to the Reverend Follis, the Brighton Express left the track and careered alongside it for a couple of minutes before hitting the other train.'

'In other words, the passengers had time to brace themselves.'

'Exactly.'

'I must speak to the Reverend Follis myself.'

'He's an interesting character.'

'I assume that the driver and fireman of both locomotives died in the crash,' said Colbeck, sadly.

'Those on the footplate of the ballast train were killed outright. The driver of the express must also be dead because he's buried beneath his engine. Until a crane arrives, we can't dig him out.'

'What about his fireman?'

'John Heddle was more fortunate,' said Ridgeon. 'He jumped from the footplate before the collision took place. He sustained a nasty head injury during the fall and was still very dazed when I spoke to him, but at least he survived and will be able to give us confirmation.'

'Confirmation?' echoed Colbeck.

'Yes – of what actually happened. The general feeling

among the passengers is that the express went too fast around a bend and jumped off the track. In short, the driver was at fault.'

'That's a rather hasty verdict to bring in, Captain Ridgeon. It's very unfair to blame the driver before all the evidence has been gathered, especially as he's not alive to defend himself.'

'I'm not sure that he *has* a defence.'

'There are recommended speeds for every stretch of the track.'

'Everyone I've spoken to says the same thing,' argued Ridgeon. 'The speed was excessive. They were *there*, Inspector. These people were in the Brighton Express at the time.'

'That's precisely the reason I'd doubt their word,' said Colbeck. 'Oh, I'm sure they gave an honest opinion and I'm not criticising them in any way. But all the passengers have been through a terrible experience. They'll be in a state of shock. You have to allow for a degree of exaggeration.'

'I talk to survivors of accidents all the time,' Ridgeon told him, eyes blazing, 'and I know how to get the truth out of them. I won't have you casting aspersions upon my methods.'

'I'm not doing so, Captain Ridgeon.'

'Well, it sounds to me as if you are.'

'I'd merely point out that there are no bends of any significance on this stretch of line. Indeed, on the whole journey from London to Brighton, you won't find dangerous curves or problematical gradients.'

Ridgeon stuck out a challenging chin. 'Are you trying to teach me my job, Inspector?'

'No, sir,' said Colbeck, trying to smooth his ruffled feathers with an emollient smile. 'I simply think that it would be unwise to rush to judgement when you're not in full possession of the facts.'

'I've garnered rather more of them than you.'

'That's not in dispute.'

'Then have the grace to bow to my superior expertise.'

'I'll be interested to read your report,' said Colbeck, meeting his stern gaze without flinching. 'Meanwhile, I'd be grateful for the names of the two drivers and the fireman who died.'

'Why?' asked Ridgeon.

'Because, over the years, I've become acquainted with many people who work on the railway,' came the reply. 'I've been summoned twice before by the LB&SCR and got to know a number of their staff.'

Ridgeon consulted the pad he was holding. 'The driver of the ballast train was Edmund Liversedge and his fireman was Timothy Parke.' He glanced up at Colbeck who shook his head. 'The driver of the other locomotive, presumed dead, was in charge of the Brighton Express for the first time, another factor that I have to take into account. Inexperience on the footplate can be fatal.'

'What was the man's name, sir?'

'Frank Pike.' He saw Colbeck heave a sigh. 'You know him?'

'I knew him quite well at one time,' said Colbeck, coming to a decision and taking a step backward. 'If you'll excuse us, Captain Ridgeon, the sergeant and I will get back to London at once. I'll take upon myself the duty of informing Mrs Pike of the death of her husband. It's the least I can do for her.'

'There's nothing to keep you here, Inspector. The investigation is in safe hands and will not need to involve the

Detective Department in any shape or form.' He flicked a hand. 'Good day to you.'

'Oh, we'll be back first thing tomorrow,' said Colbeck, resenting the curt dismissal. 'I want to make a closer examination of the site.' He gave a disarming smile. 'You'll be amazed how different things can look in daylight.'

CHAPTER THREE

The Round House was a vast and intricate structure of wrought iron and brick, built to accommodate the turntable used by trains belonging to the London and North Western Railway. Situated in Chalk Farm Road, it was always filled with clamour and action. Since its erection in 1847, it had attracted many visitors but few of them were female and fewer still were as handsome as Madeleine Andrews. In effect, she was a human turntable, making the head of every man there veer round sharply when she entered.

Many engine drivers had taken their young sons to view the interior of the Round House. Caleb Andrews, a short, wiry man whose fringe beard was speckled with grey, was the only one who had taken a daughter armed with a sketch pad. Taller than her father, Madeleine was an alert, intelligent, spirited young woman who had taken over the running of their Camden house when her mother died. Andrews was known at work for his acid tongue and trenchant opinions but his daughter had tamed him at home, coping easily with his shifting moods and taking the edge off his irascibility.

'There you are, Maddy,' he said, raising his voice over the din and making a sweeping gesture. 'What do you think of it?'

She gave a shrug. 'It's magnificent,' she agreed, running her eye over the interior. 'It's like an industrial cathedral. It's even bigger than it looks from outside.'

'Bigger and noisier – I've lost count of the number of times I've driven on to that turntable. It must be hundreds.'

'Do you think anyone would mind if I made a few sketches?'

'They wouldn't *dare* to mind,' said Andrews, distributing a warning glare around the circle of railwaymen. 'Any daughter of mine has special privileges.'

'Does that mean I can stand on the footplate while an engine is being turned?' she teased.

He laughed. 'Even I can't arrange that for you, Maddy.'

Fiercely proud of her, Andrews stood there with arms akimbo as she began her first quick sketch. Her interest in locomotives was not a casual one. Having discovered an artistic talent, Madeleine had developed it to the point where it had become a source of income. Prints of her railway scenes had been bought by several people. What she had never drawn before, however, was a turntable in action. That was why she had asked her father to take her to the Round House.

Aware of the attention she was getting, she kept her head down and worked swiftly. It was left to Andrews to explain what she was doing and to boast about her modest success as an artist. Any talent she possessed, he was keen to point out, must have been inherited from him. While he chatted to his friends, Madeleine was sketching the locomotive that had just been driven on to the turntable before being swung round so that it could leave frontward. A simple, necessary, mechanical action was carried out with relative ease then the locomotive left with a series of short, sharp puffs of smoke.

Madeleine's pencil danced over the paper and she scribbled some notes beside each lightning sketch. When she turned her attention to the structure itself, she craned her neck to look up at the domed roof. It was inspiring. The fact that the whole place was bathed in evening shadows somehow made the scene more magical and evocative. She was so absorbed in her work that she did not notice the man who came into the building and spoke earnestly to her father. After his jocular conversation with the others, Andrews was now tense and concerned, plying the newcomer with questions until he had extracted every last detail from him.

On their walk home through the gathering gloom, Madeleine noticed the radical change in her father's manner. Instead of talking incessantly, as he usually did, he lapsed into a brooding silence.

'Is anything wrong, Father?' she asked.

'I'm afraid that it is.'

She was worried. 'You're not in trouble for taking me there, are you? I'd hate to think that I made things awkward for you.'

'It's nothing like that, Maddy,' he told her with an affectionate squeeze of her arm. 'In fact, it's nothing whatsoever to do with the LNWR. While you were drawing in there, Nat Ruggles passed on some disturbing news to me. There's been a bad accident.'

'Where?'

'On the Brighton line.'

'What happened?'

'According to Nat, there was a collision between two trains

the other side of the Balcombe tunnel. I suppose the only consolation is that it happened in open country and not in the tunnel itself.'

'Nor on the Ouse Viaduct,' she noted.

'That would have been a terrible calamity, Maddy. If the viaduct was destroyed in a crash, the line would be closed indefinitely. Nobody would be able to take an excursion train to the seaside,' he pointed out. 'As it is, there are bound to be deaths and serious injuries. The Brighton Express would have been going at a fair speed and you know how poor the braking system is.' He showed a flash of temper. 'All that those brainless engineers think about is making trains go faster and faster. It's high time someone designed a means of stopping them.'

He fell silent again and Madeleine left him to his thoughts. She knew how upset he was at the news of any railway accidents. He was always uncomfortably reminded of how hazardous his own job was. Andrews had courted disaster on more than one occasion but always escaped it. There was a camaraderie among railwaymen that meant a tragedy on one line was mourned by every rival company. There was no gloating. With regard to the LB&SCR, Caleb Andrews had even more reason for alarm. He had many friends who worked for the company and feared that one or more of them had been involved.

When they reached the house, they let themselves in. Having met his daughter at the end of his day's shift, Andrews was still in his working clothes. He removed his cap and slumped into a chair.

'I'll make some supper,' offered Madeleine.

'Not for me.'

'You have to eat something, Father. You must be starving.'

'I couldn't touch a thing, Maddy,' he said with a grimace. 'I don't think I'd be able to keep it down. Just leave me be, there's a good girl. I have too many things on my mind.'

It was late evening when Robert Colbeck arrived at the house and he was pleased to see a light in the living room. After paying the cab driver and sending him on his way, he knocked on the door. When it was opened by Madeleine, she let out a spontaneous cry of delight.

'Robert! What are you doing here?'

'At the moment,' he said with a warm smile, 'I'm enjoying that look of surprise on your face.' He gave her a token kiss. 'I'm sorry to turn up on your doorstep so late, Madeleine.'

'You're welcome whatever time you come,' she said, standing back so that he could step into the house. She closed the front door behind him. 'It's lovely to see you so unexpectedly.'

'Good evening, Mr Andrews,' he said, doffing his top hat.

Deep in thought, the engine driver did not even hear him.

'You must excuse Father,' said Madeleine in a whisper. 'He's been upset by news of an accident on the Brighton line. Let's go on through to the kitchen, shall we?'

'But it was the accident that brought me here,' explained Colbeck. 'As it happens, I've just returned from the site.'

'What's that?' asked Andrews, hearing him this time and getting up instantly from his chair. 'You know something about the crash?'

'Yes, Mr Andrews.'

'Tell me everything.'

'Give Robert a proper greeting first,' chided Madeleine.

'This is important to me, Maddy.'

'I appreciate that, Mr Andrews,' said Colbeck, 'and that's why I came. If we could all sit down, I'll be happy to give you the full details. I don't think you should hear them standing up.'

'Why not?'

'Just do as Robert suggests, Father,' said Madeleine.

'Well?' pressed Andrews as he resumed his seat.

Sitting on the sofa, Colbeck took a deep breath. 'It was a head-on collision,' he told them. 'Six people were killed and dozens were badly injured.'

'Do you know who was on the footplate at the time?'

'Yes, Mr Andrews. The driver of the ballast train was Edmund Liversedge. His fireman was Timothy Parke.'

Andrews shook his head. 'I don't know either of them.'

'Their families are being informed of their deaths, as we speak.'

'What about the express?'

'The fireman was the only survivor on the footplate. He managed to jump clear before the crash. His name is John Heddle.'

'Heddle!' repeated the other. 'That little monkey. I remember him when he was a cleaner for the LNWR. He was always in trouble. In the end, he was sacked.' He scratched his beard. 'So he's made something of himself, after all, has he? Good for him. I never thought John Heddle would become a fireman.'

'What about the driver?' said Madeleine.

'It appears that he was killed instantly,' said Colbeck. After looking from one to the other, he lowered his voice. 'I'm afraid that I have some distressing news for you. The driver was Frank Pike.'

Madeleine was shocked and her father turned white. Frank Pike was more than a friend of the family. Andrews had been seriously injured during the train robbery that had brought Robert Colbeck into his life. The fireman that day had been Frank Pike and Colbeck had been impressed by his loyalty and steadfastness. He had been even more impressed by Madeleine Andrews and what had begun as a meeting in disturbing circumstances had blossomed over the years into something far more than a mere friendship.

'I felt that you ought to know as soon as possible,' Colbeck went on. 'It seemed to me that you and Madeleine might prefer to be there when I break the news to his wife. Mrs Pike is sure to be sitting at home, wondering why her husband has not come back from work. She's going to need a lot of support.'

'Then Rose will get it from us,' promised Madeleine. 'This will be a crushing blow. She was so proud when Frank became a driver.'

'It's the reason he left the LNWR,' recalled Andrews, sorrowfully. 'They refused to promote him. The only way he could be a driver was to move to another company so that's what he did. Frank Pike was the best fireman I ever had,' he said, wincing. 'I'll miss him dreadfully.' His eyes flicked to Colbeck. 'Do you know what caused the accident?'

'No,' replied the detective, 'and I was very sceptical about the one theory that was put forward. It was suggested that the express train went too fast around a bend and came off the rails as a result. Is that the kind of thing you'd expect of Frank Pike?'

'Not in a hundred years!' said Andrews, red with anger. 'Frank would always err on the side of safety. I should know – I *taught* him.' He jumped up and struck a combative pose. 'Who's been spreading lies about him?'

'It's just a foolish idea starting to take root.'

'It's more than foolish – it's an insult to Frank!'

'Don't shout, Father,' said Madeleine, trying to calm him.

'Isn't it enough that the poor man has been killed doing his job?' yelled Andrews. 'Why do they have to blacken his name by claiming that the accident was his fault? It's wrong, Maddy. It's downright cruel, that's what it is.'

'I agree with you wholeheartedly, Mr Andrews,' said Colbeck, 'and I'm sure that Pike will be exonerated when the full truth is known. Meanwhile, however, I don't believe you should let this idle speculation upset you and I strongly advise you against making any mention of it to his widow.'

'That's right,' said Madeleine. 'We must consider Rose's feelings.'

'Shall we all go there together? I know that she lives nearby.'

'It's only minutes away, Robert.'

'This is a job for Maddy and me,' announced Andrews, making an effort to control himself. 'It was good of you to come, Inspector, and I'm very grateful. But I know Rose Pike well. She'll be upset by the sight of a stranger. She'd much rather hear the news from friends.'

'I accept that,' said Colbeck.

'Before we go, I'd like to hear more detail of what actually happened. Don't worry,' Andrews continued, holding up a palm, 'I won't pass any of it on to Rose. I just want to know whatever you can tell me about the accident. You don't have to listen to this, Maddy,' he said. 'If it's going to upset you, wait in the kitchen.'

'I'll stay here,' she decided. 'I want to hear everything.'

'In that case,' said Colbeck, weighing his words carefully, 'I'll tell you what we discovered when we got to the scene.'

Since he had been spared the ordeal of spending a night way from his family, Victor Leeming made no complaint about the early start. He and Colbeck were aboard a train that took them to Balcombe not long after dawn. It was a fine day and the sun was already painting the grass with gold. Watching the fields scud past, Leeming thought about the present he ought to buy for his wife's forthcoming birthday, hoping that he would be able to spend some of the occasion with her instead of being sent away on police business. Colbeck was reading a newspaper bought at London Bridge station. As he read an account of the train crash, his jaw tightened.

'Someone has been talking to Captain Ridgeon,' he said.

The sergeant turned to him. 'What's that, Inspector?'

'This report lays the blame squarely on the shoulders of Frank Pike. I just hope that his widow doesn't read it.'

'Isn't it possible that the driver of the Brighton Express *was* at fault?' suggested Leeming.

'I think it highly unlikely, Victor.'

'Why?'

'Pike had an unblemished record,' said Colbeck. 'If there had been any doubts at all about his skill as an engine driver, he would never have been allowed to take charge of the Brighton Express.'

'We all make mistakes from time to time, sir.'

'I'm not convinced that a mistake was made in this case.'

'How do you know that?'

'I don't,' admitted Colbeck. 'I'm working on instinct.'

'Well,' said Leeming, 'for what it's worth, my instinct tells me that we're on a wild goose chase. In my view, we could be more usefully employed elsewhere. We should let the railway company do their job while we get on with ours.'

'I think you'll find that the two jobs may overlap.'

'Is that what Captain Ridgeon told you?'

'Far from it, Victor,' said the other with a grim chuckle. 'The inspector general inclined to your view that we have no business at all being there. It was a polite way of saying that we were treading on his toes.'

'So why are we bothering to go back, sir?'

'We need to find out the truth – and if that involves stamping hard on both of the captain's feet, so be it. We must establish whether the crash was accidental or deliberate.'

'How do we do that?'

'In two obvious ways,' said Colbeck. 'First, we inspect the point at which the express actually left the track to see if there's any sign of criminal intent. Second, we speak to John Heddle. He was on the footplate at the time so will be an invaluable witness.'

'I wonder why the driver didn't have the sense to jump off.'

'We may never know, Victor.'

Transferring to a cab at Balcombe station, they spent the rest of the journey in a more leisurely way. When they reached the site of the accident, they saw that considerable changes had taken place. Passengers were no longer strewn across the grass and all the medical assistance had disappeared. Work had continued throughout the night to clear the line so that it could be repaired. Fires were still burning and timber from the wreckage was being tossed on to them. Hoisted upright by cranes, the two battered locomotives stood side by side like a pair of shamefaced drunkards facing a magistrate after a night of mayhem. The body of Frank Pike had been removed.

Picking a way through the vestigial debris, the detectives reached the track for the up trains and walked along it in the direction of Balcombe. Beside them was a deep channel that had been gouged out of the earth by the rampaging Brighton Express. The rails of the parallel track had been ripped up and bent out of shape.

'You can see what happened,' noted Colbeck. 'One side of the train was running on bare earth while the wheels on the other side were bouncing over the sleepers.'

'It must have been a very bumpy ride, sir.'

'Yes, Victor. On the other hand, the ground did act as a primitive braking system, slowing the express down a little and lessening the force of impact. This long furrow saved lives.'

'But not enough of them,' said Leeming under his breath.

They strolled on for over a quarter of a mile before they came to the point where the train had first parted company with the track. Four men in frock coats and top hats were clustered around the spot. As the detectives approached, the youngest of the men broke away to exchange greetings with them. Captain Ridgeon forced a smile.

'Your journey is in vain, gentlemen,' he said. 'As we suspected, the Brighton Express left the rails here. It is, you'll observe, on the crown of a bend. The indications are that the train was travelling too fast to negotiate the bend properly.'

'This is not what I'd call a real bend,' said Colbeck, studying the broken rail then looking up the line beyond it. 'It's no more than a gentle curve. High speed would not have caused a derailment.'

'Then what would have done so?' challenged Ridgeon.

'The most likely thing is an obstacle on the line.'

'Where is it? We'd surely have found it by now. Besides, John Heddle, the fireman, would have noticed any obstacle in the path of the train and he swears that he saw nothing.'

'I'd like to speak to Heddle myself.'

'He'll only tell you what he told us, Inspector. Nothing was blocking the line. We had an accident near here some years ago when a goods train hit a cow that had strayed on to the track. Since then, both sides have been fenced off.'

Colbeck was not listening to him. Crouching down, he ran a hand along the section of flat-bottomed, cast iron rail that had sprung away at an acute angle from the track. The section was curved but more or less intact. Colbeck stood up and gazed around.

'What are you looking for, Inspector?' asked Leeming.

'The fishplates that held this rail in place,' said Colbeck.

'They would have been split apart when the train left the track,' said Ridgeon, irritated by what he saw as the detective's unwarranted interference. 'It was going at high speed, remember.'

'In that case, they would have been bent out of shape but still fixed to the sleeper. Yet there's no sign of them, Captain Ridgeon.' Colbeck pointed a finger. 'You can see the holes in the timber where the bolts used to be.'

'Then they were obviously ripped out by the train.'

'I disagree. I fancy that they were removed beforehand.'

'That's a preposterous notion!' said Ridgeon with scorn. 'You'll be telling me next that someone deliberately levered the rail away.'

'I may be telling you exactly that, sir,' said Colbeck.

After examining the rail again with great care, he signalled to Leeming and the two of them began to scour the immediate area. Ridgeon and the other men looked on with ill-concealed disdain. Having made up their minds about the cause of the accident, they resented being told that they might have made a mistake. The search was thorough but fruitless and Leeming spread his arms wide in despair. It was a cue for Ridgeon to resume his conversation with the others. They turned their back on the two interlopers.

Colbeck, however, did not give up easily. Widening the search, he removed his hat so that he could poke his head into the thick bushes that bordered the track on one side. Leeming joined him with patent reluctance. They burrowed away in the undergrowth. While the inspector made sure that he did not damage his clothing in any way, however, the sergeant scuffed the knees of his trousers and snagged his coat on a sharp twig. Leeming was also stung by a lurking nettle.

Captain Ridgeon, meanwhile, finished his discussion with his colleagues and made some notes on a pad as the others walked away. He was still writing when he heard footsteps approaching and he looked up to see Colbeck coming towards him. The inspector was holding a fishplate in each hand.

'We found these,' he said, passing them to Ridgeon. 'As you'll see, they're not bent or damaged in any way. That's because the bolts were removed so that these plates could be lifted away and tossed into the bushes.'

'That proves nothing,' said Ridgeon, defiantly.

'It proves that they were not torn apart by the force of the train. Victor found one of the bolts. That, too, was undamaged. It was taken out by someone who knew what he was doing. My guess is that the section of line was then prised away, making a derailment inevitable.'

Ridgeon was icily polite. 'I'm grateful to you for your opinion, Inspector Colbeck,' he said, 'but, in essence, that's all it is – a personal, unsought, uninformed opinion. On the basis of what I've seen and heard, I still believe that a fatal error was made by the driver, Frank Pike.'

'How can I change your mind?'

'It would be foolhardy of you even to try.'

'A crime was committed here.'

'Yes – and the man who perpetrated it was a careless driver.'

'Inspector!' bellowed Leeming.

The two men looked across at a large bush that was shaking violently. After a moment, the sergeant emerged out of it, scratched and dishevelled but wearing a triumphant grin. In his hands, he was carrying a pickaxe. He waved it in the air.

Colbeck turned slowly to confront the inspector general.

'Perhaps you can explain that away, sir,' he said.

CHAPTER FOUR

John Heddle was a restless patient. Propped up on two pillows, he sat in bed and constantly shifted his position. His head was swathed in blood-stained bandaging, his face covered with abrasions, his body bruised all over and one of his ankles was badly sprained. Aching and itching, he was in continual discomfort but the main source of his pain was the memory of what had happened the previous day. He was tormented by guilt. Heddle could not forgive himself for abandoning the Brighton Express and letting Frank Pike go on alone to a hideous death.

His wife, Mildred, a pale, thin, nervous, wide-eyed young woman, stood beside the bed and watched him with growing alarm. Her pretty face was disfigured by a frown and every muscle was tense. She indicated the large cup on the bedside table.

'Drink some tea, John,' she pleaded.

'Take it away.'

'Your mother said it would do you good.'

'I spent years being forced to drink my mother's beef tea,'

he said with disgust, 'and it tasted like engine oil. I never want to touch a drop of that foul poison ever again.'

'Then why don't you try to get some sleep?'

'How can I, Mill? I'm hurting all over.'

'If only there was something I could do,' she said, wringing her hands. 'Can I put some more ointment on your face?'

'Just leave me alone,' he advised with distant affection. 'I know you mean well but I'd rather suffer on my own. I'm sure you've got plenty of housework to do.'

'I want to look after you, John. I want to help.'

'Then take that beef tea away. The very sight of it scares me.'

She picked up the cup and saucer then ventured to give him a tender kiss on the side of his head. Heddle managed a wan smile of gratitude. He could not have had a more loving and attentive nurse. When there was a knock on the front door, his smile became a scowl.

'If that's my mother,' he instructed, 'tell her I'm asleep.'

'I can't lie to her,' she said.

'Protect me from her, Mill. I can't face Mother today.'

Biting her lip, Mildred gave him a sympathetic stare then went out of the room. He heard her clack down the wooden steps. The house was in a backstreet in Southwark. Though it was small, neglected and part of a dismal terrace, it had seemed like a haven when they moved in six months earlier to escape the ordeal of living with Mildred's parents. Heddle had been full of plans to improve their home but long working hours for the LB&SCR had left him little time to start on the house. He had not even mended the broken window or repaired the roof over the privy at the end of the tiny garden.

Voices rose up from below. Since one of them belonged to

a man, he was at once relieved and wary, glad that it was not his mother yet afraid that it might be someone from the railway company, demanding that he return to his duties. Two pairs of feet began to ascend the staircase. Mildred entered the bedroom first, shaking with fear. She touched her husband softly on the shoulder.

'This gentleman is a policeman, John,' she said, voice trembling. 'Whatever have you done wrong?'

'Nothing at all, Mrs Heddle,' Colbeck assured her, stepping into the room. 'I just need to speak to your husband about the accident.'

He introduced himself to the patient then shepherded Mildred gently out of the room. After asking Heddle how he was feeling, Colbeck lowered himself on to the chair beside the bed.

'How much do you remember of what happened?' he asked.

'Not very much, sir,' confessed Heddle. 'I had a bang on the head and I still can't think straight. All I remember is that Frank yelled at me to jump and I did.'

'So it was Mr Pike's suggestion, was it?'

'He stayed on the footplate. Nothing would have made Frank abandon the train. He'd have seen that as a betrayal.' Heddle hunched his shoulders. 'That's why I feel so bad about it. I mean, when I leapt off like that, I betrayed *him*.'

'That's not true at all,' said Colbeck. 'You obeyed his order so you have no need to reproach yourself.' He leant in closer. 'Let's go back to the moment when you first realised there was danger.'

'But I *didn't*, Inspector.'

'Oh?'

'To be honest, I'm still in the dark.'

'Go on.'

'Well,' said Heddle, rubbing a sore elbow, 'it was like this, see. We'd crossed the Ouse Viaduct and were steaming along nicely when Frank saw something ahead that frightened him.'

'What was it?'

'That's the trouble, sir, I've no idea. I just couldn't see what Frank had seen but I knew we had a big problem. I could tell by the tone of his voice. The next minute, we'd left the track and all we could do was to pray. Then we both saw another train coming towards us. Frank saved my life. When he told me to jump, I hurled myself off the footplate straight away.' His eyes moistened. 'If only Frank had done the same. I loved working with him. He was a good driver and one of the kindest men I know.'

'Yes,' said Colbeck, 'I met Frank Pike. He seemed a thoroughly decent man. Everyone speaks well of him, especially Caleb Andrews.'

Heddle gave an involuntary shiver. 'Have you been talking to that old tyrant?' he said. 'When I worked for the LNWR, Mr Andrews put the fear of death into me. He was always boxing my ears if I didn't clean his engine the way he wanted. I'll tell you something, Inspector, I'd hate to have been *his* fireman. Though fair's fair,' he added, 'Frank used to worship Caleb Andrews.'

'So you saw no obstruction on the line?'

'No, sir, and that's what I told Captain Ridgeon.'

'Yes,' said Colbeck, 'I've encountered the inspector general. He and I take a rather different view of what happened.'

'He thinks Frank was driving too fast,' said Heddle, defensively, 'but that wasn't true at all. He *never* went above the speed limits. I was the one who wanted to go faster, not Frank Pike.' He narrowed his lids to peer at Colbeck. 'What's going on, Inspector? Why are you so interested in the crash? Accidents happen on the railway all the time but we don't usually get anyone from Scotland Yard involved.'

'This was no accident, John.'

'Then what was it? I wish someone would tell me.'

'What I believe Pike saw,' explained Colbeck, 'was a section of rail that had been levered away on purpose so that the train would come off the line.'

Heddle was aghast. 'That's dreadful!' he exclaimed.

'It was a criminal act.'

'Why would anyone *do* such a vile thing?'

'That's what we intend to find out,' said Colbeck with quiet determination. 'Pike and the others were not killed in an unfortunate accident. They were, in effect, murder victims.'

Heddle was on the verge of tears. Unable to cope with the news, he quaked and gibbered. It was bad enough to lose a dear friend in an accident. The thought that someone had deliberately set out to kill and maim innocent people was utterly appalling. Engines, carriages and rolling stock had also been destroyed. Heddle was rocked. As he tried to take in the sheer magnitude of the crime, his head pounded. Horror eventually gave way to a deep bitterness.

'That was no blessing,' he said, curling his lip.

'What do you mean?'

'There was this clergyman on the platform at London Bridge. Before we set off, he told us he wanted to bless the train. He said that he always did that when catching the express.'

'That must have been the Reverend Follis,' decided Colbeck.

'I don't know what his name was and I don't *want* to know. He was a holy menace. That wasn't a blessing he gave us,' said Heddle with rancour. 'If you ask me, it was a bleeding curse.'

The Reverend Ezra Follis was a regular visitor to the county hospital in Brighton. Whenever one of his parishioners spent time there, he made a point of calling on them to check on their condition and to bring them some cheer. What made his visit different on this occasion was that he looked as if he himself should have been detained in the hospital as a patient. His clothing hid most of his cuts and bruises but his hat failed to conceal the bandaging around his skull, and his face still bore some livid scars. A blow to the hip received during the crash had left him with a pronounced limp. He refused to use a walking stick, however, and, in spite of his aches and pains, he was as affable as ever.

He arrived at the main entrance as one of the patients was about to leave. Giles Thornhill was in a frosty mood. One arm in a sling and with a black eye as the central feature in a face that was liberally grazed, he was moving very slowly towards a waiting cab, each step a physical effort. Standing beside him was a member of the local constabulary.

'Good morning, Mr Thornhill,' said Follis, chirpily. 'I'm glad to see that you're well enough to be discharged.'

'I prefer to rest in my own bed,' said Thornhill. 'There's no privacy in the hospital. I was made to share a ward with the most unspeakable people. It was so noisy that I didn't get a wink of sleep.'

'Then you're in a position to institute some improvements. As a Member of Parliament, you have a lot of influence here.

You could put pressure on the Board of Trustees to provide additional funds for the hospital so that they can build an annexe with single rooms. While patients are recovering, they need peace and quiet.'

'I have other things to worry about at the moment.'

There was a muted resentment in his voice. While Thornhill had sustained a broken arm and picked up some ugly gashes in the crash, Follis had been relatively unscathed. The politician had been knocked unconscious. The first thing he saw when he came to was the face of the little clergyman, bending over him and muttering words of comfort in his ear. It had irritated him. In intense pain and a degree of panic, all that Thornhill had wanted was to be taken to hospital instead of being bothered by Ezra Follis.

When he reached the cab, however, he felt obliged to turn back.

'How are your own injuries?' he asked with formal politeness.

'Oh,' replied Follis, displaying his bandaged hands. 'My head and my hands took the punishment so I came off rather lightly. God moves in mysterious ways, Mr Thornhill. I believe that I was spared in order to help others. Divine intervention was at work.'

Thornhill grunted. 'I saw no sign of it,' he said.

'You survived. Isn't that a reason to be grateful to the Almighty?'

'I'd have been more grateful if He'd kept the train on the rails.'

Helped by the policeman, Thornhill got into the cab. Both men were then driven away. Follis waved them off before going into the hospital. One of the nurses directed

him to a ward where some of the other survivors were being
kept. Sweeping off his broad-brimmed hat, he went into the
room and looked along the beds. The patients were subdued
and two of them, with appalling injuries, were comatose.
Of the other six, most had splints on their arms or legs. One
man, in the first bed, had broken both lower limbs. The
clergyman recognised the red face and mutton-chop
whiskers.

'Good day to you, my friend,' he said, pleasantly. 'My name
is Ezra Follis, Rector of St Dunstan's. We sat opposite each
other on the train – at least, we did until our seating positions
were suddenly rearranged by the crash. To whom am I
speaking?'

'Terence Giddens,' said the other, grasping him by the wrist.
'Do you know what's going on in here?'

'The hospital is doing its best to cope with victims of the
worst train crash in years, that's what is going on, my good
sir. Everyone is working at full stretch.'

'They won't tell me anything, Mr Follis.'

'What is it that you'd like to know?'

'I'm not even sure if everyone in our carriage survived,' said
Giddens. 'All I've gathered is that six people were killed.'

'Seven,' corrected Follis. 'A young lady died from her
wounds shortly after reaching the hospital. I was here when it
happened.'

Giddens blenched. 'It was not the young lady from our
carriage, I trust?'

'No, no, she was badly injured but, as I understand it, her
life is not in danger. None of our other travelling companions
met their deaths, Mr Giddens. Most are in here or being
looked after elsewhere. In fact,' he recalled, 'Mr Thornhill,

one of Brighton's two Members of Parliament, felt well enough to go home.'

'That's what I must do.'

'You're hardly in a condition for release,' said Follis, detaching the man's hand from his wrist and glancing at the broken legs. 'You need the kind of care that only a trained medical staff can give.'

'I can't stay *here*,' insisted Giddens.

'You have no choice.'

'There must be some way to get me back to London.'

'Well, it certainly won't be by train. The line is still well and truly blocked. And a coach would turn the journey into an ordeal for you as it bounced and bucked its way over the roads. I'm sorry, Mr Giddens, you'll just have to resign yourself to staying here.'

'Can't you persuade them to discharge me?'

'The hospital has a good reputation. You'll be safe here.'

'But I need to be in London as a matter of urgency.'

'Why is that, may I ask?'

'I'm the manager of a large bank,' said Giddens, pompously. 'I have important decisions to make. I can't instruct my clerks from fifty miles away.'

'There's an excellent postal service between here and the capital,' argued Follis. 'Besides, you can't possibly return to work when you're unable to walk. I know that it's difficult, Mr Giddens, but you have to accept the situation as it is. You'll be here in Brighton for a little while yet.'

Terence Giddens bit back an expletive and turned his head away. Trapped and helpless, he frothed with impotent rage. The pain in both legs suddenly became a searing agony.

* * *

Superintendent Edward Tallis was seated at his desk in Scotland Yard, scrutinising a report. In response to a knock on his door, he barked a command and Robert Colbeck entered.

'Good afternoon, sir,' he said.

'Ah!' said Tallis, looking up. 'I was wondering when you would deign to appear, Inspector. I thought you had perhaps forgotten your way here.'

'I was investigating the train crash, Superintendent, but I found time to write an interim report for you and made sure that it was delivered early this morning.'

'It's right here in front of me. Your handwriting is graceful as ever but that's the only compliment I feel able to make. The report is full of unsubstantiated guesswork. What it lacks are hard facts.'

'I'm here to present those to you now, sir.'

'Not before time,' said Tallis raising a censorious eyebrow. 'Well, since you're finally here, you may as well sit down.'

Colbeck sat on the chair in front of his desk and waited patiently while the superintendent pretended to read the report again. Relations between the two men had always been always strained. Tallis was a thickset man in his fifties with short grey hair and a neat moustache. A military man with the habit of command, he expected instant obedience and did not always get that from the inspector. He disapproved of Colbeck's flamboyant attire, his debonair manner and his idiosyncratic methods of detection. Tallis was also envious of the fact that Colbeck tended to receive adulation in the press while he, a senior officer, was rarely mentioned unless as a target for criticism.

'Your report hints that a heinous crime has been committed,' said Tallis, setting the paper aside and sitting back. 'Is this another typically wild conjecture on your part?'

'No, sir – Victor and I found proof positive of villainy.'

'What is it?'

Colbeck told him about their discoveries at the site of the accident and about his conversation with John Heddle. He exonerated Frank Pike from the charge of speeding. The superintendent listened carefully, his face expressionless. When Colbeck had finished, Tallis fired questions at him like a stream of bullets.

'Who was responsible for this outrage?' he demanded.

'A former employee of the railway,' answered Colbeck.

'What makes you think that?'

'Consider the choice of time and location, sir. Anyone could find out the departure time of the Brighton Express by looking at a copy of *Bradshaw* and could therefore estimate its likely arrival on the stretch of line concerned. But only someone who had worked for the LB&SCR would know when goods trains would be running on the up line. They were *meant* to collide. Whoever planned this crash wanted to achieve maximum death and destruction.'

'Why?'

'Revenge.'

'Against what or whom?'

'I fancy that the person we are after bears a grudge against the railway company.'

'What sort of grudge?'

'Perhaps he feels he was unfairly dismissed or has another reason for wanting to get his revenge. I've asked Victor to track down the names of anyone who may have left the company under a cloud in recent times. That's our starting point, sir.'

Tallis stroked his moustache while he pondered. He shook his head. 'I'm not entirely convinced that the culprit was a railwayman.'

'That's because you didn't see the way that the bolts and fishplates had been removed so that a section of the rail could be levered away. It was the work of an expert,' said Colbeck. 'Anyone else wanting to derail a train would simply have put a large obstacle on the line. The problem with that was that it would have been seen by the driver from some distance away, allowing him to shut off steam and brake much earlier. Frank Pike only noticed the damaged rail when the express had almost reached it.'

'Does the inspector general agree with your conclusions?'

'No, sir – Captain Ridgeon is finding it difficult to abandon his earlier assessment that it was an accident caused by human error.'

'His opinion should be treated with respect.'

'He's an army man,' observed Colbeck, dryly. 'Once he's made a decision – however mistaken it may be – he defends it to the hilt.'

Tallis bristled. 'There's nothing wrong with service to Queen and Country,' he said, huffily. 'I was proud to do my duty and found it an excellent training for police work.'

'That's because you're an exception to the rule, Superintendent. You are known and admired for the flexibility of your mind.'

Colbeck spoke with his tongue firmly in his cheek. Tallis, in fact, was renowned for his dogged inflexibility. Depending on the circumstances, it could be either his strength or his weakness, a single-mindedness that was a positive asset or an inability to look at case from more than one angle. Unsure if he was being mocked or receiving a compliment, Tallis settled for a non-committal grunt.

'I don't think you should disregard Captain Ridgeon's opinion altogether,' he warned. 'I'd be interested to meet the fellow.'

'I'm certain that you will, sir,' said Colbeck. 'Sooner or later, he'll be coming here to complain about the way he believes Victor and I are hampering him. The captain is not accustomed to having any of his decisions questioned.'

'That's the privilege of being an officer.'

'He's no longer in the army, Superintendent. It's time he adjusted to civilian life, as you have done so successfully.' Tallis heard the light sarcasm in his voice and was about to interrupt. 'There are, of course, two other possibilities,' Colbeck added quickly. 'The first has to be mentioned if only to be discounted.'

'Why?'

'Because it's one that other people may seize upon without realising that it will only mislead them.'

'What on earth are you talking about, man?'

'The fact that the culprit may work for a rival company,' said Colbeck, 'and that he attacked the LB&SCR out of spite. It's an obvious supposition.'

'Then why dismiss it?'

'There's no precedent for rival companies stooping to such extreme methods. Passions run high among people vying for the right to control a particular line and they'll resort to all manner of unfair tactics to secure their ends. But they'll draw back from causing a serious accident,' he continued. 'Apart from anything else, a crash on one line affects the whole railway system. It makes the travelling public more wary of using trains. In short, it's very bad publicity. It's therefore in the interest of all companies to avoid accidents.'

'You said that there were two other possibilities,' noted Tallis. 'What, pray, might the second one be?'

'It's a theory I have, Superintendent.'

'Ah, I was waiting until you trotted out another of your famous theories. It was only a question of time.'

'Actually, sir, it was Victor Leeming who had this idea.'

'So you've infected the sergeant with your disease, have you?' said Tallis with a sneer. 'One theoretician is more than enough in the Detective Department. We can't have two of you coming up with mad hypotheses that have no factual basis.'

'This is not a mad hypothesis.'

'Then what is it?'

'An idea that merits consideration,' said Colbeck. 'What Victor suggested was that the crash was caused in order to kill a particular individual who was on the Brighton Express.'

'But there's no guarantee that the intended victim *would* be killed,' contended Tallis. 'There would, however, certainly be other deaths. If a man is set on murder, he would surely stalk and kill his victim instead of going to such elaborate lengths as this.'

'I agree, sir, but take the idea a stage further.'

'I'd rather disregard it entirely.'

'It's really an extension of my original belief that the LB&SCR was the designated target,' reasoned Colbeck. 'Supposing that the villain wished to kill two birds with one stone, so to speak?'

'You've lost me, Inspector,' complained Tallis.

'The man wanted both to damage the railway company and

cause the death of someone on that train, someone who was closely associated with the LB&SCR. Do you see what I mean, sir? What if, for the sake of argument, an individual embodied the railway company in some way? To murder him in a dark alley would have been far easier but it would have lacked any resonance. A public assassination was needed, involving widespread destruction in a train crash.'

'Stop!' ordered Tallis, slapping his desk with an angry palm. 'I'll hear no more of this fanciful nonsense. Such a person as you portray does not even exist.'

'Then perhaps you will peruse this, sir,' said Colbeck, extracting some sheets of paper from an inside pocket and placing them on the desk. 'It's a list of the passengers who were injured on that express.' Tallis snatched it up. 'It's rather a long one, unfortunately. May I direct your attention to the names at the top of the first page? Among them you will find a gentleman called Horace Bardwell. Can you pick him out, Superintendent?'

'Of course,' growled Tallis, 'but so what?'

'Mr Bardwell is a former managing director of the LB&SCR. He still retains a seat on the board and acts as its spokesman. Kill him,' said Colbeck meaningfully, 'and you deprive the railway company of a man who personifies all that it stands for.' Tallis began to grind his teeth. 'Do you still think that it's fanciful nonsense, sir?'

CHAPTER FIVE

Victor Leeming was nothing if not tenacious. Given a task, he stuck at it with unwavering commitment until it was completed. Since he had been told to find the names of anyone dismissed by the LB&SCR in recent months, he badgered the staff in the railway company's London office until he had all the details available. On the cab ride to Scotland Yard, he reflected on how much his job had changed since he had joined the Detective Department. As a uniformed sergeant, he had seen and enjoyed a great deal of action on the dangerous streets of the capital. Catching thieves, arresting drunks, organising night patrols and keeping the peace had taken up most of his time.

Detective work tended to be slower and more painstaking. What it lacked in vigorous action, however, it atoned for in other ways, chief among them being the privilege of working beside Robert Colbeck. Every day spent with the Railway Detective was an education for Leeming and he relished it. He might have to travel on the trains he detested but he had the consolation of investigating crimes of a far more complex and heinous nature than hitherto. Breaking up a fight in a rowdy tavern could not offer him anything like the satisfaction he got from helping to solve cases that dealt with murder, arson, kidnap and other serious crimes. The present investigation promised to be the most challenging yet and he was not certain that the culprit would be found in due course.

Leeming arrived at Scotland Yard to find Colbeck in his office, poring over the list of casualties from the train crash. Pleased to see him, the inspector got to his feet at once.

'Come on in, Victor. Did you discover anything of interest?'

'Yes, sir,' said Leeming, taking a notepad from his pocket, 'I discovered that I could never work for the LB&SCR – not that I'd even *think* of being employed by a railway company, mind you.'

'What's the problem? asked Colbeck.

'There are too many ways to get sacked. Men have been booted out for being drunk, violent, lazy, slow, sleeping on duty, being late for work, not wearing the correct uniform, disobeying an instruction, telling lies, using bad language, playing cards, pretending to be ill, stealing company property and for dozens of other offences.' Opening his notebook at the appropriate page, he handed it over. 'As you'll see, a porter at Burgess Hill was dismissed when ash from his pipe fell accidentally on to the stationmaster's newspaper and set it alight.'

'I think we can eliminate him from our enquiries,' said Colbeck, scanning the list, 'and most of these other names can be ruled out as well. The majority seem to have been with the company a very short time so they did not put down any roots in it.'

'I wonder how some of them were taken on in the first

place. I mean, there's a fireman on that list who used to toss handfuls of coal off his engine at a place along the line then collect it later and take it home. That was *criminal*, Inspector.'

'Caleb Andrews would never have allowed that. If any fireman of his tried to break the law, he'd have lashed the man to the buffers.' Colbeck looked up. 'Talking of Mr Andrews, you'll recall that I asked him and his daughter to break the news of Frank Pike's death to his wife.'

'Yes, sir,' said Leeming. 'It was very considerate of you.'

'You need good friends beside you at such a time.'

'The widow must have been distraught.'

'She was grief stricken,' said Colbeck, 'but she did volunteer one useful piece of information.' He indicated a letter on his desk. 'Miss Andrews was kind enough to pass it on to me. Mrs Pike remembers her husband telling her that he saw a man using a telescope to watch the trains go past. The sun glinted off it, apparently.'

'Where did this happen, sir?'

'It was between Balcombe and Haywards Heath.'

'That's exactly where the accident happened.'

'Frank Pike spotted the man on two separate occasions as he drove past,' Colbeck went on, 'and in two slightly different locations. He could well have been looking for the ideal point at which to bring the Brighton Express off the line.' His eyes flicked back to the notepad. 'You've done well, Victor. This list is very comprehensive.'

'The trouble is,' said Leeming, 'it gives us too many suspects.'

'I'm not so sure about that. Only three names look really promising to me. Their respective owners all left fairly recently and, according to your notes, may have cause to resent their dismissal.'

'Who are they, Inspector?'

Colbeck picked them out with an index finger. 'I'd plump for Jack Rye, Dick Chiffney and Matthew Shanklin.'

'The one that I'd put first is Shanklin. Before he lost his job, he had a senior position in the company and had held it for a number of years. It must have been galling to be fired from such a well-paid post. Shanklin's mistake was to fall out with one of the directors.'

Colbeck's ears pricked up immediately. 'Do you happen to know *which* director it was?' he asked.

'Yes, sir,' replied Leeming. 'It was Horace Bardwell.'

Horace Bardwell still had no idea where he was and what had actually happened to him. Having suffered compound fractures, he lay in the county hospital with an arm and a leg in splints. Because of a severe head wound, his whole skull was covered in a turban of bandaging and his podgy face was largely invisible. Bardwell was a corpulent man whose massive bulk made the bed look far too small for him. Most of the day had been passed in a drowsy half-sleep. Whenever he surfaced, he was given a dose of morphine to deaden the pain. He began to believe that he had died and gone to Hell.

Someone sat beside his bed and leant in to speak to him.

'Good evening,' said Ezra Follis. 'How are you feeling now?'

'Are you a doctor?' murmured Bardwell.

'I cure men's souls rather than their bodies so I can lay claim to being a medical man of sorts. We've travelled on the Brighton Express a number of times, Mr Bardwell, and exchanged a nod of greeting. I am Ezra Follis, by the way,

Rector of St Dunstan's. I'm trying to speak to everyone with whom I shared a carriage yesterday.'

Bardwell was bewildered. 'Yesterday?'

'Our train collided with another one.'

'I remember nothing of that.'

'Then a hideous memory has been kindly wiped from your mind by a benign Almighty. I wish that I, too, could forget it.'

'I'm hurting all over,' bleated Bardwell.

'The doctor will give you something to soothe the pain.'

'But how did I get it in the first place and why can't I see?'

Follis knew the answers to both questions. Before talking to the patient, he had checked on his condition beforehand with a member of the medical staff. Bardwell had been unfortunate. Apart from taking punishment to his head and body, he had been blinded. Though a doctor had tried to explain to him the full extent of his injuries, Bardwell had been hopelessly unable to understand. Touched by the man's plight, Follis sought only to offer solace and companionship. He talked softly until Bardwell drifted off to sleep again then offered up a prayer for the man's recovery.

As he left the ward, he saw an imposing figure striding towards him. Colbeck recognised the wounded clergyman and introduced himself, explaining his reason for being there. Follis was surprised and deeply upset to hear that someone might have deliberately caused the accident.

'That's unforgivable!' he exclaimed.

'I agree, sir.'

'It's utterly sinful! Look at the devastation that was caused. I cannot believe that any human being could be capable of such wanton cruelty. So many lives were lost or wrecked.'

'What you did yesterday was truly impressive,' said

Colbeck, recalling his visit to the site. 'Though you had injuries of your own, you still found the strength and willpower to help others.'

Follis smiled. 'I found nothing, Inspector,' he argued, hand on heart. 'In my hour of need, God came to my aid and enabled me to do what I did. As for my own scratches, they are very minor compared to the injuries of other passengers. Being so short and slight has its advantage. When the crash occurred, I presented a very small target.'

'That should have made no difference.'

'It's an incontrovertible fact. Look at Mr Bardwell, for instance.'

'Would that be Horace Bardwell?'

'The very same,' confirmed Follis, nodding. 'He must be a foot taller and almost three times my size. In other words, there was more of him to hit. That's why he suffered so badly.' He sucked in air through his teeth. 'In addition to his many other injuries, alas, the poor fellow has lost his sight.'

'That must be very distressing for him.'

'It will be when he finally comprehends it.'

'Oh?'

'Mr Bardwell doesn't know what day it is, Inspector. I've just spent time at his bedside, trying to talk to him. His mind is so befuddled that it's impossible to establish any real contact. When the truth does eventually dawn on him,' he added with a sigh, 'it will come as a thunderbolt.'

'I was hoping to speak to Mr Bardwell myself,' said Colbeck.

'He'll hear precious little of what you say.'

'The doctor seemed to think he was slightly better today.'

'Only in the sense that he is much more alive,' said Follis. 'Had you seen him immediately after the crash, you'd have thought he was at death's door. Happily, he survived and his body will heal in time. Whether or not his mind will also heal is another matter.'

Follis stood aside so that the detective could see into the ward. The clergyman pointed Bardwell out. Since the patient's eyes were covered by a bandage, it was difficult to determine if he was asleep but his body was motionless. Colbeck glanced around the ward and saw that everyone else there had serious injuries.

'How many of them will make a complete recovery?' he asked.

'None of them, Inspector,' said Follis. 'The memory of the crash will be like a red-hot brand burnt into their brain. It will torture them for the rest of their lives.'

'Have there been any more fatalities?'

'Two people have died here in hospital.'

'That will bring the total number to eight.'

'I fear that it will climb higher than that.' He noticed movement in Bardwell's bed. 'I fancy that he may be stirring again, Inspector. This may be your only chance to speak to him but be prepared for a disappointment.'

'Why?'

'He's in a world of his own.'

Colbeck thanked him for his advice and went into the ward. A nurse was bending over one patient, trying to coax him to drink. In another bed, a man was coughing uncontrollably. A third patient was groaning aloud. Attended by a nurse, a doctor was examining someone in the far corner. When he eventually stood up, the doctor shook his head sadly and the nurse pulled the bed sheet over the patient's face. Another victim of the crash had passed away.

Sitting beside Bardwell, Colbeck touched his shoulder.

'Are you awake, Mr Bardwell?' he enquired.

'Who are you?' muttered the other.

'My name is Detective Inspector Colbeck and I'm investigating the crash that took place on the Brighton line yesterday.'

'Give me something to take this pain away.'

'I'm not a doctor, sir.'

'What's this crash you mentioned?'

'You were on the train at the time, Mr Bardwell.'

'Was I?'

'That's how you received your injuries.'

'My mind is a blank,' said Bardwell, piteously.

'You must remember something.'

'It's all a blur. I feel as if I've broken every bone in my body. My head is on fire and I've got something tied over my eyes.'

'You need rest, sir.'

'I want a doctor.'

'I'll call one in a moment,' Colbeck promised. 'I just want to ask you one thing.' Raising his voice, he spoke with deliberate slowness. 'Do you recall a Matthew Shanklin?'

The question produced an instant reply. Bardwell let out a gasp of horror and his body started to twitch violently. Colbeck held him down with gentle hands until the convulsions had ceased. Then he summoned a doctor. His conversation with Bardwell had been brief but, as he left the hospital, Colbeck felt that his journey to Brighton had not been in vain.

Matthew Shanklin had been out of work for a couple of months before finding another post. Discharged by one railway company, he was now employed by another and it was in the main office of the London and North West Railway that Leeming tracked him down that evening. Shanklin gave him a guarded welcome. He was a bald-headed man in his forties, short, thin and stooping. On the desk in front of him were piles of documents.

'You're working late this evening, sir,' observed Leeming.

'I have no control over my hours, Sergeant,' said Shanklin, coldly. 'In my previous situation, I had a more senior position and a degree of autonomy. That, I regret to say, is no longer the case.'

'It's your previous job that brought me here, Mr Shanklin.'

'What do you mean?'

Leeming told him about the investigation and Shanklin's back arched defensively. He peered at his visitor through a pair of wire-framed spectacles. Careful not to interrupt the narrative, he paused for a full minute when it was finally concluded.

'In what possible way can I help you, Sergeant?'

'I'd like to hear why you left the LB&SCR,' said Leeming.

'I didn't leave of my own volition,' admitted Shanklin. 'I was summarily dismissed, as I'm sure you know. Is that what brought you here?' he went on angrily. 'You believe that I had something to do with that terrible accident?'

'No, sir.'

'Then why bother me?'

'Inspector Colbeck thought you might be able to assist us, Mr Shanklin. Having worked for the company, you must have been very familiar with the rest of the management and with the directors.'

'I was there a long time, Sergeant.'

'Would you describe it as a happy company?'

'As happy as most, I daresay,' replied Shanklin. 'Every

company has its inner tensions and petty rivalries – I'm sure that you have some of those at Scotland Yard.'

'We certainly have plenty of tension,' conceded Leeming as an image of Superintendent Tallis popped into his mind. 'I think it's a means of keeping us on our toes. And, of course, there's always rivalry between the uniformed branch and the plain clothes division. But,' he continued, one eye on Shanklin, 'at least we don't have a board of directors breathing down our necks.'

'Then you are supremely fortunate.'

'You say that with some bitterness, sir.'

'I've good cause to do so.'

Leeming waited for him to explain what he meant but Shanklin remained silent. Sitting back in his chair, he folded his arms in what looked like a mild show of defiance. He was clearly unwilling to talk about his past. Leeming had to chisel the facts out of him.

'You were well-regarded at the LB&SCR, I hear,' said Leeming.

'I earned that regard.'

'Six months ago, you had another promotion.'

'Deservedly,' said Shanklin.

'Then it's odd that the company should let you go.'

'It was odd and unjust.'

'Why was that, sir?'

Shanklin flicked a hand. 'It doesn't matter.'

'It does to me,' insisted Leeming.

'I'd rather forget the whole thing, Sergeant. It was painful at the time, especially as I was given no chance to defend myself. I have a new job in another company now and that's where my loyalties lie.'

'What did you think when you heard the news of the crash?'

'I was profoundly shocked,' said Shanklin, 'as anyone would be at such horrific news. Deaths and injuries on the railway always disturb me.'

'The very thought of them terrifies me,' said Leeming.

'When I worked for the LB&SCR, my job entailed responsibility for safety on the line. If there was even the slightest mishap, I felt it as a personal failure.' He bit his lip. 'I'm just relieved that I was not still with the company when this disaster occurred.'

'Did you know anyone who might have travelled on the express?'

'Probably.'

'Could you give me their names, please?'

'No,' said Shanklin, curtly.

'But you do know people who travel on that train regularly?'

'What are you trying to get at, Sergeant Leeming?'

'Could one of them, perhaps, be Mr Horace Bardwell?'

Shanklin took refuge in silence once more, staring fixedly at his desk and fiddling nervously with a sheet of paper. Leeming could see how concerned the man was. He did not, however, press him. He watched and waited until Shanklin was ready to speak.

'Tell me, Sergeant,' he began, turning to look up at him. 'Have you ever been certain of a man's guilt yet unable to prove it?'

'That's happened to me a number of times, sir,' said Leeming, ruefully. 'I've often had to watch guilty men walk free from court because I was unable to find enough evidence to convict them.'

'Then you'll understand *my* position with regard to Mr Bardwell.'

'I don't follow.'

'I lacked sufficient evidence.'

Leeming blinked. 'Are you accusing Mr Bardwell of a crime?'

'Yes,' said Shanklin, gloomily, 'and a lot of good it did me. I lost my job, my friends and my reputation at the LB&SCR. Mr Bardwell saw to that. *He's* the person who should have been ousted – not me.'

'What charge would you lay against him, sir?'

'Fraud.'

'That's a very serious accusation.'

'I had good reason to make it, believe me. It was my misfortune to stumble upon a document written by Horace Bardwell, a man whom I had always respected. Well,' said Shanklin, grinding his teeth, 'I don't respect him now.'

'Why is that, sir?'

'What I had seen was an attempt to falsify our share prospectus, to lure investors into parting with their money on the strength of bogus promises. I need hardly tell you that the Railway Mania of the last decade led to all kinds of financial upheavals.'

'Yes,' said Leeming. 'People no longer think that investing in a railway company is a licence to print money.'

'Dividends are shrinking on all sides, Sergeant. I doubt if the LB&SCR will be able to pay its shareholders more than six per cent next year, possibly less.'

'I assume that Mr Bardwell was offering much more.'

'He was trying to defraud people,' said Shanklin with disgust. 'The prospectus was full of misleading statements and downright lies. I was so outraged that I confronted him about it.'

'How did he react?' wondered Leeming.

'First of all, he pretended that it was not his handwriting. Then, when that excuse wouldn't work, he claimed that it was a first draft that he intended to change substantially. I refused to accept that and Mr Bardwell became angry. He threatened to ruin me.'

'Why didn't you report your findings to the other directors?'

'That's exactly what I did, Sergeant,' replied Shanklin. 'They asked me to produce evidence but the document in question had already been destroyed by Mr Bardwell. It was his word against mine.' He ran a hand over his bald pate. 'I was dismissed on the spot.'

While he was not convinced that he had heard the whole story, Leeming did not ask for more detail. What he had uncovered was a justifiable grudge against Bardwell, one strong enough, perhaps, to impel Shanklin to seek revenge against the man.

'Horace Bardwell was injured in that crash,' said Leeming. 'How would you feel if you learnt that he had, in fact, been killed?'

Shanklin was forthright. 'I'd be absolutely delighted.'

During his visit to the hospital, Colbeck took the opportunity to speak to a number of the survivors of the crash, comparing their estimates of the speed at which the train was travelling and the way they had reacted when it came off the rails. Several spoke gratefully of the way that the Reverend Ezra Follis had helped them in the immediate aftermath, though one man had been highly alarmed by the sight of the clergyman, fearing that he had come to perform last rites. Colbeck found two people who had actually shared Follis's carriage. Terence Giddens, the red-faced banker, was still desperate to be discharged from the hospital. He kept glancing anxiously at the door as if afraid that an unwanted visitor would walk through it.

Daisy Perriam had been the only woman in the carriage but the beauty that had attracted her travelling companions was now masked by ugly facial cuts and bruises. She had sustained cracked ribs during the crash and a broken wrist. The injury that really distressed her, however, was the crushed foot. She would never walk properly again. When Colbeck pointed out that she was lucky to survive, she burst into tears.

'I'd rather have died,' she wailed, tears streaming down her cheeks. 'What kind of a life do I face now? It will be a nightmare.'

'Do your family know what happened to you?' asked Colbeck.

'No, Inspector, and I hope that they never do.'

On that mystifying note, Colbeck left the hospital and made his way to the railway station, a striking piece of architecture. It was late in the evening when he at last returned to Scotland Yard. The distinctive whiff of cigar smoke from the superintendent's office told him that Edward Tallis was still there. A confirmed bachelor with scant interest in a social life, Tallis had dedicated himself completely to the never-ending fight against crime. Colbeck tapped on his door, entered in response to a brusque command and caught the superintendent in the act of stubbing out his cigar in an ashtray.

'Ah,' said Tallis, sarcastically, 'the Prodigal Son returns!'

'Does that mean you have a fatted calf roasting on the spit, sir?'

'No, Inspector.'

'Then perhaps you should read your Bible,' suggested Colbeck.

Tallis sat up indignantly. 'I study it every day and am well-acquainted with its contents,' he affirmed. 'If everyone in this blighted city was as devout and God-fearing as me, there'd be no need for a Metropolitan Police Force.'

'I beg to differ, sir. You'd need hundreds of constables to control the masses fighting to get into the churches.'

'Are you being facetious, Colbeck?

'Light drollery was the most I was attempting.'

'It has no place whatsoever in a criminal investigation.'

While Colbeck disagreed, he knew that it was not the moment to debate the subject. Tallis believed that a sense of humour was a sign of weakness in a man's character. If he ever found something even remotely amusing, the superintendent made sure that nobody else ever found out about it. Waving Colbeck to a chair, he picked up a sheet of paper from his desk.

'This is a report from Sergeant Leeming,' he declared.

'Thank you, sir,' said Colbeck, taking it from him. 'I'll be very interested to see it. Victor and I were dealing with two ends of a problematical relationship. While he was calling on Matthew Shanklin, I was visiting Horace Bardwell at the county hospital in Brighton.'

'How is he?'

'He's very poorly, I'm afraid. He's lost his sight as a result of the accident and took such a blow to the head that he's in a state of great confusion.' As he was talking, Colbeck was reading Leeming's account of the interview with Shanklin. 'This could be significant,' he went on. 'Victor has probed quite deeply.'

'I want to hear about Mr Bardwell.'

'Then you shall, superintendent.'

Colbeck told him about his fleeting encounter with Bardwell and what he had gleaned from other patients. He emphasised the number of people who had praised the work of Ezra Follis.

'Disasters produce victims,' said Tallis, grimly, 'but they also create heroes. It sounds to me as if the Reverend Follis is one of them.'

'There's no question of that, sir. One of the doctors told me that he should be in hospital himself instead of carrying on as if nothing had happened to him.'

'Christian stoicism – we can all learn from his example.'

'Strictly speaking,' said Colbeck, 'Stoics were members of an ancient Greek school of philosophy, holding that virtue and happiness can only be attained by submission to destiny and natural law. I'm not sure that it can be aligned to Christianity.'

'Don't be so pedantic!'

'Nevertheless, I see and appreciate what you were trying to say.'

'I was not *trying* to say anything, Inspector – I was saying it.'

'And your point was crystal clear,' said Colbeck, suppressing a smile. 'To return to Horace Bardwell, do you accept that his presence on that express train may – and I put it no higher than that – have been the reason it was derailed?'

'I reserve my judgement.'

'You've read Victor's report and heard how Mr Bardwell reacted when I mentioned the name of Matthew Shanklin to him. Are you still not persuaded, sir?'

'I'm persuaded that there might, after all, be something in your extraordinary notion that the train crash was intended to kill a particular individual,' said Tallis, eyebrows forming a bushy chevron, 'but I very much doubt if his name was Horace Bardwell.'

'Who else could it possibly be?' said Colbeck.

'The gentleman who sent me this letter earlier today,' replied the other, jabbing a finger on the missive. 'According to this, he's had two death threats to date and is sure that he is being followed. When he discharged himself from hospital, he did so under police guard.'

'May I know his name, Superintendent?'

'It's Giles Thornhill, a Member of Parliament for Brighton.'

Colbeck was decisive. 'I'll call on him tomorrow morning, sir.'

CHAPTER SIX

When he finished his shift that Saturday evening, Caleb Andrews had left Euston station with his fireman, drunk a reviving pint of beer in his favourite public house then walked briskly home to Camden. His daughter, as usual, was waiting to make his supper.

'Have you had a good day, Father?' asked Madeleine.

'No,' he answered, removing his cap and hanging it on a peg. 'I keep thinking about Frank Pike. I miss him, Maddy. I like a man who takes his job as seriously as he did. Frank *listened* to me. He was ready to learn.' He nestled into his armchair. 'How was Rose today?'

'I only spent an hour with her. Rose's parents were there and so was Frank's mother. The house was rather crowded.'

'Is she bearing up?'

'She's trying to be brave,' said Madeleine with a sigh, 'but, every so often, the pain is too much for her and she breaks down. I've told her that she can call on me at any hour of the day or night.'

'It's Sunday tomorrow – my rest day. I'll pay Rose another

visit myself. She needs someone to tell her what a good man Frank was.'

'She found that out for herself, Father.'

'Yes,' he said, 'I'm sure that she did.' He looked up quizzically. 'Is there any word from Inspector Colbeck?'

'No,' she replied, 'but that's not surprising. You know how busy Robert always is. He works all the hours God sends him. I imagine that he's still looking into the accident.'

'That's why I asked, Maddy. There's a nasty rumour flying around that it might not have been an accident. I mean, why should the Railway Detective take an interest in it unless a crime had been committed?'

'Robert said nothing about a crime when he was here.'

'He'd only paid a short visit to the site and had no time to find out what really happened. If it turns out that some black-hearted devil caused that crash,' he went on with sudden rage, 'then he should be hanged, drawn and quartered. And *I'd* volunteer to do it.'

Madeleine was shocked. 'That's a terrible thing to say!'

'It's a terrible thing to do, Maddy. Can you think of anything worse than derailing a train like that? Supposing it had happened on the LNWR,' he said, hauling himself to his feet. 'Supposing that *I* was driving an express when it came off the line and was hit by another train. Rose Pike would have been here to comfort *you* then.'

'Perish the thought!'

'This monster must be caught and put to death.'

'It's not even certain that someone *did* cause the crash,' she said, trying to calm him down. 'I think you should wait until we know the truth.'

'I already know it,' he asserted. 'I feel it in my bones.'

'It's only a rumour.'

'Look at the facts. Trains come off the track for three main reasons – the driver makes a bad mistake, there's a landslip or a stray animal on the rails, or someone sets out to cause a disaster. You can forget the first reason,' he said, dismissively, 'because Frank Pike never made mistakes. As for the second, Inspector Colbeck made no mention of an obstruction on the line. In other words, this simply *has* to be the work of some villain.'

'That's a frightening thought.'

'It's one we're going to have to get used to, Maddy.'

'Well, I hope, for Rose's sake, that you're wrong,' she said, concerned for the stricken widow. 'If she found out that Frank and the others had been deliberately killed, Rose would be in despair.'

Andrews was disgusted. 'I can't think of any crime worse than this,' he said with vehemence. 'As long as this man is at large, we're all in danger. He could strike anywhere on the railway. Doesn't he have a conscience? Doesn't he have any human decency?'

'There's no point in getting yourself worked up, Father.'

'There's every point. What he did was pure evil.'

'Then leave the police to deal with it,' she urged. 'If there's even a suspicion of a crime, Robert will investigate it thoroughly. He loves the railway as much as you do. You could see how troubled he was about this crash.'

'Every railwayman in the country is troubled.'

'Our job is to help Rose Pike through her torment. She doted on her husband. Now that he's gone, Rose is in a dreadful state.'

'We owe it to Frank to find his killer.'

'There were other people on that train,' she reminded him, 'and some of them died horrible deaths in the crash.'

'Frank is the only one that matters to me.'

Madeleine was roused. 'Then you should be ashamed of yourself, Father. Have you no sympathy for the families and friends of the other victims? And what about all those who were badly injured? Some have been maimed for life,' she said, reproachfully, 'yet you don't care a jot about them.'

'Of course, I do, Maddy,' he said, apologetically.

'As for the person who may or may not have been responsible for the crash, leave Robert to worry about that. He's a detective. He knows what to do. If the crash was deliberate,' she assured him, 'then Robert will be searching for the man who caused it right this minute.'

Crime had no respect for the Sabbath. Since villains continued unabated, the Metropolitan Police could not afford to take a day off and let it thrive unchecked. Robert Colbeck had long ago learnt that, if an investigation demanded it, he would be required to work on the Lord's Day with the same application as in the rest of the week. It was an aspect of his job that he had accepted without complaint. Victor Leeming, by contrast, never ceased to moan about it.

'I should be taking my family to church,' he grumbled.

'I'm sure they'll say a prayer on your behalf, Victor.'

'It's not the same, Inspector. They want me *there*.'

'Given the importance of this case,' said Colbeck, 'I'm certain that they'll understand your absence. And in the fullness of time, your wife and children will be very proud of you for helping to catch a ruthless criminal. With luck, he should be in custody before too long, allowing you to have next Sunday free.'

'I hope so,' said Leeming. 'It's Estelle's birthday.'

'Then I'll do everything in my power to make sure that you'll be able to share it with her. A word of warning, however,' Colbeck went on with a twinkle in his eye. 'It might be more tactful not to mention the forthcoming event to the superintendent. He doesn't believe in family celebrations.'

'But he must have a birthday of his own, sir.'

'Must he?' asked Colbeck with a wicked smile. 'To tell you the truth, Victor, I have grave doubts about that. Superintendent Tallis was not born by natural means. I fancy that he was issued like a military regulation.' Leeming burst out laughing. 'I trust you to keep that idea to yourself.'

It was early in the morning and the two men were in Colbeck's office at Scotland Yard. The aggrieved sergeant had just arrived to get his instructions. A full day's work lay ahead of them. Having read his colleague's report of the interview with Matthew Shanklin, Colbeck pressed for more detail. As Leeming gave him an account of what had transpired, he interrupted with pertinent questions. At the end of it all, there was only one thing he wanted to know.

'Should we regard him as a suspect?' asked Colbeck.

'Yes and no, sir.'

'The two are quite different, Victor.'

'Let me explain,' said Leeming. 'Yes, Mr Shanklin despises Horace Bardwell enough to want him dead but no, he did not lever that rail out of position. He never left his office on Friday. I made a point of checking that. If he did plan the collision, then he employed a confederate to do his dirty work.'

'So we should keep an eye on Matthew Shanklin?'

'Most definitely.'

'Then we'll do so,' said Colbeck. 'We may, of course, be barking up the wrong tree altogether.'

'What do you mean, Inspector?'

'It seems that Mr Bardwell was not the only man aboard that train to provoke extreme hatred. Someone travelling, coincidentally, in the same carriage had actually received death threats.'

'Who was that?'

'Mr Giles Thornhill.'

Leeming's brow creased. 'That name sounds familiar.'

'It should do, Victor. It often appears in the newspapers. Mr Thornhill is a Member of Parliament and a fairly outspoken one at that. He's always championing causes of one kind or another.'

'You know my view of politicians, sir. They're all as bad as each other. If ever I'm allowed to vote, I'll try my best to put an honest man into Parliament for a change.'

'That's what those of us who *do* have a vote attempt to do,' said Colbeck. 'But I agree that the system might work better if it were truly democratic instead of being based simply on property.'

'We arrested two politicians for embezzlement last year and one for assault. That shows you the kind of people who get elected."

'Don't forget Lord Hendry. When his horse lost the Derby at Epsom earlier this year, he not only shot one of his rivals dead, he committed suicide on the spot. That's not something you expect of a peer of the realm.'

'Guy Fawkes had the right idea,' said Leeming with a rare mutinous glint. 'The Houses of Parliament ought to be blown up.'

'Not with Her Majesty, the Queen inside it, I trust?'

'No, no, sir – it's the politicians I loathe.'

'That's a rather unchristian thought for a Sunday, Victor. I don't think I'll bother to share it with Mr Thornhill. It might constitute a third death threat.' He gave Leeming a playful pat on the shoulder. 'While I travel to the south coast again, you can search for the other people whose names on our list – Jack Rye and Dick Chiffney. Do you have addresses for them?'

'Yes, Inspector,' said Leeming. 'They both live in London.'

'That will save you the ordeal of a train journey then.'

'Thank the Lord for small mercies!'

'I'll speak to Mr Thornhill and, while I'm in Brighton, I might even take the opportunity to call on the Reverend Ezra Follis.' He moved to the door. 'Off we go, Victor. We must not slacken the pace.'

'One moment, sir,' said Leeming, blocking his path, 'I wonder if I might ask your advice on a personal matter.'

'What is it?'

'Estelle's birthday is only a week away but I've no idea what I should buy her. Do you have any suggestions?'

'I know what your wife would appreciate most.'

'Well?'

'The company of her loving husband for the entire day,' said Colbeck. 'Solve this crime quickly and that's exactly what she will get.'

Leeming needed no more incentive than that.

The train crash had filled pews throughout Brighton that Sunday but nowhere more so than at St Dunstan's, a small church on the very edge of the town. News of the tragedy brought people in from far and wide to pray for the victims and to view the man who had made a miraculous escape from the disaster. They could not believe that their rector would be able to take the service but there he was, standing before them, ignoring the obvious discomfort from his wounds and managing to produce his customary beatific smile.

The Reverend Ezra Follis was determined not to let his parishioners down. Over his cassock, he wore a spotless white linen surplice with a stole draped around his shoulders. People gasped when they saw the scars on his face and the bandaging on his head and his hands. He looked so small and frail. There was no frailty in his voice, however, and it rose to full power when he struggled up into the pulpit and delivered his sermon.

Follis was a born orator, able to inspire the minds and arouse the emotions of those who heard him. As he described the way in which – it was his unshakable conviction – he had been saved from death by the compassionate hand of the Almighty, he had several people reaching for their handkerchiefs. It was a powerful sermon, lucid, thoughtful, well-phrased and pitched at exactly the right level. Follis did not indulge in high-flown rhetoric. He knew how to make important points simply and effectively.

Among those hanging on his words was a woman in her late twenties who sat in one of the front pews with her two elderly aunts. Plain, plump and dressed with the utmost respectability, Amy Walcott stared at him with a mixture of wonder and adoration. She knew that Ezra Follis was a great scholar – he was a former chaplain of an Oxford college – but he showed no disdain or condescension to those of lesser intelligence. He had the gift of reaching everyone in the church both individually and as a group. Amy watched him intently, admiring his resilience yet noting undeniable signs of the physical strain he was under.

When morning service was over, Follis took up his usual position at the church door so that he could have a brief word with each member of his congregation as he bade them farewell. The effort of standing on his feet for so long slowly began to tell on him. Leaving the churchwardens to tidy everything away, he waved off the last of his parishioners then adjourned to the vestry. Alone at last, he sank down on a chair and gritted his teeth as he felt sharp twinges in his legs and hips and back. All of his bruises throbbed simultaneously.

Staring at the crucifix on the wall, he offered up a prayer of thanks for being given the strength to get through the service without collapsing. It was several minutes before he felt well enough to rise to his feet again. He crossed to a desk, unlocked a drawer with a key and took out a bottle of brandy. After pouring a generous amount into a small glass, he took a sip and let it course through him. Then he locked the bottle away again. Another sip of brandy was even more restorative and gave him the energy to remove his stole and surplice. When they had been put away in a cupboard, he sat down again to rest and to reflect on his sermon.

The churchwardens and the verger had been told not to disturb him once he retired to the vestry so they went about their business then let themselves out of the church. Follis heard the latch click as the door closed behind them. With nobody else there, he felt able to relax completely, stretching himself and reaching for the brandy. It was almost a quarter an hour before he was finally ready to depart. Opening the vestry door, he stepped out into the chancel.

Expecting to find the church empty, he was surprised to see that someone was still there, using a metal can to pour fresh water into the vases. Amy Walcott, responsible for organising the flower rota, made sure that her own name was on it with increasing frequency.

'I didn't realise you were still here, Amy,' he said, wearily.

'I needed to rearrange some of the flowers,' she explained, 'and I wanted to thank you for the sermon you gave today. It was uplifting.'

Follis nodded gratefully. 'I try my best.'

'It was very brave of you even to turn up at church today. You should have been lying in bed back in the Rectory. I couldn't help noticing how exhausted you looked at times.'

'Oh dear!' he exclaimed. 'And there I was, thinking that I had contrived to deceive everybody. On the other hand,' he added, taking a step closer to her, 'you are far more perceptive than anyone else in the congregation. You have a sharp eye, Amy.'

'I was worried about you, Mr Follis.'

'There's no need to be – I'm fine now.'

'Is there anything I can do to help?' she asked.

'I don't think so. I must get on home. Mrs Ashmore will have luncheon waiting for me.'

'There must be *something* I can do.'

It was a heartfelt plea and Follis could not ignore it. He was fond of Amy Walcott and had given her unfailing support during the long period of mourning after her mother's death. From that time on, she had dedicated herself to the church and its rector, giving freely of her time and energy. Tired as he was, Follis believed that it would be cruel to refuse her offer.

'Perhaps there is something you could do, after all,' he said.

She smiled eagerly. 'Is there?'

'You have such a beautiful voice, Amy.'

'Thank you.'

'The tragedy is that I never get to hear it reading beautiful words. It's the harsher voices of men that read the epistle and the gospel, and I sometimes long for the softer tones of a woman. It would please me greatly if you could read something to me.'

'Gladly, Mr Follis,' she said with delight. 'What shall I read?'

'Let's start with one of the Psalms, shall we?' he decided, opening his Book of Common Prayer and leafing through the pages with a bandaged hand. 'And where better to begin than with the first of them?'

Finding the page, he handed the book to her then motioned for her to stand at the lectern. As he settled into the front pew, he gazed up at Amy Walcott and raised a hand.

'Whenever you're ready,' he said. 'I'm going to enjoy this.'

Giles Thornhill lived in a palatial country mansion a few miles outside Brighton. Set in rolling countryside, it commanded glorious views on every side. After admiring it from afar, Robert Colbeck was driven up to the gatehouse in a cab and had to identify himself before he was allowed into the property. As the cab rolled up the long drive, he saw the gates being locked behind them by a man with a rifle slung across his back. The house was being guarded like a fortress.

Seated at a table in his library, Thornhill made no attempt to get up when Colbeck was shown into the room. The politician's arm was still in a sling and the black eye was still acting as a focal point on his face. He looked as haughty and cold as the marble busts that were dotted between the rows of bookshelves. Thornhill was disappointed that a detective inspector had been sent to interview him.

'I expected Superintendent Tallis,' he said, frostily, 'if not the commissioner himself.'

'I'm in charge of the investigation into the train crash, sir,' said Colbeck, firmly, 'and I'm interested in anything whatsoever that may have a bearing on it. I've already established to my satisfaction that the collision was no accident so I've turned my attention to the likely motive behind this crime.'

'You may be looking at it, Inspector.'

'Indeed?'

'Sit down and I will explain.'

Colbeck took a chair at the other end of the table and glanced around the library. It was a large, rectangular, high-ceilinged room with bookshelves on three walls. Light flooded in through the windows on the other wall and made the marble busts gleam and the crystal chandelier above Colbeck's head sparkle. Before resuming, Thornhill subjected his guest to a searching glare.

'The true motive for what happened on Friday will not even have crossed your mind, Inspector,' he said, 'because it would never occur to you for a moment that the accident was intended to kill someone who was travelling on the express.'

'You malign me, I fear,' Colbeck told him. 'I considered that possibility as soon as I learnt that Mr Horace Bardwell was a passenger on the train. He struck me as being a potential target for someone in search of revenge.'

Thornhill was peeved. 'Bardwell was not the target,' he insisted, resenting the very notion of a competitor. 'That crash was engineered to kill *me*. Don't you understand, Inspector Colbeck? It was a clear case of attempted murder.'

'Attempted and actual murder, sir,' corrected the other.

'To date, there have been nine murder victims.'

'They were incidental casualties.'

'I don't think their friends and families will take any comfort from that thought,' said Colbeck, pointedly.

'If anyone was supposed to die, it was me.'

'Do you have any evidence to support that, sir?'

'You must have read my letter to the superintendent. I laid out the evidence in that. I've had two death threats. Whenever I've been in London, I've been followed, and I always travel on the Brighton Express on Friday evenings. I'm a creature of habit,' said Thornhill. 'Somebody must have been studying those habits.'

'May I see the death threats you received?'

'No, Inspector – I tore them to pieces.'

'That was unwise of you, sir. They could have been valuable evidence. Were they both written by the same hand?'

'Yes – and it was elegant calligraphy at that. It made them even more menacing somehow.'

'Can you remember the actual wording of the missives?'

'Both were short and blunt, Inspector. The first simply warned me that I had weeks to live. The second told me to make my will.'

'What precautions did you take?' asked Colbeck.

'Only the obvious ones,' replied Thornhill. 'I made sure that I never travelled alone and remained vigilant at all times. The problem is that, until the train crash, I wasn't entirely sure that the threats were serious. As a politician, I'm rather used to mindless abuse. Those were not the first unpleasant letters to be delivered here.'

'So they were sent to your home?'

'Yes, Inspector – that's what unsettles me. Most of my

mail is addressed to the House of Commons.'

'Were the letters sent from Brighton?'

'No – they bore a London postmark.'

'Can you think of anyone who may have written them?'

'I have a lot of enemies, Inspector,' said Thornhill with a touch of pride, 'because I'm a man of principle and always speak robustly in Parliament. Politics, I daresay, is a closed world to you.'

'On the contrary,' said Colbeck, 'a few years ago, it fell to me to arrest Sir Humphrey Gilzean, who organised a train robbery. I believe he was a close friend of yours.' Thornhill shifted uncomfortably in his seat. 'Since then, I've taken a close interest in the activities of the House of Commons. I know, for instance, that you were highly critical of Sir Robert Peel when he repealed the Corn Laws and that you broke with his wing of the Conservative party. Since his death, you've aligned yourself with Mr Disraeli.'

'What our late prime minister did was unpardonable,' snapped Thornhill. 'As for Gilzean, he was never more than an acquaintance who happened to share my views. He was certainly not an intimate of mine. I was thoroughly shocked by what he did.'

'There may be something of a parallel here,' suggested Colbeck, noting how keen he was to distance himself from Gilzean. 'Sir Humphrey was so obsessed with his hatred of railways that he was driven to commit dreadful crimes. It could well be that we are dealing with another case of obsession – a person consumed with hatred of a particular individual.'

'And that individual,' said Thornhill, 'appears to be me.'

'I'd need more proof before I accepted that conclusion, sir.'

'It's as plain as this black eye of mine, Inspector. I'm warned, I'm watched then I'm wounded in that horrifying train crash.'

'The same things may have happened to Mr Bardwell.'

'This is nothing to do with him!'

'He's a director of the LB&SCR.'

'I have the honour of representing Brighton in Parliament so I am identified far more closely with the town than Horace Bardwell. Also, I have political rivals who would be very happy to see me dead.' He slid a piece of paper across to Colbeck. 'I've made a list of them for you. Forgive my shaky writing. With my right arm in this sling, I had to use my left.'

'The names are perfectly legible,' observed Colbeck, eyeing them with interest. 'It's a rather long list of suspects, sir.'

'I didn't become a politician to make myself popular.'

'That's palpably true.'

'I suggest you make discreet enquiries about every man there.'

'I have my own methods,' said Colbeck, evenly, 'and I'll stick to those, if you don't mind. Meanwhile, you seem to be perfectly safe here. I can't think you'll be in any danger in your own home.'

'That's why I discharged myself from the county hospital. As long as I was there, I was vulnerable to attack. In the event,' said Thornhill, 'the attack turned out to be a written one.'

'In what way?'

'See for yourself, Inspector Colbeck.' He slid another piece of paper across the table. 'This was delivered to me in hospital. I regard it as incontestable proof that the train crash was arranged solely for my benefit.'

Colbeck read the mocking obituary of the politician.

Giles Thornhill MP was killed in a railway accident on Friday, August 15th, on his way back to his constituency in Brighton. His death will be mourned by his family but celebrated joyously by those of us who know what a despicable, corrupt and mean-spirited person he was. May his miserable body rot forever in a foul dunghill!

'Well,' said Thornhill, 'have I convinced you now?'

CHAPTER SEVEN

Victor Leeming's search began badly. The first person he had to find was Jack Rye, a porter from London Bridge station who had been dismissed on suspicion of theft in spite of vociferous protestations of innocence. The address that Leeming had been given was in one of the poorer quarters of Westminster. When he called there, he learnt that Rye had quit the premises months earlier. As the city echoed to the sound of church bells, a long, arduous trudge ensued through some of the rougher districts of the capital as the sergeant went from tenement to miserable tenement. Rye had kept on the move, changing his accommodation as often as his job. Time and again, he had departed with a landlord's curse ringing in his ears.

When Leeming finally tracked his man down to one of the rookeries in Seven Dials, he discovered that Jack Rye could not possibly have caused the train crash because he had been stabbed to death in a tavern brawl a week before the tragedy occurred. The very fact that Rye had ended up living in such a vile slum was an indication of how low his fortunes had fallen. It was a relief to cross one name off the list. Leeming was grateful to get clear of Seven Dials and of the jeering children who threw stones at his top hat.

Dick Chiffney was also elusive. A plate-layer for the LB&SCR, he had been sacked for punching his foreman. His address at the time was that of a hovel in Chalk Farm, a relic of the days when the area was predominantly agricultural. Industry had slowly encroached upon it, houses had been built for the burgeoning middle classes and the arrival of the railways had completed the dramatic change to an urban environment. Chiffney was no longer there but the little house did still have an occupant. Arms folded, she confronted Leeming at the door.

'Who are you?' she demanded.

'My name is Detective Sergeant Leeming,' he replied.

'Is that why you've come – to tell me the bastard is finally dead?'

'I'm looking for Dick Chiffney.'

'And so am I,' she said, baring the blackened remains of her teeth. 'I've been looking for him all week.'

Josie Murlow was a fearsome woman in her thirties, tall, big-boned and with red hair plunging down her back like a hirsute waterfall. Her face had a ravaged prettiness but it was her body that troubled Leeming. She exuded a raw sexuality that seemed quite out of place on a Sunday. As a uniformed constable, he had arrested many prostitutes and had always been immune to their charms. Josie Murlow was different. He could not take his eyes off the huge, round, half-visible, heaving breasts. Leeming felt as if he were being brazenly accosted in broad daylight.

'Are you Mrs Chiffney?' he asked, making a conscious effort to meet her fiery gaze.

'I'm Mrs Chiffney in all but name,' she retorted. 'I cooked for him, looked after him and shared his bed for almost two years then he walks out on me without a word of warning. It's not bleeding right.'

'I quite agree.'

'Who gave him money when he lost his job? Who nursed him when he was ill? Who kept him in drink? *I* did,' she stressed, slapping her chest with such force that her breasts bobbed up and down with hypnotic insistence. 'I done everything for that man.'

'When did you last see him?'

'Over a week ago.'

'Did he have a job at the time?'

'Dick's been out of work since he knocked his foreman to the ground when he was laying some new track on the railway. We had to get by on what I bring in.'

Leeming did not have to ask what she did for a living. Even though she was now wearing crumpled old clothes and had no powder on her florid cheeks, Josie Murlow was patently a member of the oldest profession. He decided that she must have catered for more vigorous clients. Only big, strong, brave, virile men would have dared to take her on. Others would have found her far too intimidating.

'Why are the police after Dick?' she said, belligerently. 'What's the mad bugger been up to now?'

'I just wished to talk to him.'

'Don't lie to me. I've had enough dealings with the law to know that you never simply want to talk to someone. There's always some dark reason at the back of it. Dick is in trouble again, isn't he?'

'He might be,' admitted Leeming.

'What's the charge this time?'

Leeming was evasive. 'It's to do with the railway.'

'The foreman started the fight,' she argued, leaping to Chiffney's defence. 'He threw the first punch so Dick had to hit him back. In any case,' she added, sizing him up, 'why is a detective from Scotland Yard bothering about a scuffle on a railway line? There's something else, isn't there?' She glared at him. 'What is it?'

'It may be nothing at all and that's the truth. I just need to speak to Mr Chiffney. Do you have any idea where he might be?'

'If I did, I wouldn't be standing here, would I? Josie Murlow is not a woman to give up easy. I've searched everywhere. What I can tell you,' she conceded, 'is where Dick likes to drink. I been to all the places but he must have seen me coming because he wasn't in any of them. You might be luckier. Dick doesn't know you.'

Taking out his notepad, Leeming jotted down the names of four public houses that Chiffney frequented. As he wrote, he kept his head down, glad of an excuse not to look at her surging bosom. Josie was well aware of his interest. When he looked up again, he saw that one flabby arm had dropped to her side while the other rested on the door jamb beside her head. Her crudely seductive pose made him take a step backwards.

'Would you like to come in, Sergeant Leeming?' she invited.

'I...don't have the time,' he stammered.

'I've got drink in the house – and a very empty bed.'

'No, thank you.'

'Josie Murlow gives value for money, I can tell you.'

'I've no reason to doubt that.'

'Then why are you holding back?' she said, putting both hands on her hips and turning sideways so that he saw her body in enticing profile. 'What better way to spend a Sunday?'

'I'm a married man,' he said, indignantly.

'So are most of them – they want something special for a change.' She gave a low cackle. 'I make sure they get it.'

'You'll have to excuse me. I'm still on duty.'

She became aggressive. 'Are you turning me down?'

'I have to find Mr Chiffney,' he said, retreating from the door.

'Well, when you do,' she yelled, 'drag him back here by the balls. I want a word with that swivel-eyed bastard.'

Returning to Brighton by cab, the first thing that Colbeck did was to find a hotel where he could buy himself a light luncheon. He then took time off to look at the town's most famous sight, the Royal Pavilion with its strange but arresting mixture of neo-classical and oriental architecture. In the previous century, the restorative properties of its sea water had helped to turn Brighton from a small fishing port into a fashionable resort. The Pavilion had added to its appeal. Built over a period of many years, it had become a main attraction well before its completion in 1823.

The brainchild of the future King George IV, it had failed abysmally to exercise the same fascination for Queen Victoria and ceased to become a royal residence. Colbeck was glad that it had been purchased by the town in 1850, allowing the public to admire its unique design and its spacious gardens. Those who flocked to the seaside in warmer months did not merely come for the pleasure of walking along the promenade, enjoying the facilities on the Chain Pier or merely reclining on the beach and watching the waves roll in. They were there to view the majestic Pavilion and to get a privileged insight into how royalty lived and entertained.

After seeing his fill, Colbeck set off on his second visit of the day. St Dunstan's Rectory was only a stone's throw from the church itself and it had been built at roughly the same time, retaining its medieval exterior while undergoing many internal renovations. Shown into the drawing room by the housekeeper, Colbeck was given a cordial welcome by Ezra Follis who pulled himself out of his high-backed chair with barely concealed pain.

'Forgive me if I don't shake your hand, Inspector,' he said. 'My hands are still somewhat tender and I had difficulty turning the pages of my Prayer Book during the service this morning. Your visit is timely. I was just about to have my afternoon cup of tea.'

'Then I'll be happy to join you, Mr Follis.'

'Thank you, Mrs Ashmore.'

A nod from the rector was all it took for the housekeeper to bustle out of the room. The two men, meanwhile, sat down opposite each other. After the grand proportions of the library he had visited earlier, Colbeck found the room small and cluttered. The low ceiling, thick roof beams and little mullioned windows contributed to the sense of restriction but the place had a snug, homely feeling about it. Follis had less than a quarter of the number of books owned by Giles Thornhill but Colbeck suspected that he had read far more of the contents of his library than the politician had of his.

'What brings you to Brighton again?' asked Follis.

'I had to speak to one of your Members of Parliament.'

'Then it must have been Giles Thornhill.'

'Yes,' said Colbeck. 'Like you, he was a survivor of the crash.'

'How did you find him?'

'I think he's still in considerable discomfort.'

Follis chortled. 'That's a polite way of saying that he was singularly inhospitable. It's no more than I'd expect,' he said. 'On the one occasion when I called at his house, Thornhill kept me waiting for twenty minutes before he deigned to see me.'

'I take it that you are not an admirer of the gentleman.'

'Voting against him at the last election gave me a sense of delight, Inspector. I despise the man. He manipulates people to his advantage. The only thing that animates him is the greater glory of Giles Thornhill.' He chortled again. 'When visitors come to Brighton for the first time, I ask them what they think of the monstrosity.'

'The Royal Pavilion?'

'No,' said Follis, 'our Parliamentary eyesore – Mr Thornhill.'

'What has he done to offend you?' wondered Colbeck.

'He's treated people with contempt as if he inhabits a superior order of creation. Then, of course,' said Follis, knowingly, 'there's the small matter of his inheritance.'

'Judging by the size of his house, I'd say that it was an extremely large one.'

'His father made his fortune in the slave trade, Inspector.'

'Ah, I see.'

'He grew rich on the suffering and humiliation of others. That may explain why Thornhill regards so many of us as mere slaves. However,' he went on, sympathy coming into his voice, 'I'm genuinely sorry that he was injured in the crash and did my best to help him at the time. Needless to say, I received no thanks.'

'Do you see Mr Thornhill often?' asked Colbeck.

'At least once a week – we catch the Brighton Express every Friday evening and often share a carriage. Though we acknowledge each other, we rarely speak.' Follis grinned. 'I fancy that he knows he can't rely on my vote.'

They chatted amiably until the housekeeper arrived with a tray. As she served the two of them with a cup of tea, Colbeck was able to take a closer look at Ellen Ashmore. She was a stout woman of medium height with well-groomed grey hair surrounding a pleasant face that was incongruously small in comparison with her body. Though she and Follis were of a similar age, she treated him with a motherly concern, urging him to rest as much as possible.

'Mrs Ashmore will spoil me,' said Follis when she had left the room. 'She did everything she could to stop me taking the service this morning. I told her that I had a duty, Inspector. I couldn't let my parishioners down.'

'I'm sure that they appreciated your being there.'

'Some of them did.' Adding sugar to his cup, Follis stirred his tea. 'Incidentally, did you manage to get anything coherent out of Horace Bardwell?'

'I'm afraid not,' said Colbeck. 'He's hopelessly bewildered.'

'We prayed for him and the other victims.'

'While I was at the hospital yesterday, I spoke to some of them. Two, apparently, were in the same carriage as you.'

'Oh? And who might they be?'

'Mr Terence Giddens and a young lady named Miss Daisy Perriam. They were both highly distressed at what happened to them.'

'That's understandable,' said Follis with something akin to amusement. 'Instead of being trapped in hospital beds, the pair of them had hoped to be sharing one.' Colbeck was taken aback. 'You didn't see them together as I did, Inspector. Had you done so, you'd have noticed that, though they pretended to be travelling alone, they were, in fact, together. That's why Giddens was so desperate to get out of the hospital.'

'He told me that his bank needed him in London.'

'I heard the same lie. The truth of it is that he was afraid that his wife would read about the crash in the newspapers and see her husband's name among the injured. The last thing that Giddens wanted was for his wife to discover that, instead of doing whatever he told her he would be doing that weekend, he had instead slipped off to Brighton with a beautiful young woman. He lives in fear that Mrs Giddens will walk through the door of his ward at any moment.'

Colbeck was impressed. 'You're a shrewd detective, Mr Follis,' he said. 'I wish I had your intuition.'

'It's something one develops,' explained Follis. 'If you'd sat by as many sad deathbeds as I have, and settled as many bitter marital disputes, and listened to as many tearful confessions of wickedness and folly, you'd become acutely sensitive to human behaviour. As it was, Giddens gave himself away at the start. When I first spoke to him in hospital, he wanted to know if Daisy Perriam had survived the crash. He was far less interested in the fate of Giles Thornhill and the others in our carriage.'

'I wish that I'd talked to you earlier.'

'Why – are you going to offer me a job at Scotland Yard?'

'No,' said Colbeck, tickled by the suggestion. 'By inclination and training, you're clearly far more suited to the

Church – though I'm bound to observe that there are very few clergymen who'd share your tolerant view of people's peccadilloes. Any other gentleman of the cloth would be scandalised by the relationship you discerned between Mr Giddens and Miss Perriam.'

'God has punished them enough for their sins,' said Follis. 'I don't feel they deserve the additional penalty of my disapproval. Given their condition, they'll get nothing but sympathy from me.'

Colbeck could not imagine that view being expressed by any other churchman. It would certainly not be endorsed by Edward Tallis, a man of high ideals and a stern moral code. In his report to the superintendent, Colbeck would make no mention of the liaison between a respected, married banker and an attractive young woman. The more he got to know Ezra Follis, the more interesting and unusual the man became. Colbeck was about to ask a question when the rector read his mind.

'The honest answer is that there *have* been occasional moments of friction,' he said, blithely 'That's what you wanted to know, isn't it? You were wondering about my relationship with my bishop.'

Colbeck blinked. 'How did you know I was going to ask that?'

'It's what most people think when they hear some of my rather eccentric opinions. They marvel why I've not been rapped over the knuckles and forced to toe the line.'

'The Anglican church has many restraints.'

'And I willingly abide by most of them,' said Follis. 'But I reserve the right to conduct my ministry according to my own promptings. I'm more concerned about the response of my parishioners than the strictures of the bishop or the dean. As long as I can preach to a congregation, I'll continue to do so in my own way.' He took a sip of tea. 'Now, tell me, Inspector – what progress have you made?'

'We're still in the early stages of the investigation,' said Colbeck, 'but I have every confidence that we'll catch the person or persons responsible for the crash. It's only a question of time.'

'That's reassuring to hear.'

'We already have some suspects in mind.'

'It must be someone with a fierce hatred of trains.'

'You could well be right,' said Colbeck, unwilling to give any more information. 'Even after all this time, railways are still not universally accepted. Whoever caused that crash wanted to inflict serious damage on the LB&SCR. He knew how calamitous the consequences would be.'

'Journeys to London have been badly disrupted,' remarked Follis, 'and that's a nuisance to those of us who go there on a regular basis. Not that I'll be doing any travelling for a while,' he went on. 'I'll have to wait until I begin to look more human.'

Colbeck sampled the tea. 'This is excellent,' he said.

'Mrs Ashmore looks after me very well. Here in the rectory, I have everything a man could desire – peace, harmony, a selection of fine books and the loving care of a woman.' He set his cup and saucer down. 'In view of your well-deserved reputation, Inspector, I've every reason to accept your judgement but I have to point out that your view is not shared by everyone. All of the passengers still believe they were victims of an unfortunate accident.'

'Until we catch the perpetrator, I'm happy for them to think that. There's no need to spread alarm, especially when the survivors are hardly in the best condition to cope with it. No,' said Colbeck, 'the official view remains that of the inspector general.'

'He puts the blame on the driver of the Brighton Express.'

'That's both wrong and unjust.'

'Is he aware that you hold a very different opinion?'

'Oh, yes,' replied Colbeck. 'Captain Ridgeon and I have already clashed once. I daresay that we shall do so again before long.'

Captain Harvey Ridgeon was in a purposeful mood when he called at Scotland Yard that afternoon. Demanding to speak to the most senior detective on the premises, he was shown into the office of Edward Tallis. After attending church early that morning, the superintendent had spent the rest of the day going through reports of the various cases that came under his aegis and making copious notes of the instructions he intended to give to his respective officers. He could see at a glance that his visitor had come to complain.

Once introductions had been made, Ridgeon was offered a seat. As former soldiers, they had similar attitudes, similar upright sitting positions and similar ways of speaking. What distinguished Tallis was that he no longer attached his military rank to his name, preferring the nomenclature conferred on him by the Detective Department.

'What can I do for you, Captain Ridgeon?' he asked.

'I'd like you to remonstrate with Inspector Colbeck,' said the other, coolly. 'I find his interference both unhelpful and annoying.'

'Then your argument is with the railway company itself. It was they who sought his assistance.'

'I need no assistance, Superintendent. As my record shows, I'm perfectly capable of carrying out an inquiry into a railway accident.'

'Nobody disputes that. The point at issue here, however, is that we are not dealing with an accident. Inspector Colbeck is certain that a heinous crime has been committed.'

'The facts are open to that misinterpretation, I agree,' said Ridgeon. 'What surprises me is that the much-vaunted Railway Detective has misread them so wilfully.'

'His report seemed convincing enough to me.'

'The real fault lies with the driver, Superintendent.'

'What about the bolts that were found in the bushes?'

'They could easily have sprung clear when the locomotive first left the rails. Think of the force involved – the train demolished the whole track as it careered along.'

'How do you explain the pickaxe found by Sergeant Leeming?'

'That was the surest proof of your officers' inexperience,' said Ridgeon. 'Both of them leapt to the same conclusion. Had they been as acquainted with the laziness of certain railwaymen as I am, they would have known that some of them conceal their tools under the bushes to save them the trouble of having to carry them to and fro.'

'But no work had been done recently on that stretch of line,' said Tallis, recalling the detail in Colbeck's report.

'Then the pickaxe was left there at an earlier stage and forgotten by the man who put it there. Or perhaps he's no longer working for the company. There's nothing sinister in that pickaxe. It's not the first implement I've found concealed near the line.'

Tallis was irritated by the mingled authority and

complacence in his voice. Unlike the superintendent, Ridgeon was not given to bluster and browbeating. He opted for a calm yet incisive approach. There was no doubting the man's credentials. Only someone of exceptional talent would have been appointed to head the railway inspectorate. For the first time, Tallis began seriously to wonder if Colbeck had made a mistake in his assessment of the crash. His instinct, however, was to support his officers steadfastly so his expression betrayed no hint of this worrying thought. He stroked his moustache meditatively.

'Well?' asked Ridgeon after a long pause.

Tallis gave a shrug. 'Well what, Captain?'

'I'm waiting for a response.'

'I put my faith in Inspector Colbeck.'

'Does that mean you're not going to reprimand him?'

'Not without good reason,' said Tallis.

'But I've just given you that good reason,' said Ridgeon. 'The inspector has contradicted my findings and reached an alternative conclusion that is both mistaken and dangerous.'

'Dangerous?'

'If the newspapers hear that a crime is suspected, they will seize on the notion and give it wide publicity. Imagine how upsetting that will be for the survivors of the crash, not to mention the LB&SCR itself. Inspector Colbeck will have caused a lot of unwarranted panic.'

'The truth is bound to come out sooner or later.'

'We already know the truth. The driver of the Brighton Express was to blame. It's the only explanation,' said Ridgeon. 'If the inspector had taken the trouble to speak to the fireman on the express, he would have discovered that there was no obstruction on the track.'

'As it happens,' said Tallis, quick to score a debating point, 'the Inspector *did* interview John Heddle. While the fireman confirmed that he saw nothing obstructing the track, he was adamant that the train had not been going at an excessive speed. Driver Pike was apparently known for his caution.'

'Even the best horse stumbles, Superintendent.'

'This was rather more than a stumble.'

'Let's not mince words here,' said Ridgeon with a touch of impatience. 'The situation is this – as long as Inspector Colbeck is looking over my shoulder, I'm unable to do my job properly. I want you to give him a formal reprimand and take him off this case.'

'Then you'll be disappointed, Captain Ridgeon, because I intend to do neither. Colbeck is a remarkable detective with a habit of knowing exactly which stones to look under.'

'He's in the way, Superintendent.'

'I believe he takes a similar view of you.'

'Damn it all, man!' protested Ridgeon, raising his voice at last. 'I'm the inspector general with a legitimate right to investigate this accident. It's not a police matter. Inspector Colbeck is trespassing on my territory and I take exception to it.'

'Your complaint is noted,' said Tallis, brusquely.

'Does that mean you'll take no action?'

'None is necessary at this stage.'

'Of course it is,' said Ridgeon, rising to his feet. 'One of your officers is making it impossible for me to do my job properly. He's making wrong assumptions on inadequate evidence and must be moved immediately out of my way. I'm not used to being disobeyed, Superintendent,' he added, pulling himself to his full height. 'I'll have you know that I was a captain in the Royal Engineers.'

'I have every respect for an army man,' said Tallis, getting up behind his desk and straightening his back. 'I was a major in the 6th Dragoon Guards.' He bestowed a glacial smile on his visitor. 'Was there anything else, Captain Ridgeon?'

Before he left Brighton, Colbeck paid another visit to the county hospital. Another of the survivors of the crash had died from his injuries, reinforcing Colbeck's determination to solve the crime. Entering one ward, he saw Terence Giddens being interrogated by a woman whose age, dress and manner identified her as his wife. Mixing sympathy with suspicion, she was asking her husband what he had been doing on a train to Brighton in the first place. Ezra Follis's assessment of Giddens as an adulterer had been correct. A collision between two trains had precipitated a marital crisis.

The journey back to London gave Colbeck time to reflect on his visit to the town. Giles Thornhill had presented a strong argument for being the real target of the train crash but Colbeck was reluctant to forget about Horace Bardwell. He felt that Bardwell's association with the railway company was a telling factor. What pleased him most was his decision to call on Ezra Follis. He had learnt a lot about Thornhill from the outspoken rector and now understood why the politician was so unpopular in certain quarters. He wondered how Follis would have reacted if he had read the fake obituary sent to the Member of Parliament. Though he had disliked the man intensely, Colbeck felt sorry for his plight. Thornhill was definitely being stalked.

Regardless of the fact that it was now evening, he knew that

Tallis would be waiting for him to report to Scotland Yard. Instead of going straight there when he reached London, however, he first took a cab to Camden to pay a more enjoyable visit. Madeleine Andrews was thrilled to see him. They embraced warmly on the doorstep and kissed once they were inside the house. Over her shoulder, Colbeck noticed the easel, standing by the window to catch the best of the light.

'What are you working on?' he asked, crossing to look.

'Oh, it's the turntable at the Round House.'

'Father took me there last week.'

'There's so much drama in the way you've drawn it.'

'I found it a very dramatic place.'

He studied the picture admiringly. 'You've got a wonderful eye for detail, Madeleine.'

'I know,' she said, subjecting him to careful scrutiny. 'I always choose subjects I like.' They shared a laugh and he hugged her again. The sound of the back door opening made them move guiltily apart. 'I'd forgotten that Father was here,' she whispered. 'He's been out in the garden.'

Caleb Andrews came in from the kitchen in his shirtsleeves and stopped when he saw Colbeck. 'Just the man I want to see, Inspector,' he said. 'I discovered that there is truth in the rumour.'

'And what rumour might that be, Mr Andrews?' asked Colbeck.

'Someone caused that accident on the Brighton line.'

'Who told you that?'

'You did,' replied Andrews. 'That's to say, you told John Heddle and he passed it on to me when I called on him today. It's a fact, isn't it? I mean, you won't deny it, will you?'

'No,' admitted Colbeck. 'It's a fact.'

'It beggars belief that anyone could be so evil,' said Madeleine. 'What is Rose Pike going to say when she learns the hideous truth?'

'How is Mrs Pike?'

'She's still in a daze, Robert. We both spent time with her today but there was little that we could do. She and Frank were so happy together. All that happiness has suddenly been snatched away from here and it's been a shattering blow.'

'Don't add to her pain by telling her that the crash was not an accident,' said Colbeck. 'The time for her to learn the truth is when we've caught the man behind the disaster. The same goes for you, Mr Andrews,' he went on, turning to him. 'I'd be grateful if you didn't spread the word about our investigation until it's been completed.'

Andrews was puzzled. 'Why not?'

'Do as Robert advises,' said his daughter.

'But I don't understand why, Maddy.'

'Apart from anything else,' said Colbeck, 'if it becomes common knowledge, it will alert the man we're after. At the moment, he has no idea that we're on his tail. I want to keep it that way.'

'Very well, Inspector – if you say so.'

'Thank you, Mr Andrews. I'd be very grateful. And I also need to thank you, Madeleine,' he said, smiling at her. 'That note you sent me contained a valuable piece of information. Frank Pike actually saw someone carrying out what looked like a reconnaissance of the line.'

'I can vouch for that,' said Andrews, seizing his cue. 'I got all the details from John Heddle. I know you spoke to him, Inspector, but you questioned him as a detective. I talked to him as another railwayman. I wanted to know the speed of the train immediately before the crash, the way the engine was performing and how well Frank was driving it.'

'Did he remember the man with the telescope?'

'He remembered more than that. He and Frank were on stopping trains both times so they were going slower than the express. The first time they saw the man,' recalled Andrews, 'they didn't pay much attention. When they saw him a second time, it was different.

'Why was that?' asked Colbeck.

'The man with the telescope wasn't alone, Inspector.'

'Is he sure about that?'

'Heddle was a cheeky lad when he worked for the LNWR as a cleaner but he had a sharp eye. He reckons that the man with the telescope was well-dressed while the other man wore rough clothing.'

'Does Heddle remember exactly where this was?'

'More or less,' said Andrews, relishing the chance to pass on what he believed was significant evidence. 'He claims it was close to the place where the express came off the track on Friday. The man with the telescope was pointing at the line as if he was giving orders to the other man. Is that any help to you, Inspector?'

'It is, indeed,' said Colbeck. 'Thank you.'

'There you are – I've told you before. When it comes to a crime on the railways, the person to turn to is Caleb Andrews. I'll help all I can and there's only one thing I ask in return.'

'What's that, Mr Andrews?'

'When you catch the men who murdered Frank Pike,' said the other, letting his fury show, 'hand the pair of them over to me!'

CHAPTER EIGHT

Facing the superintendent on his own when he had little progress to report was something that Victor Leeming chose to evade, preferring to have Robert Colbeck at his side during the ordeal. Instead of going straight to Scotland Yard that evening, therefore, he lurked in the Lamb and Flag, the public house nearby, and enjoyed a pint of beer while standing at the window. He had almost finished his drink when he saw Colbeck arrive by cab. Downing the last mouthful in one gulp, he put the tankard aside and rushed out. Colbeck saw him coming and waited at the door.

'Good evening, Victor,' he said, understanding very well where the sergeant had been. 'I'm glad that we have a chance to compare notes before we see Mr Tallis. Did you have any luck?'

'None at all,' replied Leeming. 'Except that I managed to dodge the urchins in Seven Dials who thought it would be a joke to knock off my top hat.'

'Let's go inside.'

In the privacy of Colbeck's office, they exchanged details of how each had spent the day. Leeming was envious. Colbeck appeared to have gathered useful evidence whereas the sergeant's efforts had been more or less futile. Apart from being hounded by ragamuffins in the rookeries, he had had to endure an indecent proposal from the daunting Josie Murlow.

'I went to all four of Chiffney's favourite taverns,' he said, morosely, 'but there was no sign of him.'

'Was he well-known to the landlords?'

'Oh, yes – they all had Dick Chiffney stories to tell. Most were about fights he'd started or times when he drank himself into oblivion and had to be carried home. He and Josie Murlow have a reputation.'

'She sounds like a potent lady,' said Colbeck.

'Overwhelming is the word I'd use, sir.'

Having discussed their respective reports, they went down the corridor to the superintendent's office. From the other side of the door, they heard the raised voice of Edward Tallis as he berated one of his officers for failure to solve a crime. A minute later, the man came out, shooting a baleful glance at Colbeck and Leeming as he did so. Tallis, apparently, was even more hot-tempered than usual. After tapping on the door, Colbeck led the way in.

'Is this a convenient time to speak, sir?' he enquired, politely.

'I expected you hours ago,' growled Tallis.

'Victor and I were unavoidably delayed.'

'Well, I hope you have more to show for your efforts than Sergeant Nelson. I've just threatened him with demotion if he doesn't improve markedly.' He pointed to the chairs and they sat down. 'I hope I don't have to issue the same threat to you.' Leeming squirmed but Colbeck responded with a confident smile. 'Let's hear from you first, Inspector.'

Colbeck was succinct. He talked about his visit to Brighton, recounting his conversations with Giles Thornhill, Ezra Follis and some of the survivors at the hospital. He omitted any reference to the Royal Pavilion. Without divulging the name of Caleb Andrews, he said that he had information from Fireman Heddle that two people had been seen watching trains go by near the spot where the crash later occurred. Colbeck felt that the use of the telescope was significant.

'If they were simply looking at trains,' he argued, 'they did not need it at all. The telescope was used to check up and down the line to make sure that there would be no witnesses if anyone levered part of the rail away. They chose that specific place with care. There are no farmhouses or cottages nearby.'

Throughout the report, Tallis made no comment. He sat there in silence, smouldering quietly like a cigar in an ashtray. When Colbeck had finished, the superintendent blazed into life.

'Why did you waste time talking to the Rector of St Dunstan's?' he said, acidly. 'The fellow is no help to us at all.'

'I believe that he was, sir,' argued Colbeck. 'Mr Follis is an excellent judge of character. More to the point, he survived the train crash and was able to describe exactly how the collision felt.'

'That has no relevance to the pursuit of the malefactor.'

'Malefactors,' corrected Leeming. 'There were two of them, sir.'

'Be quiet, man!'

'According to Fireman Heddle...'

'Don't you recognise an order when you hear one?'

demanded Tallis, interrupting him. 'The sight of two men looking at trains on the Brighton line is not, in my view, conclusive evidence that they are anything to do with the disaster. For all we know, they may even have been railway employees, surveying the line.'

'With respect, sir,' said Colbeck, 'John Heddle has seen enough surveyors in his time to be able to identify one. He thought their presence was odd. Driver Pike felt the same because he told his wife that someone had been watching the trains.'

'Come to the crux of your evidence, Inspector. Are you still firmly of the belief that the accident was caused to kill a particular individual on board?'

'I am, superintendent.'

'Then the choice would seem to be between Horace Bardwell and Giles Thornhill. Which one would you select?'

'Mr Bardwell.'

'Yet it's Mr Thornhill who has been receiving death threats.'

'They could relate to his political activities,' said Colbeck. 'He's supported many unpopular causes in Parliament and is leading the fight for a Sunday Trading Bill. It would mean the closure of all shops and public houses on the Sabbath.'

'That would be cruel!' protested Leeming.

'It's eminently sensible and long overdue,' said Tallis.

'But if people work hard for six days a week, sir, surely they're entitled to the pleasure of a drink on Sunday.'

'Strong drink leads to drunkenness and that, in turn, leads to crime. It would greatly relieve the pressure on our police if there was one day when they did not have to deal with violent affrays in public houses or people in the streets being drunk and disorderly. But there's an even stronger reason why the

Sunday Trading Bill should be passed,' continued Tallis, sounding a reverential note. 'It shows respect for the Lord's Day and for people's spiritual needs.'

'I still think it will cause a great deal trouble if it's ever put forward,' said Leeming. 'It might even lead to a riot.'

'The point is,' observed Colbeck, rescuing the sergeant from Tallis's stony glare, 'that the Bill is highly controversial. It will stir up a lot of opposition, as other legislation sponsored by Mr Thornhill has done. I fancy that he's being menaced by a political enemy. Mr Bardwell, on the other hand, embodies the LB&SCR in several ways. That's a salient point in my opinion. As far as I know, Mr Thornhill has no connection with the railway company.'

'Then you are not as well-informed as you should be,' said Tallis, savouring the opportunity to embarrass Colbeck for once. 'While you and the sergeant went gallivanting off today, I did not sit idly here. I took it upon myself to call on the London office of the LB&SCR and I made an interesting discovery.'

'What was that, sir?' asked Colbeck.

'Searching through the list of their major shareholders, I came across the name of Giles Thornhill. He has a large financial stake in the company. You should have found that out, Inspector.'

'I agree, sir, and I'm grateful that you did so on my behalf.'

'It tips the balance of probability in favour of Mr Thornhill. If, that is,' added Tallis with beetle-browed scepticism, 'your theory about the crime is correct.'

'Do you have an alternative theory, Superintendent?'

'No, but Captain Ridgeon certainly does. He called here today.'

'I daresay that he wanted to complain about me,' said Colbeck.

'You upset him, Inspector, and I fear that I upset him even more by supporting you to the hilt.' He leant forward across his desk. 'I hope you won't make me regret that support.'

'We won't, sir. Victor and I owe you our thanks.'

'Yes, sir,' agreed Leeming, picking up his cue. 'We need you to back us. Captain Ridgeon didn't like what we were doing.'

'I'm not sure that I do,' said Tallis, twitching his moustache. 'You may have identified the intended target of the crash but are no nearer finding those who seem to have engineered it.' His gaze fell on Leeming. 'What new information have *you* garnered today, Sergeant?'

Leeming cleared his throat before launching into his report. It was short, apologetic and delivered with breathless speed. Tallis reacted with a mixture of sarcasm and outrage.

'What have you been *doing* all day?' he asked. 'Twelve hours of detective work have yielded precisely nothing. If the Sunday Trading Bill had become law this year, at least you'd have been spared the chore of running pointlessly from one public house to another.'

'I think you're being unfair in Victor,' said Colbeck. 'Because he was a plate-layer, Dick Chiffney has to be a major suspect.'

'Then *find* the man, Inspector.'

'We will, sir.'

'And track down his accomplice – if such a person exists.'

'I'm certain that he does,' said Colbeck. 'From everything that Victor learnt about Chiffney, it seems clear that he'd never be capable of planning and carrying out the work on his own. Someone far more calculating has been giving the orders.'

'It could be Matthew Shanklin,' suggested Leeming.

'I don't want to know who it *could* be,' said Tallis, scornfully. 'Tell me who it actually *is* and produce the evidence to prove it.'

'We'll start by locating Dick Chiffney,' decided Colbeck.

'That won't be easy, Inspector,' warned Leeming. 'If the woman he lives with can't find him, what chance have we got?'

'We'll catch him, Victor.'

'Then we need to do so before Josie Murlow gets hold of him, sir, or there'll be nothing left of Chiffney to question.'

Josie Murlow was dozing in a chair when she heard the noise. It brought her awake instantly. When a second stone hit the window of the living room, she struggled up, ready for combat, flinging open the front door and peering into the half-dark. Through the gloom, she could pick out a familiar shape.

'Is that you, Dick Chiffney?' she challenged. 'Don't think you can come back here with your snivelling excuses.'

'I've brought no excuses, my love,' said Chiffney, taking a few tentative steps forward. 'But I've brought a flagon of gin.'

Her manner softened. 'Where have you been, you devil?'

'I'll explain that later, Josie.'

'You left me high and dry.'

'I was sworn to secrecy, my love. I was working for a gentleman and he paid me well.' He came closer, allowing her to see that he was wearing a new suit. 'Do you like the look of this?'

'How could you afford that?'

'I can afford a lot more, Josie, and you'll share in my good luck.' He gave a sly smile. 'If you want to, that is.'

Chiffney was only yards away now. He was a hulking man with broad shoulders and massive fists. A broken nose and a squint turned an ugly, misshapen face into a grotesque one. He had even fewer teeth than she did. Josie took time to make her decision, remembering the lonely nights without him and aching to take revenge. At the same time, she was a practical woman. A man with money in his pocket was always welcome and – whatever his reasons for leaving – Chiffney had come back to her at last. She spat on the ground before speaking.

'What kind of gin is it?' she asked.

'The very best, my love,' he said.

'And is it paid for?'

'Everything is paid for, including the present I brought you.'

She was tempted. 'You've got a present for me?'

'I couldn't come back empty-handed now, could I?' he said with a leer. 'As soon as I saw it in the shop, I thought of you.'

'What is it?'

'Invite me in and I'll show you.'

She folded her arms. 'I swore that you'd never cross this threshold again.' Chiffney lowered his head in disappointment then turned to walk away. 'But since you're here,' she added, quickly, 'you may as well come in.'

Chiffney rallied, turned around and rushed to embrace her. As they went into the house, Chiffney kicked the door shut behind them then muffled the questions she hurled at him with passionate kisses. When he broke away from her, he felt in a pocket and whisked out a string of garnets on a gold chain. The necklace sparkled in the light from the candles. Josie was thrilled with the gift. Nobody had ever bought her anything so expensive before. He helped her to put it on.

'It's wonderful, Dick,' she cried, looking in a mirror.

'So are you, my love.'

'Let's get some glasses,' he said, going into the kitchen.

Josie followed him. 'Who needs glasses?' she said, snatching the flagon from him and uncorking it to take a long swig. 'Did you miss me, Dick Chiffney?'

'Every second I was away.'

'Show me how much.'

Chiffney cackled with joy. After taking a swig of gin himself, he put the flagon aside, tore off his coat and reached for her. Big as she was, he lifted Josie up in his arms and carried her upstairs to the bedroom. Lowering her onto the bed, he flung himself on top of her and they kissed away their differences. Josie soon forgot about his apparent desertion of her and his inability to forewarn her of his movements. All that mattered now was that Chiffney had lots of money and an overwhelming desire for her. Josie laughed joyously. Her man was back.

Later on, as they had a supper of cheese and gin, Chiffney gave her a partial explanation of where he had been, unable to tell her the whole story or to name the man who had employed him.

'What I can tell is this, my love,' he confided, swallowing a hunk of cheese. 'There could be more money to come.'

'Could there?'

'I was paid for one job but there's another to be done now.'

'It's against the law, though, isn't it?' she guessed.

Chiffney sat back in his chair. 'Who cares?' he said airily. 'One day's work will bring in a lot more money and nobody will be any the wiser. It's against the law but it's safe.'

'No, it isn't,' she cautioned, remembering her visitor earlier that day. 'You'd better take care, Dick.'

'Why do you say that?'

'Because someone come looking for you,' she told him. 'It was a detective from Scotland Yard.'

He was jerked out of his complacency. 'Are you sure, Josie?'

'His name was Sergeant Leeming.'

'What did he want?'

'All he'd tell me was that he needed to speak to you. He said it was something to do with the railway.'

Chiffney got to his feet. 'That's impossible!' he exclaimed. 'How could he possibly know?'

'Know what?' she asked.

'Nothing, my love,' he said, reaching for his coat. 'I've got to get out of here. Don't worry,' he went on as she tried to stop him. 'I'll send word where I am when I've found somewhere to hide. But I can't be caught here when there's such a big pay day to come. If I get that money,' he promised, pausing to take a guzzling kiss, 'then the two of us can afford to get out of this place.'

'Why are the police after you, Dick?'

But she was talking to thin air. Chiffney had already fled through the back door and left it wide open. Josie closed it and leant against it as she mused on how fleeting happiness could be. Then she felt the necklace around her fleshy neck and noticed the flagon of gin still standing on the table. There were compensations.

When his unexpected visitor called, Captain Harvey Ridgeon was studying reports in the office loaned to him by the railway company. He rose to his feet and offered Colbeck a subdued welcome.

'I should have thought you'd be out looking for ruthless

villains, Inspector,' he said with a slight edge.

'I wanted to speak to you first, sir.'

'What use can I be? I don't believe that the people who caused that accident even exist. They're phantoms of your imagination.'

'We must agree to differ on that,' said Colbeck, pleasantly. 'It seems to me that, though we take opposing views, we are both striving for the same result – namely, to find out what caused that disaster.'

'You know my view, Inspector Colbeck.'

'Given your position, I respect it. I have the feeling that you might respect my position a little more if you were aware of the evidence on which it's based.'

'I doubt that.'

'At all events,' said Colbeck, mildly, 'I felt that you had the right to know how our investigation was proceeding even though you did your best to bring it to a completely halt yesterday.'

'There's not room for two us in the inquiry,' asserted Ridgeon.

'I believe that there is, Captain. What's more, we have a greater chance of learning the full truth if we pool our resources, so to speak. Yes,' he said before Ridgeon could interrupt, 'I know that you feel a police investigation is an irritating irrelevance but I hope to convince you to think again. I've come here in the spirit of cooperation. Is it too much to ask for a small amount of your time?'

'Superintendent Tallis showed no spirit of cooperation.'

Colbeck smiled. 'He and I have somewhat different approaches to these situations, sir. I trust that you'll find mine less abrasive.'

Ridgeon studied him warily for a moment then relaxed slightly. 'I'm sure that I will, Inspector,' he said. 'Why don't we both sit down then you can say your piece?' As they each took a seat, Ridgeon pulled a face. 'I must say, that I don't envy you one bit, working under the superintendent.'

'Mr Tallis is a fine detective,' replied Colbeck, loyally, 'and it needs someone with his experience of command to keep the rest of us in order. You must have realised that he was an army man.'

'Oh, he made that abundantly clear.'

Ridgeon gave a first smile as he remembered the confrontation with Tallis at Scotland Yard. Though he had left feeling disappointed, he admired the superintendent for standing unequivocally by his officers in the teeth of a protest about their behaviour. For his part, Colbeck sensed an easing of the tension between the two of them. In meeting the man, he was acting on his own initiative and had seen no need to forewarn Tallis of his plan for fear that it might be overruled. As an enemy, Ridgeon would be a continuing nuisance. As an ally, Colbeck reasoned, he might prove extremely useful.

'Well, Inspector,' invited Ridgeon with a gesture, 'why don't you present your case?'

It was something in which Colbeck was well-versed. Before joining the Metropolitan Police, he had been a barrister and had presented a case in court on numerous occasions. He knew how to marshal his facts to the best advantage. Eschewing the histrionics he used before a jury, he spoke directly and persuasively as he reviewed the evidence that had so far been gathered. Ridgeon was an attentive listener who blinked in surprise more than once. He was not, however, entirely won over by the argument.

'It's an ingenious theory,' he admitted, 'but it owes more to the liveliness of your imagination than to the known facts. Whenever an accident occurs on the railway, one of the first things I look for is human intervention. There were, I grant you, signs of it in this case but not enough of them to be convincing. As for the notion that the object of the crash was to kill a single individual on the express, I find that too ludicrous to accept.'

'Look at how carefully chosen the scene of the crash was,' said Colbeck. 'A great deal of thought went into it.'

'I disagree, Inspector. Far more damage could have been caused had the collision taken place on the Ouse Bridge or in the Mertsham Tunnel – and, I would suggest, more people might have been killed as a result. As it was,' he continued, 'the death toll was mercifully low. In similar crashes, dozens of passengers have perished.'

'The intention was to have one man among the victims.'

'Yet there was no guarantee that he would be killed.'

'There was every chance that he might be,' said Colbeck. 'Horace Bardwell was in the carriage immediately behind the locomotive, the one that would suffer the full force of the impact.'

'What about your other potential target?' asked Ridgeon.

'Giles Thornhill was in the next carriage, again near the front of the train. Like Mr Bardwell, he always travelled first class.'

'So do lots of other people, Inspector.'

'Most of them don't have dangerous enemies.'

'I see no criminal intent behind this accident.'

'Then we'll have to convince you otherwise, Captain.'

'I defy you to do so.'

Colbeck took up the challenge. 'It's only a matter of time before we banish all your doubts,' he said. 'If we do, how will you respond?'

'By being honest enough to concede that I was mistaken,' said Ridgeon. 'I'll also shake your hand in apology. Somehow,' he added with a thin smile, 'I don't think an apology will be necessary. You talk of two men watching trains go by – a harmless event in itself – as if it's proof of conspiracy to derail a train. Yet you have absolutely no idea who those men were.'

'That's not true, sir,' said Colbeck. 'As a matter of fact, Sergeant Leeming could well be talking to one of them at this moment.'

Matthew Shanklin was not at work that morning. Hearing that the man had sent a note to say that he was ill, Victor Leeming asked for his address and went to visit him. The house was an Italianate villa in St John's Wood, indicative of the high salary Shanklin had once commanded as a manager with the LB&SCR. Admitted by a maid, Leeming was surprised to find Shanklin fully dressed and seated in his drawing room with a newspaper.

'I was told that you were unwell, sir,' said Leeming.

'I suffer from migraines, Inspector,' explained Shanklin, putting a hand to his head. 'First thing this morning, I was in agony.'

'I'm glad to see that you've made something of a recovery.'

Invited to sit down, Leeming lowered himself on to a settee but he refused the offer of refreshment. After his encounter with Josie Murlow on a doorstep, he found it reassuring to be able to conduct an interview with a civilised man in such pleasant surroundings. He had to remind himself that Shanklin was a suspect.

'This won't take long, sir,' he began, taking out his notebook. 'I just wanted to hear a little more about your relationship with Mr Bardwell.'

'It came to an abrupt end,' said Shanklin, sullenly.

'Since you were part of the management, you must have seen a lot of each other at one time. What sort of man was he?'

'He was self-important and dictatorial.'

'Yes,' said Leeming as the face of Edward Tallis was conjured up before his eyes, 'it can be difficult working for someone like that.'

'Our job was to run the company efficiently. Mr Bardwell's job was to ensure that we had sufficient funds to do so and that we showed a healthy profit. There was no call for him to interfere in what we were doing.'

'Why do you think he did so?'

'It was partly force of habit, I suppose,' said Shanklin. 'He likes to exercise complete control. But the main reason was a financial one. He was always urging us to find ways to cut costs and increase our income. Needless to say, as the managing director, he always got the largest dividend each year.'

'So there was a long history of strife between the two of you?'

'You could put it that way.'

'Hostility built over a period of time.'

'Listen,' said Shanklin, irritably, 'I've already told you that I disliked him. I've given you my reasons for doing so. What more do you want me to say?'

'What interested me was Mr Bardwell's reaction to your name, sir. When my colleague, Inspector Colbeck, visited him in hospital, he found Mr Bardwell in a serious condition.'

'I hope you're not asking for sympathy from me.'

'In fact, he was so bad that it was impossible to talk to him. Mr Bardwell's mind kept wandering. Until, that is,' said Leeming, 'your name was mentioned. It caused him to go into convulsions.'

'I'm pleased to hear it,' said Shanklin with a grim smile.

'Why should he respond like that, sir?'

'I found him out for the scheming fraud that he was.'

'Was that the only reason?'

'You'll have to ask Mr Bardwell.'

'Until he recovers his senses,' said Leeming, sadly, 'that's rather difficult. I can see that you gave him a fright by uncovering his attempt to defraud investors but that scare was long behind him. I wondered if there was a more personal reason why he reacted so violently.'

'It was pure guilt, Sergeant – no more, no less.'

'Yet you gave me the impression that Mr Bardwell was an unscrupulous man with no conscience whatsoever. If he felt guilty over what he had tried to do, he would surely have resigned from the board altogether.'

'Horace Bardwell should be in prison for what he did.'

'Was there some other crime in addition to the fraud?'

Shanklin composed himself before speaking. 'Yes, Sergeant,' he said. 'He was making wrong decisions about the running of the company and bullying the rest of the board into accepting them. We had to implement those decisions even though we knew that they were detrimental to the LB&SCR.'

'Such decisions were not exactly criminal, sir.'

'They were to me.'

Leeming wrote something in his notebook then changed his tack. He watched Shanklin closely as he fired a question at him.

'Have you ever met a man named Dick Chiffney, sir?'

'I don't believe that I have, Sergeant.'

The reply was too quick and defensive for Leeming and it was accompanied by a shifty look in Shanklin's eye. Realising that he had aroused suspicion, he tried to negate it at once.

'I *may* have met someone of that name,' he confessed, 'especially if the man worked for the LB&SCR. The names of hundreds of our employees used to pass before my eyes and I met several of them in person, far too many to remember individually. Well,' he said with a feeble attempt at jocularity, 'can you recall the names of everyone you've arrested?'

'As a matter of fact, I can,' attested Leeming.

'Then you have a better memory than I, Sergeant.'

'I need it where villains are concerned.' The pencil was poised over the notebook again. 'Let's go back to Horace Bardwell, shall we?'

Horace Bardwell had slowly improved, gathering strength, sleeping less and finally managing to get a grasp of what had happened. By the time that Ezra Follis got to him that morning, Bardwell was sitting up in bed and looking more alert. A large number of cards and letters lay on his bedside table, most of them unopened. After asking his health, Follis volunteered to open his mail for him.

'I'd be most grateful,' croaked Bardwell. 'I still can't see. My wife read some of them to me but I can only concentrate for a little while. So many friends have sent their best wishes.'

'They have, indeed,' said Follis.

'Read very slowly, if you please.'

'I will, Mr Bardwell. The moment you tire, tell me to stop.'

Follis took a card from the first envelope and read the message inside. Bardwell was touched. Next came a short letter from his nephew, sending him love and praying for his speedy recovery. Other letters were from friends or business associates, all expressing sorrow at his injuries and hope that he would soon be fully fit again. Follis then extracted a black-edged card from an envelope. Startled by the message inside, he elected not to read it out.

'What does it say?' asked Bardwell.

'Nothing at all,' replied Follis.' Someone was so keen to send you his best wishes that, in his haste, he forgot to write anything. Now this one is very different,' he went on, unfolding three pages from the next envelope he opened. 'We have a veritable novel, here.'

Bardwell did not get to hear it. Halfway through the recitation, he fell gently asleep. Follis slipped the letter back into its envelope and replaced it on the table but he made sure that he took the funeral card with him. After speaking to all the other patients in the ward, he went back out into the corridor. The first person he saw was Amy Walcott, carrying a large basket filled with posies of flowers. Her face lit up when she recognised him.

'I came here because of that sermon you gave yesterday,' she said. 'When you told us about the survivors of the crash, I had to do something to ease their suffering.'

'So you brought some flowers for the ladies,' he noted. 'That was very kind of you, Amy. You have such a sweet disposition.'

'Some of the injuries I've seen are frightening.'

'Not everyone was as fortunate as I, alas.'

'I thank God that you were not badly hurt,' said Amy. 'I couldn't bear it if you'd been seriously wounded like some of the other victims. As it is, those bandages of yours distress me. You must be in such pain, Mr Follis.'

'It's nothing that I can't happily endure.'

'Oh, by the way,' she went on, brightening, 'I've had so much pleasure from that book you gave me.'

'Tennyson is a magical poet.'

'I've read some of the poems time and time again.'

'Good,' he said, beaming at her. 'I'm glad you appreciated them, Amy. You must read them to me some time.'

'I'd love that, Mr Follis.'

'Then it must be very soon.'

Amy bade him farewell and went off to visit another of the female wards. After watching her go, Follis took out the funeral card sent to Horace Bardwell. He looked at the message once more and gave a shiver.

CHAPTER NINE

In view of Victor Leeming's experience with her, Colbeck did not feel he could ask his sergeant to pay a second visit to Josie Murlow. It would not have been a tempting assignment for him. Showing his habitual compassion, Colbeck therefore took on the task himself, travelling to Chalk Farm by cab and alighting outside the little hovel. When he knocked on the door, there was no reply. After waiting a couple of minutes, he used a fist to pound on the timber. Still there was no response. Colbeck was on the point of leaving when a window creaked open above his head and an angry female face appeared.

'Who the hell is that?' she roared.

Colbeck looked up. 'Am I speaking to Josie Murlow?'

'Who wants to know?'

'My name is Detective Inspector Colbeck,' he told her. 'I believe that you spoke to a colleague of mine yesterday.'

She peered at him through bleary eyes. Having been roused from a drunken stupor, she needed time to understand what he had said. As the fog in her brain cleared a little, she recalled the visit of Sergeant Leeming. The memory made her grimace.

'I got nothing to say to you,' she told him.

'All I ask is a chance to speak to you briefly,' he said, removing his top hat so that she could see him properly. 'You're not in any trouble, I assure you. I just need to ask a few questions.'

'The other one did that. You'll get no more from me.'

His voice hardened. 'I'm making a polite request, Miss Murlow,' he warned. 'If you spurn it, I'll have to get a warrant to enter your premises and, if you refuse to speak to me then, I'll have no option but to place you under arrest.'

'I done nothing!' she clucked, indignantly.

'Then you have nothing to fear.'

Josie's eyes were fully open now and she was able to take a better look at the man on her doorstep. He was far more handsome than his predecessor from Scotland Yard and he had none of the other's diffidence. What worried her was his rank. Josie had had enough brushes with the law to know that someone who had risen to the level of an inspector would not bother with trivial offences. He was there in connection with a serious crime.

'Well,' he called up to her, 'are you going to let me in?'

The fact that he was willing to come into the house set him immediately apart from Leeming. She had unsettled the first detective. Josie could see that she would not have the same effect on the second one. After weighing up the possibilities, she capitulated.

'Wait there,' she said at length. 'I need to dress.'

Colbeck stood patiently outside the door. When it eventually opened, Josie was wearing a voluminous gown of pink satin, badly faded and speckled with food and other stains. Her feet were bare, her face flushed and her red hair was an unkempt torrent surging over one shoulder and disappearing down her cleavage like water gurgling between two giant boulders.

He could see why Leeming had found her overwhelming. At a glance, he was also able to make certain assumptions about Dick Chiffney. Only a hefty man with boundless energy and strength of character could partner such a forbidding creature for any length of time. Lids narrowed, Josie regarded him suspiciously.

'There's nothing I can tell you,' she said, stubbornly.

'May we talk inside, please?' asked Colbeck.

'What are you after?'

'I think you know that.'

'Dick is not here.'

'I'd still like to speak to you.'

After looking him up and down, she stood reluctantly aside and let him step into the house. The first thing he noticed was the stink, a compound of rancid food, household filth and the reek from the vast unwashed body of Josie Murlow. The room was small, cluttered and sparsely furnished. A tattered carpet lay over the flagstones. Colbeck had to duck under the cobweb-covered beam.

'Well, now,' she said, tossing her hair back over her shoulder to expose her new necklace, 'you *are* a fine gentleman and no mistake. Josie Murlow doesn't have many like you under her roof.'

'When did you last see Mr Chiffney?'

'I told the sergeant that – it was over a week ago.'

'Did he give any indication where he was going?'

'I'd have stopped the bastard if he had. Dick was my man.'

'Had he ever gone off before?' said Colbeck.

'He wouldn't have *dared* to,' she said, huffily, 'because he knew what would happen when I caught up with him.'

'Yet he had the courage to go this time. Why did he do that?'

She became defensive. 'Well, it wasn't because of anything I did or said, Inspector,' she insisted. 'I gave him everything a man wants. We lived here as close together as any man and wife – a lot closer, judging by some of the miserable faces on the men I see in this part of the city,' she went on, meaningfully. 'Their wives keep a cold bed. My bed is as warm as toast.'

'Did Mr Chiffney always work on the railway?'

'When he could get a job,' she replied. 'Dick worked for a lot of different railway companies over the years. He's good at what he does, Inspector, there's no two ways about that. But he hates taking orders and always has a row with someone or other. Dick is a bit too ready to use his fists. Mind you,' she stipulated, 'he was always provoked.'

'How long had he worked on the Brighton line?' said Colbeck.

'I think it was a year or more.'

'If he had such a record of violence, why did they employ him?'

'He knew someone who got him the job,' she explained. 'Dick liked the work so he was on his best behaviour. It was only when that foreman hit him that Dick lost his temper.'

'Has he tried to work on the railways since then?'

'Nobody would touch him now the word's got round about him looking for a fight. Listen,' she said, squaring up to him, 'why are you and that Sergeant Leeming so interested in Dick Chiffney? What's he supposed to have done?'

'He may have done nothing at all,' Colbeck assured her. 'We just need to eliminate him from our enquiries. That's why we're so anxious to speak to him – as I'm sure *you* are.'

'I'm very anxious, Inspector.'

She spoke with feeling but with none of the raging fury that Victor Leeming had reported. Colbeck wondered what had brought about the change in her manner. Josie Murlow had softened in a way that could not wholly be attributed to the effect of gin, the fumes of which he could still detect. He moved slightly so that he could look into the kitchen, noting the cheese left on the table along with two plates. Somebody else had been there recently.

'May I ask you a favour?' he said.

'You can ask anything you like, Inspector,' she replied, running both hands over the contours of her body, 'and it won't cost you a penny. I'd have charged the sergeant but he ran away. I've got a flagon of gin upstairs if that takes your fancy.'

'As it happens,' said Colbeck, meeting her bold gaze, 'I never touch it. You're obviously a woman of experience in these matters so I don't need to remind you of the penalty of offering blandishments to a member of the Metropolitan Police.'

She was defiant. 'They don't all refuse, I can tell you!'

'The favour I wish to ask is this. If and when Mr Chiffney does return, please advise him that it's in his best interests to get in touch with me at Scotland Yard. That way, his name can be cleared.'

'You still haven't told me what you think he's done.'

'It's a railway matter.'

'Has Dick been punching another foreman, then?

'No,' answered Colbeck, 'it's a little more serious than that.'

Dick Chiffney loaded the pistol again and took careful aim at the empty bottle standing on the tree stump. When he pulled the trigger, there was a loud report then the glass exploded into a thousand shards. Birds took wildly to the sky in an unrehearsed symphony of protest. Chiffney grinned at his success and set another bottle on the stump.

He was deep in the woods, far away from the nearest human habitation and therefore free from the possibility of any interruption. This time, he stood a few yards farther away from his target. Apart from his companion, his only witnesses were the birds. When he had loaded the weapon again, he took aim, peered along the barrel then fired. The bullet struck its target a glancing blow, detaching a small piece of glass and causing the bottle to spin crazily round before falling on to the ground. Chiffney was annoyed at his failure.

The man who had been watching him handed over a rifle.

'Try with this next time,' he ordered. 'You may not get close enough to use the pistol.'

Robert Colbeck arrived back at his office to find Victor Leeming waiting there for him. The sergeant described his second interview with Matthew Shanklin and added what he felt was a telling detail.

'As I was shown out of the house,' he said, 'I spoke to the maid.'

'Go on.'

'I asked her if Mr Shanklin had ever possessed a telescope and she told me that he did.'

'Good work, Victor,' said Colbeck. 'That was astute of you. I had a feeling that you'd unearth something interesting if you paid Shanklin a second visit. Did you believe his claim that he suffered from migraines?'

'No, sir,' replied Leeming. 'I think he simply wanted a day off. It's just as well that he isn't a detective. The superintendent doesn't believe in using sickness as an excuse. He'd have us on duty if we were suffering from double pneumonia.'

'In fairness to Mr Tallis, he applies the same rule to himself. Nothing short of complete paralysis would keep him away from here. What you learnt this morning,' Colbeck went on, 'could be very significant. There's patently a link between Shanklin and Chiffney.'

'They could be accomplices, sir.'

'It's something we must bear in mind.'

'Did you visit Chalk Farm?' asked Leeming, eagerly.

'Yes, Victor, I had a most diverting time.'

He gave a full account of his conversation with Josie Murlow. Leeming was astonished at his bravery in actually going into the hovel to question her. Colbeck made Josie sound like a different woman to the one who had unnerved him.

'Didn't she rant and rage, then?' he said.

'I think she's mellowed since you were there, Victor.'

'Mellow or not, sir, I'd rather steer clear of her.'

'Unfortunately, you won't be able to do that,' said Colbeck. 'I want you to keep a close watch on the lady.' Leeming spluttered. 'Have no fear – you won't have to meet her face to face, and you certainly won't go there dressed like that. You'll be in disguise, Victor.'

'I'll need a suit of armour to feel safe near that woman.'

'She was hiding something. When I mentioned Chiffney's name, she didn't curse and threaten as she did when you spoke to her. She was more concerned to find out why we were after him. Evidently, someone had been at the house recently,' said Colbeck. 'Two people had supper there and Josie Murlow was wearing a garnet necklace. Do you think she usually goes to bed with that on?'

'I'm not familiar with her sleeping habits, sir,' said Leeming with a tremor, 'and I've certainly no wish to be.'

'She's not the sort of person you'd expect to own an expensive piece of jewellery, and her clients are hardly likely to be able to afford such an item. So,' asked Colbeck, 'who do you think could have given her the necklace?'

'Dick Chiffney must have been back there.'

'That was my guess – the necklace was a peace offering.'

'Then why wasn't he still there this morning?'

'For one simple reason,' said Colbeck. 'She warned him that you'd been looking for him. He probably fled at once.'

'That *proves* he was involved in the crime.'

'All that it proves is that he's not willing to talk to us and there could be any number of reasons for that. We'll only find out the truth when we run him to ground. That's why I want you to keep Josie Murlow under surveillance. If Chiffney *was* there last night,' he said, 'it means that the two of them are reconciled. Since he won't go to her house again, they'll have to meet elsewhere. You'll follow her.'

'Well, it will be from a safe distance, Inspector.'

'You'll be dressed in rough clothing.'

'I'm not looking forward to this,' admitted Leeming, gritting his teeth 'but I know it has to be done. I'll get changed and make my way back to Chalk Farm.'

Before he could leave, however, there was a tap on the door and a constable entered with a letter that had just been delivered. Colbeck thanked him, sent him on his way then looked at the envelope.

'It's been sent by hand,' he observed, opening it to take out a letter. He unfolded it swiftly. 'It's from the Reverend Follis,' he said as he read the contents. 'He must have dictated it because he could never write with that injured hand of his.'

'What does he say, sir?'

'He's enclosed a card that was sent to Horace Bardwell.' Opening the envelope again, Colbeck fished out the black-edged funeral card. He read the words inside it with disgust. 'I can see why Mr Follis was so anxious for me to see this.'

'Why is that?'

'Look at the message, Victor.'

Taking the card, Leeming read it aloud. '*Please die soon and make me happy.*' He looked up. 'I'd hate to get something like that if I was lying in hospital. It must have been a real shock to Mr Bardwell.'

'Fortunately,' said Colbeck, 'he never read it. Mr Follis was able to keep it from him. It looks as if I shall have to go to Brighton yet again,' he decided. 'According to the letter, Mr Bardwell is able to sit up and talk now. I need to speak to him.'

Until she had met Colbeck, Madeleine Andrews had never imagined that she had anything more than a facility for drawing. Her sketches were merely a pleasant way of spending what little leisure time she had. As soon as Colbeck saw them, however, he discerned signs of a real artistic talent and urged her to develop it. Where other artists might favour portraits, landscapes or seascapes, Madeleine's preferred subject was the steam locomotive. If nothing else, it helped her to stand out from the main pack.

Over a period of a couple of years, she had refined her technique, extended her range and gained confidence. To discover that her work actually had a commercial value gave her an immense fillip. It was one of many reasons she had for being grateful to Robert Colbeck. Standing at her easel, she was so absorbed in her work on the Round House that she did not hear the cab pull up outside. It was only when Colbeck's face appeared at the window that she realised she had a visitor.

Breaking away excitedly from her work, she ran to open the door. Colbeck took her hands in his and kissed her.

'Am I interrupting you, Madeleine?' he asked.

'Yes – but it's a very welcome interruption. Are you coming in?'

'I'm rather hoping that you'd come out.'

'*Now?*' she said in amazement.

'Unless you have a dislike of Brighton,' he said. 'If you can give yourself a rest from your easel, I'll take you to the seaside. I'll explain why on the way.'

Waving aside her excuses about not being properly dressed, Colbeck went into the house and admired the painting while she was getting ready. Minutes later, they were climbing into the cab and heading for London Bridge station. Colbeck linked arms with her.

'This is the last thing I expected, Robert,' she said.

'I'm glad that I still have the capacity to surprise you.'

'Why do you need to go to Brighton?'

'It's the latest stage in our investigation, Madeleine. There are certain people I need to see.'

'Are they suspects?'

'Quite the reverse – both gentlemen were victims of the train crash. I have to question them.'

'Won't I be in the way?' she asked, worriedly.

'You could never be in the way,' he said, gallantly. 'Besides, while I'm busy with one the gentlemen, I'm hoping that you'll be having tea with the other one.'

Madeleine was puzzled. 'Who might that be?'

'The Rector of St Dunstan's.'

Since the accident, Ezra Follis had learnt to conserve his energy, balancing the need to appear alert in public by snatching regular periods of rest in private. His housekeeper had to do some shopping in the market that afternoon. The moment that Mrs Ashmore had left the house, Follis sat down in an armchair and drifted immediately off to sleep. It was over half an hour before he was roused from his slumbers by the insistent tinkle of the doorbell, though it seemed like a matter of minutes to him. Shaking himself fully awake, he opened the front door and saw Amy Walcott, standing there with a smile on her face and a book under her arm.

'I wondered if this was a good time to read to you,' she said.

'It's not the ideal time, Amy,' he said then he relented, 'but why don't you come in for a moment?'

He stood back to let her in then closed the door behind her. Clutching the book, Amy moved to the centre of the room. The sun slanted through the window to make her hair glisten and to lend her dull features an attractive sheen.

'I can't thank you enough for these poems,' she said with a nervous laugh. 'This is the best book you've ever given me, Mr Follis.'

'There is a much better one,' he said, teasingly.

'Is there?'

'Yes, Amy.' He picked up a copy of the Bible from the table. 'This is the best book ever written – though Tennyson has his own charms. I'll be the first to concede that.'

'His poems have such *feeling*.'

'Perhaps you could read just one to me.'

She was elated. 'Which one shall it be?'

'Choose your favourite,' he said, resuming his seat. 'As long as it's not *In Memoriam* – I don't think I'm in the right mood for that at this precise moment.'

'Then I'll read you *The Lady of Shalott*.'

Amy was to be cruelly disappointed. Before she could even find the page, someone rang the doorbell. She was deeply hurt.

'That can't be Mrs Ashmore already,' she said, flustered. 'She always goes to the market on a Monday.'

'I see that you know our domestic routine here at the rectory,' said Follis with a fond smile. 'Mrs Ashmore has a key, of course, so she would never ring the bell. Excuse me a moment.'

Getting up from his chair, he went out to answer the door. Amy heard him talking to someone then he reappeared with a tall, elegant man and a pretty young woman. Resenting the strangers, she was at the same time relieved to see that they were not fellow-parishioners.

'Allow me to introduce our Flower Lady,' said Follis, indicating her. 'Thanks to Amy Walcott, our church is always a floral delight.'

'We're pleased to meet you, Miss Walcott,' said Colbeck, noting the absence of a ring on her left hand. 'We're sorry to intrude. My name is Robert Colbeck and this,' he went on, turning to his companion, 'is Miss Madeleine Andrews.'

'Good afternoon,' said Madeleine.

'Delighted to make your acquaintance,' mumbled Amy, nodding at them and wishing that she had such a lovely complexion as Madeleine's. 'I didn't know that the rector was expecting visitors.'

'Nor more did I,' said Follis with a chuckle. 'I'm afraid that we'll have to postpone the reading until a more appropriate time, Amy. What Mr Colbeck failed to mention is that he's a Detective Inspector at Scotland Yard. He's doubtless come to discuss the train crash with me so *The Lady of Shalott* will have to wait her turn.'

'Of course,' said Amy, moving to the door. 'I understand. Don't bother about me. I'll let myself out.'

She left the room so swiftly that none of them had time to see the tears forming in her eyes. By the time she walked past the church, they were streaming down her cheeks.

Dick Chiffney used a piece of chalk to draw the rough outline of a man on the trunk of the tree. A crude circle was placed where he thought the heart might be. Walking thirty paces away, he picked up the rifle and went down on one knee. He put the butt of the weapon into his shoulder and took aim, making sure that he was steady before he pulled the trigger. When he did so, the bullet missed the tree altogether and spent its fury in the undergrowth.

'You need more practice,' said his companion.

'I'm much better with the pistol.'

'Whichever weapon it is, there must be no mistake. He's escaped with his life once already. That must never happen again.'

'It won't, sir,' said Chiffney, obsequiously.

'Bide your time until you find the right moment.'

'Yes, sir.'

'And don't fail me,' warned the man. 'I take a poor view of people who let me down.'

'You can count on me.'

'Then why wasn't he killed in the train crash?'

'He was lucky, sir. Next time it will be different.'

The man pointed to the target. 'Keep practising,' he ordered. 'I want to see you hit that tree time and again.'

Chiffney licked his lips. 'When do I get paid, sir?'

'When he's dead,' was the reply.

Having left Madeleine Andrews at the rectory, Colbeck went off to the county hospital. He first sought out the doctor in charge of Horace Bardwell and discussed the case with him. It emerged that the patient would be there for at least a week before being allowed home. There was a degree of safety in a crowded hospital but not enough to discourage a determined assassin. Colbeck realised why Giles Thornhill, under threat, had been so keen to return to his own house.

Though Bardwell was awake, he looked pale and distraught. It took him a few moments to gather his thoughts when Colbeck spoke to him. He wondered why a detective had come to see him.

'This is our second conversation, sir,' said Colbeck.

'Is it? I don't remember you.'

'I'm trying to find out what actually happened,' said Colbeck.

'A goods train collided with the express,' muttered Bardwell. 'At least, that's what they tell me. It's all rather hazy to me.'

'How do you feel now, Mr Bardwell?'

'I'm so tired. My wife, my son and some of my friends have been here to see me. It was very heartening but it's left me so weary.'

'Then I won't stay too long,' promised Colbeck. 'Last time I was here, I mentioned a name that appeared to upset you.'

'Did it? Who was it?'

'Matthew Shanklin.'

Bardwell shuddered. 'Don't mention that fiend!' he gasped.

'Why is that, sir?'

'Because he did everything he could to ruin me.'

'I believe that he used to work for the LB&SCR.'

'Then you're mistaken – Shanklin worked *against* the company. You must have men under you, Inspector.'

'Several of them,' said Colbeck.

'Then you'll know that the first thing you demand of them is unquestioning loyalty. It's an essential prerequisite, don't you agree? Matthew Shanklin betrayed me.'

'In what way, sir?'

'I don't want to go into the details,' said Bardwell, plucking at the bandage around his eyes. 'It would only distress me. Suffice it to say that he made false allegations against me that led, in time, to the loss of my position as Managing Director of the Board.'

'Mr Shanklin claims that you caused him to lose *his* job.'

'That was the least he deserved.'

'Were you dissatisfied with his work?'

'He should never have been employed by the company.'

'Yet he held a post with you for some years,' argued Colbeck, 'so he must have been competent. My colleague, Sergeant Leeming, spoke to some of those who worked alongside Mr Shanklin. To a man, they said that he had been a very able manager.'

'They didn't know him as well as I did!'

'You parted on bad terms, by the sound of it.'

'The worst kind,' said Bardwell, shaking with anger. 'When I got him dismissed, the fellow had the gall to threaten me with violence. That's the kind of person Matthew Shanklin is.'

Even though it was a hot summer's day, Madeleine Andrews felt a slight chill as they stepped into the church. It was alleviated by the warm sunshine streaming in through the magnificent stained glass window above the door. Ezra Follis guided his visitor to a spot where she could bathe in the sunlight while carrying out her inspection. The interior of St Dunstan's was larger than she had imagined. The nave was bisected by a wide aisle separating ranks of oak pews. There were two lady chapels, a large vestry at the rear of the chancel and a bell tower that housed five large cast iron bells.

Follis was in his element, describing the main features of the church and giving Madeleine a concise architectural history. In a medieval building that had survived well over the centuries, the item of which he was proudest was, paradoxically, a modern one. It was a list of former incumbents, drawn up like an illuminated manuscript and framed to hang on a stone pillar.

'You see,' he said, pointing to the first name on the list, 'it all started way back in 1244 when Ebenezer Marmion became rector and there's been continuous worship here ever since. I'm honoured to be part of such an illustrious tradition.'

'Yet your own name is not here, Mr Follis,' she noted.

'I have to move on or die before that happens.'

'But that means you never get to see it.'

He laughed. 'Oh, I'm sure that sheer vanity will make me look down from heaven to take a peep at it.' He gestured at the flowers in the chancel. 'What do you think of Amy's handiwork?'

'What lovely arrangements!' she said, admiringly. 'It's not simply a question of putting flowers into a vase. There's a real art to it.'

'Amy Walcott is on her way to perfecting that art.'

'I agree.'

'This is where I address my flock,' he said, patting one of the elaborate carvings on the front of the pulpit. 'When I climb up there I'm four feet above contradiction. It gives me a wonderful sense of power and responsibility. Over here,' he continued, moving across to it, 'is our lectern, donated to the church in 1755 so it's almost a hundred years old.'

Made of brass that glinted in the sunlight, the lectern was in the shape of an eagle with its wings spread wide to hold the Bible. Madeleine was struck by the sharpness of the bird's beak and the ferocity in its eyes. Follis stepped up behind it.

'Read something to me,' he invited.

She was taken aback. 'But I've never read in church before.'

'That's because you've never been given the opportunity. You have a lovely voice, Miss Andrews, soft and melodic. It's well-suited to Holy Writ. Here,' he said, flipping over the pages with some difficulty. 'Let me hear you read from the

First Epistle of Paul the Apostle to the Corinthians. Chapter Thirteen will, I'm sure, be familiar to you.'

Madeleine was discomfited. Though she attended church every Sunday, she was accustomed to sitting in a pew at the rear of the nave with her father. Like other women there, she had taken no active part in the service itself. To be asked to read from the Bible – albeit with a congregation of one – was unsettling. At the same time, she did not feel that she could refuse. Ezra Follis had been kind and charming to her. In obeying his wish, she would be thanking him for his hospitality.

While the rector sat down a few yards away, she took her place at the lectern. Madeleine needed a little time to read through the passage and to control the sudden beating of her heart. After using her tongue to moisten a dry mouth, she began. Her voice trembled at first but quickly grew in confidence. Madeleine read clearly and mellifluously without fully understanding the import of the words. Follis watched her intently throughout. When she came to the final verse, he spoke it in unison with her.

'And now abideth faith, hope and charity, these three; but the greatest of these is charity.'

Relieved to have got through it, Madeleine raised her eyes. The person who caught her attention, however, was not Ezra Follis, seated contentedly before her, but Robert Colbeck, striding down the aisle.

'Thank you, Madeleine,' he said, 'It was a privilege to have heard that. I'm glad that I arrived in time.'

'So am I, Inspector,' declared Follis, getting up and turning round. 'The passage was beautifully read. The female voice is so much kinder on the ear than the rasping diction of men.

Thank you for lending me such a delightful reader.'

Madeleine was embarrassed. 'I don't think I read it *that* well.'

'Let *us* be the judge of that, my dear.'

Follis led them out of the church and swung the heavy oak door shut behind them. Sensing that Colbeck wanted to speak to the rector alone, Madeleine drifted away to examine the inscriptions on some of the tombstones. She was also grateful for some time alone to reflect on what had happened in church. Reading from the Bible had been both a trial and a pleasure. It had left her heart beating louder than ever.

Colbeck, meanwhile, was telling Follis about his visit to the county hospital. He described Bardwell's reaction to the name of Matthew Shanklin. Follis shook his head.

'I've never heard that name before,' he said.

'He worked as a manager for the LB&SCR,' Colbeck told him. 'He made an allegation of impropriety against Mr Bardwell.'

'Well, he won't have been the only one, Inspector.'

'What do you mean?'

'You've only seen the man in a hospital bed. Any of us would look rather pitiable in that state. Until last Friday,' said Follis, 'Horace Bardwell was a robust gentleman with a fondness for throwing his considerable weight around. Since he lives here in Brighton, his antics are often reported in the local newspaper.'

'What sort of antics?'

'He's always complaining about the speed at which the town is growing – we have a population of almost 70,000 now – even though his railway is chiefly responsible for the growth. He's always thrusting his opinions down everyone's throat. To his credit,' he pointed out, 'Mr Bardwell has always been a generous man. He's given thousands of pounds to worthy causes. The problem is that he thinks his money also buys him influence.'

'What allegations have been made against him?'

'There are strong rumours of bribery and corruption – not that I've seen any proof of either myself. People claim that Mr Bardwell has some civic leaders in his pocket, and he certainly exerts power over the *Brighton Herald*. His articles appear in it so often that you'd think he was the editor. What I'm telling you, Inspector,' he went on, 'is that Horace Bardwell is a deeply unpopular man here.'

'He and Giles Thornhill are birds of a feather, then.'

'In one sense, yes,' agreed Follis. 'But they're hardly kindred spirits. Mr Thornhill has lofty aspirations, grappling with national problems. He despises Mr Bardwell for dabbling in local politics.'

'From what you say,' remarked Colbeck, 'he does more than dabble. As for the funeral card, you didn't send me the envelope in which it came. From where was it sent, Mr Follis?'

'It had a London post mark.'

'I'll keep the card, if you don't mind.'

'I can give you the envelope as well,' said Follis. 'The main thing is that Mr Bardwell doesn't hear about it. More than one person in Brighton would approve of the sentiments in it but that card would upset him greatly when he's feeling so weak and vulnerable.'

'One last question,' said Colbeck.

'Ask as many as you wish, Inspector.'

'Which man is the more unpopular here – Horace Bardwell or Giles Thornhill?'

'There's a simple answer to that.'

'Is there?'

'Yes,' said Follis with a merry chortle. 'The most hated man in this whole county is, without a shadow of doubt, Mr Thornhill.'

Tempted by the warm weather, Giles Thornhill sat at a table on the terrace and dictated letters to his secretary, a tall, angular man in his thirties. Though Parliament was in recess, there was much for the politician to do as he sought support for various Bills that were in the offing or looked for opportunities to attack the coalition government in power at the time. His final letter was destined for the *Sussex Express,* a newspaper that was used to printing his trenchant views. When his secretary had finished penning it, he exchanged a few pleasantries with his employer before taking his leave.

Thornhill was left alone to bask in the sun and wonder how long it would take his broken arm to heal. The inconvenience of being unable to use it was frustrating and the nagging pain never went away. It was not long before the gentle breeze stiffened and made the flowers dance. Leaves began to rustle in the wind and the weathervane on the roof of the gazebo twisted to and fro. Thornhill decided that it was time to go indoors.

He stood up and turned sideways just in time. At that very moment, a shot rang out and a bullet whistled past, missing him by inches before hitting the window behind him and shattering the glass.

CHAPTER TEN

Disguise was a weapon that Colbeck had used many times and he had taught Victor Leeming its value. Accordingly, the sergeant kept a couple of changes of clothing at his office in case they were needed. Off went his frock coat, smart trousers, waistcoat, shirt, cravat and shoes and on went a crumpled shirt, a smelly old coat frayed at the edges, a pair of baggy trousers and two boots in urgent need of repair. When he replaced his top hat with a ragged cap, Leeming looked like a costermonger down on his luck. After checking his appearance in a mirror, he felt ready to venture out.

Since few cab drivers would stop for someone so blatantly down-to-heel, Leeming made his way to Chalk Farm by means of a horse-drawn omnibus, collecting disdainful looks and murmured complaints from the other passengers. Josie Murlow's hovel was at the end of a cul-de-sac. As he walked along the pavement towards it, he kept his head down and cultivated a lumbering walk. Choosing a spot from which he could keep the house under observation, he pretended to read the newspaper he had brought with him.

Leeming was unhappy. Apart from the danger of meeting Josie Murlow again, he feared that his vigil would be pointless. Dick Chiffney might already have come and gone to the house or sent an intermediary on his behalf. Its formidable owner might not even be there. He was certainly not minded to find out. All in all, it promised to be a long, tiring, uneventful and futile assignment.

It did, however, give him time to brood once more on what he should buy his wife as a birthday present. A garnet necklace was beyond the reach of his wallet and, since Josie Murlow sported such an item of jewellery, he would not even consider it. A small silver brooch was a possibility or even a ring of some kind. What his wife had talked about needing most was a new dress but that was something he could only buy with Estelle's cooperation, and he wanted to enjoy the pleasure of watching her face as she opened a gift that came as a total surprise.

Thoughts of his wife inevitably led to a comparison with the woman whose house he was keeping an eye on. Estelle Leeming was everything that Josie Murlow was not. She was short, dark-haired, slight of build and, even though she had given birth to two children, she had retained something of the youthful bloom that had first won Leeming's heart. Most of all, she was thoroughly wholesome. The same could not be said of the raddled denizen of the nearby hovel, a gross woman whose occupation had reduced her to a waddling mound of flesh and exposed her to the constant threat of assault and hideous diseases.

An hour soon passed and he shifted his position to stretch his legs and to avoid the disapproving glare of the man outside whose house he was standing. Crossing to the other side of the road, he opened his newspaper once more and stared unseeingly at one of the inside pages. There was a consolation. Because he was in a cul-de-sac, people could only come from one direction. Leeming could not miss anyone who went to Josie Murlow's house. As another half an hour slid past, he moved back across the road and took up a different stance, trying to recall when he had last wasted so much time maintaining such an unproductive surveillance. Colbeck might make few mistakes but Leeming felt that he was the victim of one of them now. He gave a first yawn of disillusion. He wanted to go home.

His disaffection was premature. Moments later, a figure came into the street and walked furtively towards him. The man was thickset, shambling and wearing the kind of threadbare suit that could never belong to anyone who lived in one of the neat and respectable villas. Since the stranger's cap was pulled down over his forehead, Leeming could not see much of the unshaven face but the man passed close enough for him to smell the beer on his breath.

Reaching the hovel, the newcomer was circumspect. He looked around to make sure that he was not seen then he banged on the door. Hidden behind his newspaper, Leeming peered around the edge and saw the door open. Josie Murlow was there, after all. From the effusive welcome she gave the man, she knew him well. Leeming felt a thrill of discovery. He might have found Dick Chiffney.

On the train to London, Colbeck and Madeleine Andrews had a compartment to themselves, allowing them to talk freely for the first time since they had left Camden.

'I hope that your father will not disapprove,' he said.

'Of course not,' she replied. 'Father trusts you as much as I do, Robert. He knows that we have an understanding and is quite happy for us to spend time alone together.'

'That's not what I meant, Madeleine. He's such a dedicated servant of the LNWR that he might object to his daughter being taken off on a line owned by another company.'

She laughed. 'He's not that prejudiced,' she said. 'Besides, he'll willingly accept anything that helps you to catch the man who killed Frank Pike and the others. Do you think you're any closer to doing that after today?'

'I hope so.'

'That was the purpose of the visit to Brighton, wasn't it? You wanted to speak to two of the survivors of the crash and that's exactly what you did. What you still haven't explained is why you took me with you.'

He kissed her. 'Do you *need* an explanation?'

'I'm serious, Robert. All that I seemed to do was to keep you company on the journey there, get a glimpse of the Royal Pavilion, take tea in the rectory, look around a church and be more or less forced to read a passage from the Bible.'

'That's why I took you, Madeleine.'

'I'm still none the wiser.'

'I wanted you to meet the Reverend Follis,' he said. 'He's such a curious fellow. I thought he might interest you.'

'He did. I found him very interesting. He's pleasant, attentive and highly intelligent. And he made me feel so welcome.'

'It's precisely why I left you alone with him. I wanted a woman's opinion of the rector. To some extent, of course,' he continued, 'I got that from Amy Walcott. She obviously adores him and was upset when we tore him away from her.'

'Did you see the flowers in the church?' she asked. 'It must have taken her hours to pick and arrange them like that.'

'She's only one doting female at his behest. Mrs Ashmore, his housekeeper, is another, as you must have noticed when she served tea. She mollycoddles him.'

'Well, that's not what *I* did, Robert,' she said, laughing.

'What happened while I was away?'

'We just talked. When the housekeeper came back from the market, she made us some tea and served scones. Then Mr Follis tried to probe me about our friendship.'

'I thought he might.'

'He was fascinated to hear how we met,' she recalled, 'and amused to discover that Father is an engine driver. The rector has an almost childish love of trains.'

'I don't condemn anyone for that,' said Colbeck, grinning.

'After tea, he asked me if I'd like to see the church. He was showing me around when he suddenly asked me to read something.'

'Were you given freedom of choice?'

'No, Robert,' she replied. 'He chose the passage for me. If it had been left to me, I'd have refused politely but I felt obliged to him. He'd been so friendly and courteous.'

'Considering that you'd never been allowed to read in church before, you did extremely well.'

'I was very nervous.'

'It didn't show, Madeleine.'

'The odd thing was that Mr Follis knew exactly what he wanted me to read. It was almost as if he had made up his mind about it before we even went into the church.' She gave a shrug. 'Why do you think he picked that passage?'

Colbeck smiled. 'I have a theory about that.'

* * *

Leeming was in a quandary. There was enough evidence to suggest that Dick Chiffney might have been involved in causing the train crash and it was important to question him. Since the man could well be inside the house, Leeming's first instinct was to knock on the door and apprehend him. He was not afraid of any resistance from Chiffney. Leeming was strong, fit and fearless, very accustomed to overpowering criminals. What made him hesitate was the presence of Josie Murlow. If she became violent – and he was certain that she would – then the arrest would be more difficult. It would also entail restraining, if not actually punching, a woman and that troubled him.

He agonised for a long time over what he should do. In the event, the decision was made for him because the door of the hovel opened and the man came out. After wiping a hand across his mouth, he came back up the street. Lowering the paper, Leeming folded it up and stuffed it into his pocket. He then took a good look at the approaching figure. The fellow was certainly big and brawny enough to be Josie Murlow's lover and he was around the same age as her. He had also been shown great affection on his arrival. It had to be Chiffney. He and his woman had been reconciled.

Careful not to forewarn the man, Leeming turned on his heel and lumbered off, moving slowly so that he would soon be overtaken. The moment that the man went past him, the sergeant pounced. He grabbed him by the shoulders, spun him round then held him by the lapels of his jacket.

'What are you doing!' protested the man.

'Dick Chiffney?'

'Let go of me!'

'Are you Dick Chiffney?' demanded Leeming.

'No, I'm not,' said the other, struggling to get away.

'What's your name?

'That's my business.'

'I'm a member of the Metropolitan Police and I just saw you going into Josie Murlow's house.'

'No harm in that, is there?'

'That depends on who you are.'

'If you must know,' said the man, exhaling beer fumes into Leeming's face, 'my name is Luke Watts and that's the truth. You can ask anyone – ask Josie, if you like.'

Leeming released him. 'Then you're not Dick Chiffney?'

Watts was offended. 'Do I *look* like him?' he said. 'Dick is the ugliest bugger in London. Don't you dare take me for that cross-eyed son of a sow. It's a bleeding insult, that's what it is.'

'I seem to have made a mistake, Mr Watts.'

'Yes – a bad mistake.'

'But if you're not Chiffney,' said Leeming with a glance at the hovel, 'what were you doing in Josie Murlow's house?'

The man smirked. 'What do you think?'

Edward Tallis had never been hampered by indecision. When action was needed, he took it instantly. Hiring a cab outside Scotland Yard, he was driven to the offices of the LB&SCR. He was immediately shown into the room occupied by Harvey Ridgeon. The captain was nonplussed to see him storming through the door.

'What brings you here, Superintendent?' he asked.

'This,' replied Tallis, tossing a copy of the evening newspaper on to the desk. 'It's the early edition – have you read it?'

'I can't say that I have.'

'It contains defamatory statements made by you about my officers. Worse than that, it brings a covert investigation into the full glare of publicity and thereby weakens its effectiveness.'

'It was ineffective enough already.'

'I demand an apology.'

'You'll get nothing at all if you try to hector me,' said Ridgeon, coolly. 'Why don't you sit down and give me a chance to see what it is that I'm supposed to have done?'

Choking back another accusation, Tallis removed his top hat and sat down opposite the desk. Ridgeon, meanwhile, opened the newspaper and saw the headline that had upset the Superintendent. POLICE CHASE PHANTOM KILLER. Highly critical of Tallis and Colbeck, the article contended that the train crash was the result of an accident caused by the driver of the Brighton Express. Ridgeon was quoted a number of times.

'You pour scorn on hard-working detectives,' complained Tallis.

'Not in the way that I'm quoted here,' said Ridgeon. 'I give you my word that I didn't actually say some of these things.'

'You spoke to the press, Captain Ridgeon, and that was fatal. They always twist what you tell them. If you'll forgive my language,' said Tallis, 'a man in your position should know that a newspaper reporter is a man who swallows nails and shits screws. This unprincipled scribbler didn't even have the courtesy to speak to me.'

'That's not true, Superintendent. According to him, he came to Scotland Yard as soon he heard about the crash and asked if the police were taking an interest in it. You told him that you were not.'

'It was an honest answer.'

'Yet you'd already dispatched Inspector Colbeck to the scene.'

'I authorised him to go in the light of a request from the railway company. At that time,' said Tallis, 'there was no indication of any criminal activity in relation to the crash. Strictly speaking, therefore, I had not set an investigation in motion. When I did so, I hoped that it could operate without the so-called gentlemen of the press looking over our shoulders. Thanks to that libellous article,' he went on, pointing to the newspaper, 'the whole world now knows about it.'

'Then they can judge for themselves whether or not a police investigation is appropriate.'

'No, they can't, Captain. People can only make a considered judgement if both sides of a case are presented to them. Only one is offered in that article – *yours*. You have no idea how much evidence Inspector Colbeck has gathered.'

'I must correct you there, Superintendent.'

'What do you mean?'

'The Inspector was good enough to reveal it to me.'

Tallis frowned. 'When was this?'

'Earlier today,' said Ridgeon.

'Colbeck made no mention of any visit to you. It was certainly not something I'd have endorsed. I felt that we'd said everything that needed to be said between us in my office.'

'The Inspector took a less inflexible view of the situation than you, Superintendent. He had the sense to see that my work might complement his own. We had a long discussion.'

'Really?' said Tallis, infuriated at being wrong-footed.

'I admired him for his candour and heard what he had to

say. His argument was very cogent. Unfortunately,' said Ridgeon, 'it was fundamentally flawed.'

'Those are the very words quoted in that article.'

'I stand by them.'

'In the fullness of time, you may be embarrassed by them.'

'I think not, Superintendent.'

Tallis glowered. 'Do you realise what you've done, sir?'

'I've given straight answers to straight questions.'

'Oh, you've done a lot more than that. You've just opened a Pandora's box. Every newspaper in London will now be baying at the door of my office. That article has not simply made a mockery of our investigation,' said Tallis, 'it's also a stark warning to the villains behind the crash that we are pursuing them. If they have any sense, they'll have left London already.'

'Yes,' said Ridgeon, unable to resist sarcasm, 'and stepped straight back into the sensational novel from which they escaped. That's where they belong, after all – in the world of imagination.'

Getting to his feet, Tallis snatched up his newspaper and left.

Colbeck had also been dismayed by the article. After sending Madeleine Andrews home in a cab, he had bought a copy of the newspaper at the railway station and read it on his way back to Scotland Yard. It made him regret his decision to speak to Ridgeon in confidence. He was wounded and disappointed by what the Inspector General of Railways had done. A difficult and complex investigation had suddenly become even more arduous.

His immediate concern was how upset Madeleine would be

when she read the article and saw the biting criticism of the
Railway Detective. Caleb Andrews was in the habit of buying
the newspaper at Euston station when he came off duty in the
evening. He, too, would be deeply hurt by the attack on
Colbeck and scandalised by the accusation of speeding made
against his friend, Frank Pike. There was a venomous note to
the article. It was almost if, having praised Colbeck for a long
record of success, the newspaper felt that it was time to go to
the other extreme. It was a crucifixion in print.

There would be repercussions. Colbeck would be dogged
by reporters from other newspapers, mocked anew in their
columns and denied complete freedom of movement. From
now on, he would be watched. There would also be one or
two colleagues at the Detective Department who, jealous of
his reputation, would derive great joy from the public censure
of him. Not everyone at Scotland Yard was ready to join in
the general adulation of Robert Colbeck.

As the cab rolled to a halt, he got out and paid the driver,
only to be set upon immediately by half a dozen reporters who
had been lying in ambush. In answer to a salvo of questions,
he told them that he had no comment to make and went
swiftly into the building. The real torment was yet to come.
Colbeck would now have to face a gruelling interrogation by
Edward Tallis and would be reprimanded for not having made
more progress in the case. Continuing success was the only
way to keep bad headlines at bay. Colbeck would be blamed
for the hostile article in the newspaper.

He went straight to the superintendent's office and tapped
on the door before opening it. Anticipating a barrage of
abuse, he was amazed to find Tallis quiescent for once, seated
at his desk in a cloud of cigar smoke. Colbeck's first thought

was that his superior had not yet read the article then he saw the newspaper lying open on the desk. As Tallis drew deep on his cigar, it glowed with life and the swirling cloud of smoke was thickened as he exhaled with calculated slowness. When he spoke, his voice was eerily soft.

'Have you read the newspaper, Inspector?'

'Yes, sir,' replied Colbeck.

'Do you have any comment to make?'

'I'm saddened that Captain Ridgeon saw fit to criticise us in such a public way, though I daresay he feels that the very fact of a police investigation is an implied criticism of *his* work.'

'That's exactly what he feels,' said Tallis, 'even if he didn't put it in those exact words. I've not long come back from seeing him.'

'What did he say?'

'Among other things, he told me that you and he had discussed the whole business in some depth but that you had failed to persuade him that the train crash was a criminal act.'

'That's true, Superintendent.'

'Why didn't you tell me you were going to see him?'

'I felt that you might advise against it,' said Colbeck. 'At the start of the investigation, you warned us to work alongside Captain Ridgeon without causing any friction. When you met him, however, you objected to his tone and refused to obey the orders he unwisely tried to give you. Victor and I expressed thanks for your support.'

'I find this very alarming, Inspector Colbeck,' said Tallis, voice still uncharacteristically soft. 'Is it your habitual practice to do things to which you know I would object?'

'Not at all, sir – this was an isolated instance.'

'What was the motive behind it?'

'I hoped that I could get Captain Ridgeon on our side.'

Tallis picked up the newspaper. 'This is the result,' he said. 'The other result is that I am made to look foolish because I was unaware that you had paid a visit to the captain earlier. Do I have to remind you that there's a chain of command here?'

'It's not possible to clear everything with you beforehand, sir,' argued Colbeck. 'Some decisions have to be made in response to a given situation. If I had to get your approval for every move I make, then my hands would be tied. That would be intolerable.'

Tallis puffed on his cigar again, filling his lungs with the smoke before blowing it out again in a series of rings. He studied Colbeck in silence through the fug. While it was too much to ask him ever to like the man, he had to respect his achievements over the years. The Railway Detective's record was unrivalled even if some of his methods were not endorsed by the superintendent. Nobody, however, was infallible. In trusting Captain Ridgeon, Colbeck had made a serious misjudgement. Tallis wondered if it was the only one.

'Are you *sure* that crash was caused by someone?' he said.

'I'd stake every penny I possess on it,' affirmed Colbeck.

'The Detective Department does not take gambles, Inspector. We deal only in certainties. Give me some of them. How, for instance, have you spent today – after you left Captain Ridgeon, that is?'

Colbeck told him about his visit to Chalk Farm and about the funeral card that had sent him haring off to Brighton. He said nothing about Madeleine Andrews, however, or her strange experience at the lectern in St Dunstan's church. It was not relevant and it would only serve to inflame Tallis.

Colbeck's conclusion was that Horace Bardwell definitely had to be considered the most likely target of those who had caused the disaster on the Brighton line.

'What does that tell you?' asked Tallis.

'Matthew Shanklin is a prime suspect,' said Colbeck. 'If, that is, my supposition is correct. Should Mr Thornhill's death turn out to be the object of the crash, then Shanklin will be exonerated. I have grave doubts that that will happen.'

'Why is that, Inspector?'

'I told Victor to speak to him again.'

He recounted the details of Leeming's visit, stressing Shanklin's reaction to the name of Dick Chiffney. The possession of a telescope was also viewed as strong evidence. He reminded the superintendent of Bardwell's bitter remarks about Shanklin. Mutual hatred existed between the two men.

'I think that Matthew Shanklin may well have sent the macabre message to the hospital,' said Colbeck.

'How can you prove that?'

'I'll compare his handwriting with that on the card, sir.'

Resting his cigar in the astray, Tallis sat back pensively in his chair. Ever since he had entered the room, Colbeck had been waiting for him to explode and to unleash the kind of vituperation for which he was so well-known. Instead, he was unusually subdued. He had been sobered by the personal attack in the newspaper and was desperate for reassurance that the crime could indeed be solved before too long.

'The first thing you must do,' he said at length, 'is to establish a connection between Shanklin and this other fellow, Chiffney.'

'Victor is trying to do that at this moment, sir.'

'Why – where is he?'

'Somewhere in Chalk Farm,' said Colbeck. 'He's keeping watch on the home of Josie Murlow.'

Victor Leeming had retreated to the end of the street, feeling that he was too conspicuous if he stayed too long in the same place. He was still chiding himself for confusing one of Josie Murlow's clients with Dick Chiffney. The confrontation with Luke Watts had made him feel stupid but he had at least learnt something about Chiffney. The man was ugly and cross-eyed. He wished he had known that before he accosted the wrong person. Leeming had lost all track of time. It seemed as if he had been there for hours and all he had seen of Josie was a fleeting glimpse. He began to despair of catching sight of her again and wondered if he should accept defeat and leave.

He decided to stroll down the street for the last time, taking a final look at the house from close quarters before quitting his vigil. Hands thrust into his pockets and head down, he walked slowly along and hoped that his next assignment would not be so boring and so fruitless. His feet were hurting, his shoulders were aching and the smell from his coat was increasingly offensive. He longed to get back into clean clothing once more.

Leeming was only twenty yards from the hovel when a small boy ran past him to slip an envelope through the letterbox before dashing away. Within a matter of minutes, the door opened and out stepped Josie Murlow. He did not recognise her at first. She had been transformed. Wearing a dark dress that verged on respectability, she had somehow tamed her hair, swept it up and hidden it completely beneath her hat. She moved along with a measure of dignity. If he had not known her true calling, he would have taken her for a servant from a large establishment.

He felt a stab of fear, thinking that she would recognise him but Josie did not even glance in his direction. Wherever she was going, she was eager to get there, ignoring everything else on the way. It made it much easier for Leeming to follow her. Turning at the corner, she went on down the main road, never once looking over her shoulder. Leeming was tingling with excitement. He believed she had received word from Chiffney and was going to meet him. All of his recriminations vanished. His visit to Chalk Farm had, after all, been supremely worthwhile.

Given her size, Josie could not walk fast but she kept up a reasonable speed as she picked her way through pedestrians coming towards her. After going for a couple of hundred yards, she turned into a side-road and continued on her way. Leeming came around the corner, checked that she was not looking back then kept up his pursuit. Confident that she was leading him to a main suspect in the investigation, he squeezed the handcuffs in his pocket, certain that they would be needed on Chiffney. A man ruthless enough to bring an express train off the rails was unlikely to surrender meekly. Even the presence of Josie did not deter Leeming now. If necessary, he would take them both on.

She eventually stopped outside the Shepherd and Shepherdess, an incongruous name for a public house in an urban district. Then, for the first time, she turned round. Leeming took evasive action, diving sideways into an alleyway. When he peeped around the corner, he saw that

Josie was walking further on. He tried to follow her but it was in vain. Before he even stepped back out into the road, he was hit on the back of head and plunged helplessly into unconsciousness.

Dick Chiffney unlocked the door and hustled her into the bedroom. Josie Murlow was so pleased at their reunion that she that threw her arms around him and held him tight. Taking off her hat, he let her hair cascade down then kissed her full on the lips. It was minutes before they finally broke apart.

'I was beginning to think you'd run out on me again,' she said.

'I gave you my promise I'd send for you.'

'Where did you spend last night?'

'Right here,' he said, indicating the room. 'This house belongs to an old friend. He let me in as a favour.'

'Why didn't you send for me earlier?'

'I had someone to see, Josie – the gentleman I'm working for.'

'Has he paid you yet?'

'I have to do the job first.'

'Well, be quick about it, Dick,' she urged. 'The police are sniffing about. I had another one banging on my door today. They want you.'

'That's why I took precautions.'

'Them instructions you give me, you mean?'

'Yes, Josie. I had a feeling you might be followed. My note told you to stop at the Shepherd and Shepherdess to look round.'

'I saw nobody,' she said. 'Not a bleeding soul.'

'Well, I did,' he said with a chuckle, taking out his pistol, 'and I give him a sore head with this.' He mimed the action of striking with the butt of the weapon. 'That will teach him not to mess with Dick Chiffney.'

Josie was anxious. 'Where did you get that gun?'

'The gentleman give it to me.'

'What for – you're not going to shoot someone, are you?'

'I told you before, Josie – you don't need to know what's going on. I've got a job to do, that's all. When it's done, I get the rest of the money and I can hand back both of the guns.'

'*Both* of them?' she echoed.

'I've got this as well,' he boasted, lifting the overhanging coverlet to reveal the rifle under the bed. She gasped in alarm. 'Don't get so upset, my old darling,' he said, letting the coverlet go and putting an arm around her. 'Everything will be all right.'

'What have you got yourself into, Dick?'

'Nothing I can't handle.'

'I don't like it,' she said. 'You told me that there was no danger at all then I get two detectives coming to my house. When I try to leave it, I'm followed by someone.'

'He was a police spy, Josie.'

'That's dreadful! I don't want policemen camped outside my house, watching everything I do. What will happen now that you attacked the man following me?' A worrying thought struck her. 'You didn't kill him, did you?'

'No,' he said, airily, 'I didn't hit him hard enough. I should've done really. The more coppers we can get rid of, the better.' He took her by the shoulders. 'Try to stay calm, my love,' he urged. 'I'm doing this for *us*.'

'All you've done so far is to bring the law down on me and I'm scared. What's happening, Dick? I don't like being kept in the dark. Most of all,' she went on, 'I don't like having my house watched.

'Then you've no need to go back there, Josie.'

'Where else can I go?'

'You can stay here, my darling,' he said, nodding at the flagon on the table, 'for the time being, anyway. We've got plenty of gin and a nice big bed – what more do we need?'

When he regained consciousness, Victor Leeming found himself lying on the ground in an alleyway close to some animal excrement. His face and body had been bruised in the fall and his head felt as if it were about to explode. It took him a little while to work out what had happened. His thick cap had prevented a bad scalp wound, leaving him with a large bump that throbbed insistently. Most people who had passed by took him for a drunk who had passed out. Nobody came to his aid. It was only when he dragged himself painfully to his feet that an old man stopped to help him.

'Are you all right?' he asked, looking at the grazes on his face.

'I think so.'

'Is there anything I can do?'

'Yes,' said Leeming, wincing at the pain. 'Find a policeman.'

'You stay here.'

When the old man went off, Leeming leant against the wall for support, annoyed that he had let himself be caught off guard. He took off his cap and ran a hand gingerly over the bump on his head. The assault had not been the work of a thief. Nothing had been taken from his pockets. Given the fact that Leeming was trailing Josie Murlow, the most likely assailant, he guessed, was Dick Chiffney.

A policeman eventually arrived and was astonished when he heard that the scruffy man in the alleyway was a detective sergeant. He hailed a cab on Leeming's behalf, helped him into it and told the driver to go to Scotland Yard as fast as he could. The juddering movement of the carriage made Leeming's head pound even more and the clatter of the horse's hooves resounded painfully in his eardrums. He could not wait to reach his destination.

By the time he finally got to Colbeck's office, he was still a little unsteady on his feet. Colbeck took charge at once, sitting him down, pouring him a glass of whisky from a bottle concealed in his desk then gently bathing his face with cold water.

'I hate to send you home to your wife in this state,' he said.

'Estelle is used to seeing me with a few bruises, sir,' said Leeming, bravely. 'Her father was a policeman, remember. She knows that it's a dangerous job.'

'You were lucky, Victor.'

'I don't *feel* lucky.'

'No,' said Colbeck, sympathetically, 'I'm sure you don't but it could have been far worse. If you were knocked out, somebody might have taken the opportunity to inflict serious wounds. Tell me exactly what happened.'

'I'm not certain that I remember it all, Inspector.'

After another restorative drink of whisky, Leeming gave a halting account of his time outside Josie Murlow's house, recalling his folly in accosting Luke Watts and his lack of concentration when he stepped into the alleyway. Colbeck seized on one detail.

'The boy delivered a warning to the house,' he decided. 'Josie Murlow was told that she should take a particular route so that anyone following her could be seen. She was probably told to look back outside that public house so that you would instinctively try to hide somewhere. Someone was waiting for you.'

'I think it was Dick Chiffney.'

'There's a strong possibility that it was, Victor.'

'Then I need to go back and search for him,' said Leeming. 'I have a score to settle with Chiffney.'

'The only place you're going this evening,' said Colbeck, 'is home to Estelle. You need rest. My advice is that you don't buy a newspaper on the way there.'

'Why not, sir?'

Colbeck told him about the article concerning the train crash and how Tallis had responded to it. He also talked about the visit to Brighton where he had spoken to Horace Bardwell and learnt more about his relationship with Matthew Shanklin. Leeming was cynical.

'One of them is lying, Inspector,' he argued. 'Mr Shanklin reckons that Mr Bardwell is a crook yet you heard him claim that Mr Shanklin is the troublemaker. Which one should we believe?'

'I'll let you know when I've talked to Mr Shanklin tomorrow.'

'At least, we know one thing for certain. The target of the train crash was Horace Bardwell.'

'That's what I thought, Victor,' admitted Colbeck, 'but I've been forced to reconsider. In the last hour, we received another message from Giles Thornhill – someone tried to kill him earlier today.'

CHAPTER ELEVEN

There was still good light when Madeleine Andrews arrived home so she began work at her easel immediately. Though she did her best to concentrate, however, her mind kept straying back to the excursion she had been on with Colbeck. She still could not understand why he wished her to meet the Rector of St Dunstan's, nor could she see why she had been asked to read a specific passage from the Bible. Colbeck had not explained his theory about the choice. Madeleine did not expect him to divulge details of his cases to her because she had no right or need to know them but there were times – this was one of them – when his reticence was irritating. She wanted to know exactly what he had meant.

She was so distracted that she eventually abandoned her work and took the Bible from a bookshelf. The well-thumbed volume had been passed down through generations of the Andrews' family and there was a long list at the front of all of her forbears. The name of her late mother had joined the list years earlier. Turning to the New Testament, she found the passage she had read in church and went through it again in search of a clue as to why Ezra Follis had chosen it. She could find none.

Madeleine was still pondering when her father came home from work. Letting himself into the house, Caleb Andrews was surprised to see his daughter reading the Bible.

'Is there something you haven't told me, Maddy?' he teased.

'Of course not, Father.'

'You don't want to enter a convent, then?'

'Heaven forbid!' she cried, laughing as she realised that it was not perhaps the most appropriate exclamation. 'I just wanted to look at something, that's all. Could *you* read this for me, Father?'

'No,' he said, firmly.

'But I'd like your opinion.'

'The time for studying the Bible is on a Sunday. That's why your mother and I always read bits of it to you when we got back from church. At this moment,' he went on, hanging his cap on a peg and flopping into his armchair, 'the only thing I want to read is the evening paper I've just bought.'

Madeleine put the Bible back on the shelf, deciding that her father would, in any case, be unlikely to help. She went into the kitchen to prepare his supper. After a short time, a howl of rage sent her rushing back into the living room.

'What's the matter?' she asked.

'This nonsense,' he replied, shaking the newspaper violently. 'There's an article here, laying the blame for the crash on Frank Pike.'

'But that's untrue.'

'I know it's untrue, Maddy. It's also unfair on a man who's not here to speak up for himself. John Heddle was on the footplate with Frank and he told me the train was going at the proper speed.'

'Does it say anything about Robert?'

'It says rather a lot,' he noted as he read through the rest of the article, 'and none of it very kind.'

'Why not?'

'According to this, there was no crime involved.'

Madeleine stiffened. 'Who's decided that?'

'Someone called Captain Harvey Ridgeon – he's the Inspector General of Railways and he has a lot to say for himself. What does *he* know about driving an express train? Precious little, I'll wager.'

'Let me see it.'

'No, Maddy, I don't think you should.

'If there's criticism of Robert, I want to read it.'

'It would only upset you.'

'Please, Father,' she insisted. 'I'm not a child. I want to see exactly what the article says about Robert and about the crash.'

'Very well,' he said, yielding up the newspaper with a long sigh, 'but don't say I didn't warn you. I think you'd be far better off reading the Bible again.'

Security at the house had been visibly improved. Colbeck arrived at Giles Thornhill's estate next morning to find three armed men on duty at the gate as well as a policeman from the local constabulary. As the cab took him up the drive, Colbeck noticed a man patrolling the grounds with a mastiff on a leash. When he reached the front door of the mansion, he was asked for proof of his identity yet again before he was permitted to enter. Thornhill was in his library once more but this time he was reclining in a leather armchair, well away from the window. His black eye had faded a little and he had slipped his broken arm and its splint out of its sling to rest in his lap. There was a crackle of deep dissatisfaction in his voice.

'You came on your *own?*' he asked.

'What did you expect, sir?'

'At the very least, I thought you'd bring a team of detectives. Someone tried to kill me in my own home, Inspector. Doesn't that merit a proper response?'

'I represent that response, Mr Thornhill,' said Colbeck, evenly. 'Our manpower is very limited and is fully deployed fighting the tide of crime in London. Besides, you seem to be extremely well guarded here so additional men are not needed.'

'I don't expect them to guard me,' Thornhill retaliated. 'What I want is to see is the villain caught and arrested. In short, I require more resources than the service of a single detective.'

'You'll be surprised what one person can achieve, sir.'

'It's what you *can't* achieve that concerns me.'

Colbeck ignored the slighting comment and sought a full account of what had taken place. Thornhill provided every detail, including the position he was in when the shot was fired. Even though the bullet had been so perilously close, he had not lost his nerve. He had taken cover and waited until some of his employees had come to his rescue. The grounds had been searched but no trace of the attacker had been found.

'What about the bullet, sir?' asked Colbeck.

'The bullet?'

'Do you still have it?'

'No, Inspector – I'm just grateful that it missed its target.'

'So it must be here on the premises.'

'Yes,' said Thornhill, 'I suppose that it must. It smashed through the drawing room window and ended up in there somewhere. I had the window boarded up immediately and have not ventured outdoors.'

'May I see the drawing room, please?'

'Is it really necessary, Inspector?'

'I believe so,' said Colbeck. 'Could someone take me there?'

Thornhill tugged on a bell rope beside the fireplace and a maidservant soon entered. Given instructions, she took Colbeck down the corridor and showed him into the drawing room. It was large, well-proportioned and filled with exquisite furniture. Since one of the windows was now blanked out, there was little natural light in that corner. Colbeck first unlocked the door and stepped out on to the terrace, sitting in the chair that Thornhill claimed to have occupied.

He stood up again, turned sideways and tried to imagine a bullet shooting past his left ear. It gave him a rough idea of the angle at which it had smashed into the window. Going back into the room, he tried to work out where the bullet might have ended up. The only clue he found was tear in the large tapestry on the far wall. When he lifted it up, he saw a hole gouged out of the wall itself and decided that the bullet must have ricocheted. Long, painstaking minutes of searching finally ended with success. After bouncing off the wall, the bullet had penetrated a thick cushion then embedded itself in the back of an ornate settee.

Thornhill was waiting for him with growing impatience.

'Well,' he demanded as Colbeck came back into the library.

'I found it, sir,' said the other, showing him a bullet whose nose had been blunted. 'I've afraid that your tapestry and one of the settees is in need of repair. The bullet was damaged when it struck the wall but I can tell you that it came from a rifle. That means it could have been fired from some distance away.'

Thornhill sneered. 'Is that supposed to make me feel safer?'

'I don't think you're in any danger now. There are too many people on guard for anyone to risk a second visit here. What I'd like to do first is to establish exactly where he was when he fired the shot. Some clue may have been left behind.'

'You're wasting your time, sir. He could have been anywhere.'

'I disagree,' said Colbeck. 'The trajectory of the bullet gives me a definite idea of the direction from which it came. All I require is your permission to search the grounds without fear of being attacked by that mastiff you have out there.'

'Search if you must,' said Thornhill, petulantly, 'but you won't find anything, I know that. The man must have fled as soon as he fired the shot.'

'That's what I'm counting on, Mr Thornhill. When people are in a great hurry to escape, they often make mistakes.'

The tender ministrations of his wife and a good night's sleep had revived Victor Leeming and sent him back to work with renewed vigour. Dressed in his normal attire, he travelled to Chalk Farm by cab and rapped on the door of Josie Murlow's hovel. There was no answer. After knocking even harder a few times, he accepted that she was not there. Leeming followed the route he had taken the previous day, turning into the main road and walking along it until he made a second turn. When the Shepherd and Shepherdess came into view, the bump on his head started to throb.

He paused at the alleyway where he had been assaulted. Narrow and twisting, it ran through to the street beyond, giving his attacker a choice of two exits. Leeming went on to the public house. Its first customers of the morning had already drifted in. Standing behind the counter was the landlord, a tubby man of medium height with a bald head offset by a drooping walrus moustache. Leeming introduced himself and described the woman he wanted to find. The landlord guessed her name at once.

'You're talking about Josie Murlow,' he said.

'You know her?'

'I know her and that cock-eyed ruffian she lives with. They're nothing but trouble, those two. I barred them from the Shepherd and Shepherdess months ago.'

'Josie Murlow was standing outside here yesterday afternoon.'

'Then I'm glad she didn't have the gall to come in.'

'I don't suppose you saw her,' said Leeming, 'or noticed which way she walked off.'

'No, Sergeant,' replied the landlord. 'As long as she and Dick Chiffney keep away from here, that's all I'm worried about. On the other hand,' he went on, looking around the bar, 'some of my regulars might have seen her through the window. Josie is not easy to miss. She'd make three of my wife.'

'She'd make four of mine.'

Leeming first spoke to a couple of men who had just entered but they were unable to help him. None of the other customers had even been there at the relevant time on the previous day. He was about to leave when he noticed an old man tucked away in a corner. Crouched over a table, he was playing dominoes on his own, moving from one seat to another and back again as he took turns, pausing only to quaff some of his beer. As Leeming came over, he fixed a pair of watery eyes on him.

'Care for a game of dominoes?' he croaked.

'You seem to be playing well enough on your own,' said Leeming with a grin. 'Who's winning?'

'*He* is,' said the old man, pointing to the empty chair.

'I'm sorry to interrupt the game, sir. I just wanted to ask if you knew a woman named Josie Murlow.'

The old man cackled. 'Everyone knows Josie.' He sat back to appraise Leeming. 'I wouldn't have thought a gentleman like you would have any time for her. She's beneath you, sir. Or is that what you want?' he added, slyly. 'Having Josie beneath you, I mean.'

'No!' denied Leeming, revolted by the notion. 'That's not what I want. I'm a detective from Scotland Yard and I wish to speak to her in connection with a crime.' The old man gabbled his apologies. 'Did you, by any chance, see her yesterday afternoon?'

The old man thought hard. 'I did, as a matter of fact.'

'Where was she?'

'Standing outside, all dressed up in her finery.'

'Did you see her through the window?'

'No,' said the other. 'I was walking along the pavement outside. Josie was lurking at the door as if she didn't know whether to come in or go away.'

'Was she on her own?' asked Leeming.

'She was at first. Then that ugly devil of hers steps out of the alleyway and rushes her away up the road.'

'In which direction did they go?'

'Towards Camden,' said the old man, 'but I only saw them for a few seconds. Dick Chiffney stopped a cab and the both got into it.' He cackled again. 'I pity the poor horse, having to pull Josie along. She must weigh the best part of a ton.'

'Are you *certain* that it was Chiffney?'

'Oh, yes. Nobody else could be as ugly as that.'

Dick Chiffney peered at his face in the mirror, twisting his head sideways as he used the razor to shave the last bristles from his chin. After washing the blade in a bowl of cold water, he dried it on a piece of cloth before closing the razor. Then he splashed his face with water and dabbed at it with the cloth. He viewed the results in the mirror. On the bed behind him, Josie Murlow slowly came out of her sleep.

'Where am I?' she said, drowsily.

'You're with me, Josie,' he told her. 'We're staying at the house of my friend for a little while.'

'Why is that?'

'You *know* why.'

'I'd rather be in my own house.'

'It could be watched.'

'But there's things I need, Dick.'

'I'll sneak back after dark and get them for you, my love,' he said. 'I can't take that chance in daylight. He might've come back.'

'Who're you talking about?' she asked, yawning.

'The policeman I knocked out yesterday.'

The reminder brought her fully awake. Josie struggled to sit up in bed, her naked breasts spilling out over the bed sheet like a pair of balloons filled with water. She rubbed a knuckle against both eyes.

'I remember now,' she said with annoyance. 'I was followed.'

'As I guessed you would be,' he bragged. 'You have to keep one step ahead of the police, Josie. I know the way they work.'

'Does that mean I can never go back to my house?'

'You may never need to, my love.'

She yawned again. 'What time is it?'

'It's time for me to go.'

'You're not going to leave me here alone, are you?' she protested.

'I have to,' he explained. 'There's breakfast waiting for you in the kitchen downstairs and I've left money if you want to send out for drink. My friend's name is Walter, by the way. Ask him for anything you need. Walter will look after you.'

'I'd rather *you* did that,' she grumbled.

Josie looked around the room with a mixture of interest and distrust. It was bigger, better furnished and very much cleaner than her bedroom at home. They were obviously in a sizeable house. The bed was extremely comfortable. She and Chiffney had tested the mattress to the limit. She watched him as he put on his jacket and did up the buttons. The new suit made him look so much smarter. She wanted to believe that the two of them were going up in the world but she was haunted by doubts.

'Everything is going to be all right, Dick, isn't it?' she said.

'Put your faith in me, my love.'

'I want to come with you.'

'No, Josie,' he said, restraining her as she tried to clamber out of bed. 'I've got business I can only do on my own. In any case, I don't want us to be seen in public again.'

She bristled. 'Are you ashamed of me, then?'

'Don't be silly.'

'Have you got someone else, Dick?' she said, accusingly.

'Yes,' he replied. 'I've got a gentleman who'll pay me more money than I've ever earned before to do one small job. You'll be fine here, my love,' he said, jokingly. 'If you have any fears for your virginity, there's a rifle under the bed. I don't need that today.'

He picked up the pistol that lay on the table and opened his coat to tuck the weapon into his belt. Slipping some ammunition into his pocket, he reached for his hat. Josie was concerned.

'How long will you be?' she asked.

'I could be away for most of the day.'

'Why – where are you going?'

'Brighton,' he said.

Robert Colbeck was away for such a long time that Thornhill assumed that he was not coming back to the house. He was already composing a letter of complaint to Scotland Yard when the detective was finally shown back into the library.

'I thought you'd abandoned me, Inspector,' he said.

'I'd never do that, sir,' Colbeck told him. 'There was a large area to search but it was worthwhile. I found the exact spot from which that shot was fired at you.' He held up a tiny piece of cloth. 'Your attacker was hiding behind a bramble bush some fifty yards away. His jacket must have caught on the spikes.'

'There's no guarantee that the material came from his clothing,' Thornhill contended. 'It might have come from anyone else who'd walked that way – from my gamekeeper, for instance.'

'I think your gamekeeper would have more sense than to stand in a bramble patch, sir. Besides, there are clear footprints there. From that position, he had a good view of the terrace.'

'What use is that information now?'

'I thought it might reassure you.'

Thornhill was perplexed. 'How could it possibly do that?'

'It proves that your would-be assassin was no marksman, sir,' said Colbeck. 'From fifty yards away, a trained rifleman would have been confident of hitting you when you were sitting down. This man waited until you got up so that you presented a larger target – and yet still he missed.'

'Only by a matter of inches,' said Thornhill.

'Someone who knew how to handle a rifle could have shot you dead from hundreds of yards away. This man had to get close and even then he failed. In your position,' said Colbeck, 'I'd draw comfort from that fact.'

'The only comfort I get is when the house is properly guarded and I'm locked up safely inside.'

'I meant to speak to you about that, sir. After today, I suggest that you stand down some of the men at the gate and those patrolling the estate.'

'That's an insane suggestion, Inspector.'

'If you want the man caught, it's the best thing to do.'

'Lay myself open to the possibility of a *second* attack?' cried Thornhill in disbelief. 'What on earth is the point of that?'

'It will tempt him to come back.'

'That's the last thing I want to do, man.'

'Then we may never find him, warned Colbeck. 'He'll melt into the crowd and stay there until you're sufficiently recovered to leave the safety of your home. It may take weeks, even months, before he strikes again – and it will be when you least expect it. If we can lure him into making a second attempt, however,' he went on, 'we can bait the trap.'

'I won't be used a target practice,' said Thornhill, hotly.

'There's no danger of that, sir. Now, you have a reputation as a public speaker. As well as taking part in Parliamentary debates, you've addressed meetings on a regular basis.'

'One has to spread the word.'

'Do you keep a record of such meetings?'

'Naturally,' said Thornhill. 'Everything is listed in my diary. As it happens, I was due to speak here in Brighton tomorrow evening.'

Colbeck was pleased. 'In that case,' he said, 'you must honour the commitment.'

'How can I when someone out there is waiting to shoot me? I've instructed my secretary to say that I've had to withdraw.'

'Has he done so yet, Mr Thornhill?'

'Yes, he's advised them to find another speaker.'

'I think you should rescind that instruction and announce that you'll address the meeting, after all. It would impress your audience greatly that you've made light of your injuries.'

'I've no wish to appear in public.'

'You may not have to, sir – just do as I ask.'

Thornhill was reluctant. 'I'll think about it.'

'Thank you, sir,' said Colbeck. 'Meanwhile, I'd be most grateful to see the list of public meetings you've addressed in recent months. When I have that in my possession, I'll go back into Brighton.'

'Why is that, Inspector?'

'I need to look at some newspapers, sir.'

* * *

If nothing else, the visit to Chalk Farm had confirmed the fact that it was Dick Chiffney who had knocked Victor Leeming unconscious in an alleyway. It served to concentrate the victim's mind. Leaving the Shepherd and Shepherdess, he turned to the next task assigned to him by Colbeck and headed for the offices of the LB&SCR. As he was about to go in, he met Captain Ridgeon on his way out.

'Good morning, Sergeant,' said Ridgeon, brightly.

'Good morning to you, sir,' returned Leeming.

'Are you still persisting in your unnecessary inquiry?'

'Yes, Captain – in spite of jibes from ill-informed sources.'

'Are you referring to my comments in the newspaper?'

'They were both harsh and unjust.'

'I was quoted incorrectly, Sergeant Leeming.'

'Does that mean you actually approve of what we're doing?'

Ridgeon stifled a smile. 'I wouldn't go that far,' he said, 'but I would ask you to believe that my remarks were not as intemperate as they appeared to be in that article.'

'It all hangs on the interpretation of the evidence,' said Leeming, 'and, in my opinion, there's nobody alive who does that better than Inspector Colbeck.'

'Unfortunately, some of that "evidence" has now disappeared.'

'Has it?'

'I can see that you haven't been to Brighton recently,' said Ridgeon. 'Once I had made my decision about the cause of the crash, it was vital to open the two lines again as quickly as possibly. Crews worked twenty-four hours a day to clear the debris and repair the track. As from yesterday, the Brighton Express is running again in both directions.'

'I wondered how the Inspector got back so early yesterday.'

Ridgeon was curious. 'What was he doing in Brighton?'

'Exactly the same as I'm doing now, sir,' said Leeming, looking him in the eye. 'He's doing his damnedest to prove you wrong.'

He went into the building, introduced himself to one of the clerks and asked to see Matthew Shanklin. After disappearing for a couple of minutes, the man returned and shook his head.

'I'm sorry, Sergeant,' he said. 'Mr Shanklin is not here.'

'Is he still indisposed?'

'Yes, sir – he's too ill to come into work this morning.'

'How do you know?'

'The manager says that he sent a letter to that effect.'

Leeming's eye lit up. 'Was it written by Mr Shanklin himself?'

'I think so, Sergeant.'

'Then I should very much like to see it.'

While nothing could have endeared the politician to Colbeck, he had to admire Giles Thornhill's industry. The man was quite indefatigable, addressing public meetings on issues of the day with a frequency that was breathtaking. When he was not facing an audience in a hall, Thornhill was, more often than not, expressing his opinions as an after-dinner speaker at various functions. Most of his work had been done in London but there were enough occasions when he had spoken in his constituency to send Colbeck to the offices of one of the local newspapers, the *Brighton Gazette*.

The editor, Sidney Weaver, was an anxious little man in his forties, his brow furrowed and his hands twitching nervously.

The Railway Detective, it turned out, was a man for whom he had the highest respect.

'I've followed your career carefully,' said Weaver, gesticulating at him. 'I know what you did on Derby Day this year and how you solved the murder of that man thrown from the Sankey Bridge. You'll get all the help you need from me.'

'Thank you,' said Colbeck, finding his praise rather tiresome. 'All I want is somewhere quiet to read back copies of your newspaper.'

'Is there anything in particular that you're looking for, sir? If so, I might be able to save you the time. I've got an encyclopaedic mind where the *Gazette* is concerned. Mr Bardwell calls me a marvel.'

'I gather that he often writes for you.'

'We always accept copy from someone of his eminence. Mark you,' Weaver went on, closing an eye, 'he's not so ready to offer an opinion when there's been an accident and that's happened once too often.' The lines in his face multiplied and deepened. 'Do you remember when the *Jenny Lind* came into service?'

'Of course,' replied Colbeck. 'It was seven years ago. She was a beautiful locomotive with those huge six-foot driving wheels and that classical fluted dome.'

'I was travelling on the express when *Jenny Lind* got into trouble. Her leading axle broke and tore off a wheel. The driver had no idea what had happened so he kept up full speed, unaware that he was ripping up the track behind him. We were aware of it,' said Weaver, hands semaphoring wildly, 'because we were shaken about every inch of the way. We were lucky to come out of it alive.'

'What was Mr Bardwell's reaction?'

'He went strangely quiet for once.'

'That same can't be said of the gentleman in whom I'm interested,' said Colbeck, taking out a piece of paper. 'These are the editions I'd like to see, Mr Weaver,' he continued, handing the list over. 'Is there somewhere private where I can study them?'

'Have the use of my office,' said Weaver, moving various items off his desk. 'It's a privilege to have the Railway Detective here.'

'Thank you.'

'I'll get one of my lads to find these for you.'

Weaver opened the door, beckoned a young man over and gave him the list. While they were waiting, he gave Colbeck a brief history of the *Gazette* and how he had come to edit it. The newspapers arrived and Weaver took them from the young man before putting them in the middle of the desk.

'If there's anything I can do, Inspector, just call me.'

'I will, Mr Weaver.'

Grateful to be left alone at last, Colbeck worked through the newspapers chronologically, searching for reports of public meetings that Giles Thornhill had addressed. Occasionally, he had shared a platform with the other sitting Member of Parliament for Brighton but Thornhill's had always been the more dominant voice. He was an unrepentant reactionary, defending the status quo and resisting any hint of radical reform. Chartists were treated with especial scorn.

In almost every speech, Thornhill had stressed his pride in his country, arguing that the British Empire was a wondrous achievement that acted as a civilising influence all over the world. On the subject of immigration – and he spoke on it more than once – his patriotism had taken on a sharper edge.

His most recent speech on the subject had been quoted in some detail. Colbeck could almost hear him declaiming the words from a platform. Folding over the page, he got up and opened the door. Sidney Weaver scurried across to him like a spaniel.

'Did you want to see anything else, Inspector Colbeck?' he said.

'It's possible,' replied Colbeck. 'There's a speech here that Giles Thornhill made about immigration.'

'He's always had great distaste for foreigners.'

'This is more than distaste, Mr Weaver.' He showed the report to the editor. 'Did you have any response to this?'

'We had a very strong response,' said Weaver with an abrupt laugh. 'Some of the letters were far too offensive to print.'

Colbeck smiled. 'I don't suppose you kept any of them, did you?'

'I kept them all, Inspector – including the one from the Rector of St Dunstan's. He was outraged by what Mr Thornhill had said.'

A meeting with the churchwardens was always an essay in sustained boredom but Ezra Follis endured it without demur. Retired, worthy, staid and lacking in anything resembling lightness of touch, the two men were pillars of the community who took their duties with a seriousness matched only by their solemnity. A couple of hours in the presence taxed even Follis's nerves and he waved them off with more than usual alacrity. The moment they disappeared, Mrs Ashmore bustled out of the kitchen.

'Is there anything I can get you?' she offered.

'Yes,' he replied, 'you can untie the bandage on the other hand.'

'The doctor said that you had to keep it on.'

'It's so *inconvenient*.'

'Your other hand is now free,' she pointed out.

'Thank goodness! I can at least start to write again.'

Flexing his right hand, he examined it. Still covered by scabs, it was no longer burning away under the bandaging. It was the left hand that was more badly damaged and it would be some time before he had free use of it again. Meanwhile, he could now catch up on the correspondence that he had to postpone.

'Will you be going to London this week?' asked Mrs Ashmore.

'I think not. I'll have to change my routine for once. Until my hands and my head are better, I'll stay here and enjoy the comforts of home.'

'I'm glad to hear that.'

'As for refreshment, Mrs Ashmore, I think that a long walk will be the best tonic for me somehow. Splendid fellows though they are, our churchwardens can lower the spirits at times – not that they must ever know that.'

'You can always rely on me, Mr Follis.'

'Your discretion is much appreciated.'

After thanking her with a smile, he took his leave and stepped out of the rectory. It was a fine day and he wished that he could wear a hat to ward off the sun but the bandaging around his skull made that impossible. Though he had told his housekeeper that he was going on a long walk, he instead took a short stroll to a terrace not far from the church. Stopping outside the corner house, he rang the bell. The door was opened by a breathless Amy Walcott, who had seen him through the window of the drawing room and scampered to meet him.

'Good morning, Amy,' he said.

'What a lovely surprise!'

'The churchwardens and I have just been talking about you.'

Her expression changed. 'There are no complaints about the way the flowers are arranged, are there?' she said, apprehensively. 'I take so much trouble over them and always check when it's been someone else's turn.'

'The flowers have earned nothing but compliments,' he told her. 'In fact, Miss Andrews, whom you met yesterday, said that you had mastered the art of flower arranging.'

'Did the young lady go into the church, then?'

'I made sure that she did.' He beamed at her. 'It's very nice standing out here on your doorstep, Amy, but I was hoping for a private word. May I come in?'

'Of course, of course,' she said, backing away.

They went into a drawing room that was cosy and inviting rather than elegant. It had a dated feel to it. Everything in it had been bought by Amy's mother before she had followed her husband to the grave. The passion for flowers was reflected in the floral pattern on the wallpaper and the landscapes on the wall, replete with fields of bluebells, daffodils and other flowers.

'Your mother left her mark on this room, Amy,' he observed.

'I try to keep it exactly as Mother left it.'

'That's why I feel so comfortable in here.' She indicated the sofa and he sat down. 'Thank you.'

'I'm sorry that I was in the way yesterday.'

'Don't talk such nonsense!'

'Inspector Colbeck came to talk about the train crash.'

'He gave me no warning of his arrival,' said Follis. 'Since he was there, I could hardly turn him away.'

'Is Miss Andrews his...fiancée?' she probed.

'I fancy that she will be in time – they are very close.'

Amy was relieved to hear it. The fact that he had taken her into the church had set off a faint pang of jealousy. At the rectory, she had felt ousted by a much prettier young woman.

'You have your own charms,' he said, settling back, 'and not even Miss Andrews could compete with you in some ways. Have you been reading Tennyson again?'

'Yes,' she replied. 'I know some of the smaller poems by heart.'

'You've always been quick to learn, Amy.'

She almost blushed. 'I've had a good teacher.'

'Then let me hear how well I've taught you.' He looked towards the door. 'Are we alone in the house?'

'The maid is in the kitchen. We'll not be disturbed.'

'Good.'

'Shall I fetch the book, Mr Follis?'

'Where is it?'

'On the table beside my bed,' she replied.

'Let it stay there for a while, Amy,' he said, using his right hand to stroke his chin. 'Why don't you recite the poems that you've learnt by heart? At this moment in time, I can't think of anything in the world I'd rather hear.'

Amy Walcott glowed with delight.

CHAPTER TWELVE

Victor Leeming had hoped that he could slip back to Scotland Yard without being spotted by the superintendent but Edward Tallis had an uncanny knack of knowing which of his officers was on the premises at any given time. No sooner had Leeming crept into Colbeck's office than the shadow of his superior fell across him. He quailed.

'Do you have the inspector's permission to come in here while he's away?' enquired Tallis.

'Yes, Superintendent, I do.'

'For what purpose, may I ask?'

'He wanted me to compare some handwriting, sir,' said Leeming. 'I believe that he showed you the funeral card received at the hospital by Mr Bardwell.'

'Yes – it was an appalling thing to send.'

'Thank heaven Mr Bardwell didn't actually know what it said. The Reverend Follis had the presence of mind to keep it from him and pass it on to us instead.'

'Everything I learn about this clergyman is to his credit,' said Tallis, warmly. 'I should like to meet the fellow some time.'

'I'd like to hear him preach in church. I fancy that he'd deliver a lively sermon. Oh, that reminds me, sir,' Leeming continued, seizing his opportunity. 'I'd very much like to have next Sunday free, if it's at all possible.'

'That depends on the state of this investigation.'

'Whatever its state, I need to be at home.'

'Why – is there some kind of domestic emergency?'

'We're having an important family event.'

'Dear God!' cried Tallis with dismay, 'are you telling me that your wife is about to give birth to *another* child? Learn to contain yourself, man,' he said, reproachfully. 'Control your animal urges. You were not put on this earth to people it indiscriminately.'

Leeming was embarrassed 'We're not expecting an addition to the family, sir.'

'I'm relieved to hear it.'

'Estelle and I are happy with the two children we already have.'

'My opinion remains unchanged,' said Tallis. 'Children are a grave distraction for any police officer.'

'You were a child once, Superintendent.'

'Don't be impertinent.'

'I'm sorry, sir.'

'What exactly is this important family event?'

'It's nothing,' said Leeming, not wishing to invite derision by explaining his request. 'I'll do whatever needs to be done to bring this investigation to a conclusion.'

'That's the attitude I expect of my men. You must have seen that vicious article in the newspaper yesterday,' said Tallis, still smarting at the personal attack on him. 'We need to vindicate our reputation and do so quickly. I rely on you and

Colbeck to put the Inspector General of Railways in his place.'

'As it happens, I met Captain Ridgeon this morning.'

'Oh – where was that?'

'At the offices of the LB&SCR,' said Leeming.

'Did he say anything to you?'

'Yes, sir – he was crowing over us.'

'We must put a stop to that,' said Tallis, vengefully. 'What were you doing there, Sergeant?'

'I'd hoped to speak to Mr Shanklin, sir. Inspector Colbeck had intended to do so but he was called away to Brighton. I went in his stead. For the second day running, Mr Shanklin was not there. But I managed to get what I went for,' said Leeming, taking a letter from his pocket. 'It's a sample of his handwriting.'

'Do you think that *he* might have sent that funeral card?'

'Why don't we find out, sir?'

Opening a drawer in the desk, Leeming took out the envelope containing the funeral card and put it side by side with the letter written by Matthew Shanklin. The looping calligraphy was almost identical. Tallis picked up both items and looked from one to the other in quick succession. He sounded a note of triumph.

'We've got him!'

'They do look very similar,' said Leeming.

'They should do, Sergeant – they're the work of the same man.' He took out the funeral card to compare it with the letter. 'There's no doubt about it. Matthew Shanklin sent this card.'

'He may have done a lot more than that, sir.'

'I'm sure that he did,' said Tallis, grimly. 'He caused that crash deliberately then sent that card to Mr Bardwell as a taunt. He was gloating.' He snapped his fingers. 'We need a warrant for his arrest. You can go to his home this morning.'

'That won't be possible, Superintendent.'

'Why not?'

'I called there on my way back from his office,' said Leeming. 'His wife told me that her husband had gone out. That was very odd because his letter claims that he was too ill to go to work. Mr Shanklin is deceiving his employers.'

'Find him, Sergeant,' ordered Tallis. 'Find him at once.'

The Brighton line was one on which Matthew Shanklin had travelled many times when he worked for the company but the present journey was different from the others. He was smouldering with residual anger at his dismissal from a post that he had expected to hold until his retirement. As the train puffed its way past the site of the crash, he was astonished to see how much of the debris had been cleared away. The scarred embankment still bore testimony to the disaster, as did the bushes flattened during the derailment but the place was no longer littered with mangled iron and shattered timber.

What did catch his eye were the wreaths that had been placed beside the line, marking the spot where lives had been lost. From the newspaper he had bought at the station, Shanklin had learnt that the death toll had now reached a dozen. His one regret was that a particular name was missing from the list. The train raced on to Brighton where it disgorged several passengers taking advantage of a glorious day to visit the seaside.

Surging out of the railway station, the crowd was oblivious

to its arresting architecture. Shanklin, however, paused to look back at the magnificent classical façade, worthy of an Italianate palace and a symmetrical tribute to the vital importance of the terminus. He had always admired stations that were both imposing and functional, soaring works of art that could yet be used daily by untold thousands of people. Brighton was a perfect example.

Cabs, omnibuses and the occasional carriage stood on the forecourt but Shanklin chose to walk. He was in no hurry. Having the day to himself, he could take his time and see some of the sights that had made Brighton so appealing. It was over an hour before he turned towards the county hospital. Shanklin was forced to wait. The person he wanted to see was being examined by a doctor. When the patient was left alone, Shanklin was thrilled to see how poorly he was. He leaned over the bed.

'Do you remember *me*?' he asked with a smirk.

Horace Bardwell began to quiver uncontrollably.

Colbeck had some difficulty in breaking free from the attentions of the over-helpful Sidney Weaver. The visit to the offices of the *Brighton Gazette* had, however, been very rewarding and its editor had been a mine of information. Among other things, he told Colbeck where to find the best gunsmith in the town. It was there that the detective took the bullet he had retrieved from the back of Thornhill's settee. Having been given a professional opinion by the gunsmith, Colbeck decided to pay another call on someone else whose opinion he valued highly. The Reverend Ezra Follis was as cordial as ever.

'This is becoming a habit, Inspector,' he said. 'Hardly a day passes when you don't come to see me. This time, alas, you've not brought the charming Miss Andrews.'

'Madeleine is working back home in London,' said Colbeck.

'Yes, she told me that she was an artist. I found it extraordinary that such a beautiful young woman should want to sketch steam locomotives.' He raised a palm. 'That's not a criticism, I hasten to say. I applaud her talent. At least,' he added with a laugh, 'I would do if I were able to clap with both hands.'

They were in the rectory and it was only a matter of minutes before Mrs Ashmore appeared magically from the kitchen with a pot of tea and a plate of biscuits. Colbeck thanked her, realising for the first time that he had not eaten since having an early breakfast.

'I'd like to think you came back to Brighton with the sole pleasure of seeing me,' said Follis, wryly, 'but I'm sure it was for a much more important reason.'

'Someone tried to shoot Mr Thornhill,' explained Colbeck.

'Saints preserve us!'

'It happened yesterday, Mr Follis.'

'Was he hurt?'

'Luckily, the bullet missed him.'

Colbeck told the rector what had happened and how he had found both the place from which the shot was fired and the bullet itself. Follis was shocked. While he was no friend of Giles Thornhill, he was distressed to hear of the attack and said that he would pray for the politician's safety.

'That explains why Mr Thornhill has withdrawn from a meeting he was due to address tomorrow,' he said. 'I thought it was because of his injuries. In view of the attempt on his life, I can appreciate the real reason why he's not willing to appear in public.'

'If he won't speak, the meeting will have to be cancelled.'

'One can't disappoint an audience, Inspector. The town hall is booked and tickets have been sold. Another speaker has been found at short notice. I could not recommend him more highly.'

'Who is going to replace Mr Thornhill?'

Follis chortled. 'As luck would have it – I am.'

'What's the title of your talk?'

'The one already advertised – The Future of Brighton.'

'I've heard rather a lot on that topic in the last couple of hours,' said Colbeck. 'I've been doing some research at the offices of the *Brighton Gazette*. The editor had much to say about the town's future.'

'How did you get on with Sidney Weaver?'

'He was extremely helpful, though inclined to fuss over me like a mother hen. I've never seen anyone look so worried.'

'Sidney is always afraid that that the *Gazette* is not as good as it should be and that the next edition may be the last. He's a slave to his anxiety. After successful years in charge of the newspaper, he still lacks confidence.'

'His knowledge of the town's history is amazing.'

'Incomparable,' said Follis. 'I've urged him to write a book about it. And, as you discovered, he has opinions about the future of the town as well. If he were not so dreadfully nervous in public, Sidney might have been approached to deputise for Mr Thornhill tomorrow.' He reached for a scone. 'Did you tell him about the shooting?'

'No,' said Colbeck. 'Neither Mr Thornhill nor I want it splashed across the newspaper. I only confided in you because

I know that you'll be discreet. Also,' he went on, 'you needed to be told the truth before you can assist me.'

'How can I help you this time, Inspector?'

'I believe you wrote to the *Gazette* a couple of weeks ago.'

'I'm always writing to newspapers,' said Follis. 'I'm a great believer in healthy debate. If there's an issue that interests me, I make sure that I offer an opinion on it. That's why I took on that speaking engagement tomorrow.' He took a first bite of the scone. 'Can you remind me about this particular letter?'

'It was in on the subject of immigration.'

'Ah, yes – that dreadful speech by Mr Thornhill.'

'You took strong exception to what he said.'

'I was disgusted, Inspector,' said Follis. 'I was sorry that I was not actually at the meeting or I'd have stood up and denounced him. Did you see what he was preaching?'

'He objects to foreigners settling in this country.'

'It's more specific than that. Though he spoke in general terms, his poisonous arguments had a very specific target. The foreigners he was attacking live right here in Brighton.'

'The town is not noted for its immigrants.'

'Mr Thornhill doesn't work in numerical terms. The fact that we have any foreigners at all here is enough to arouse him, especially when they better themselves by dint of sheer hard work.' He put his scone back on the plate. 'Do you remember 1848?'

'I remember it very well,' said Colbeck. 'Sergeant Leeming and I were in uniform at the time, deployed, along with the rest of the Metropolitan Police Force, to resist the threat of a Chartist uprising. Happily, that threat never materialised.'

'It did elsewhere in Europe, Inspector. There were revolutions in France, Germany, Austria and elsewhere.

Countries were in turmoil, governments were overthrown and the streets ran with blood.'

'I know, Mr Follis. Many people fled to this country for safety.'

'Some of them came to Brighton and liked it so much that they settled here. These are frightened refugees whom we should welcome with open arms,' said Follis with passion. 'All that Mr Thornhill can do is to stir up hatred against them. He has two main arguments. The first is that they are simply not British – an accident of Fate over which they have no control – and the second is that they've prospered in their new country. Foreigners, he argues, are taking opportunities that rightly belong to people who were born here.'

'Judging by the report, his speech was almost inflammatory.'

'It arose from a twisted patriotism, Inspector, and more or less incited people to join in a witch hunt. The wonder is that it didn't provoke our immigrant population to react.'

'I suspect that it did,' said Colbeck, taking the bullet from his pocket and holding it on his palm. 'This was intended to kill Giles Thornhill. According to the gunsmith I consulted, it did not come from a British rifle. It was fired from a foreign weapon.'

The funeral was a sombre affair. It was at Kensal Green Cemetery that Frank Pike was laid to rest. Wearing mourning dress, Caleb Andrews held back tears as he watched the coffin being lowered into the ground. The wooden box contained the unrecognisable remains of a friend he had loved and respected for many years. The thought that he would never see him again was like a bonfire in his brain. Andrews was grateful that Rose Pike was not there to see the last agonising minutes of her husband's funeral.

Dressed in black like the others, Madeleine had stayed at the Pike household to make refreshments for those returning from the cemetery. She could see how deeply moved her father was. He was one of a number of railwaymen who had forfeited a day's wages to pay their last respects to Pike. Now recovered, John Heddle was among them. All of them offered commiserations to the widow. What nobody did, Madeleine was relieved to see, was to refer to the newspaper article blaming the dead man for the train crash. To draw that to the attention of the widow would be like driving a stake through her heart.

On the journey back home, neither Madeleine nor her father spoke a single word. The bruising experience of the funeral had left them feeling hurt and bereft. Madeleine had been uncomfortably reminded of the death of her own mother and of its destructive impact on the family. Years after the event, it remained fresh and unbearably painful. She could understand the searing anguish that Rose Pike must be feeling and vowed to offer what succour she could in the future. Widowhood was a trial for any woman. The circumstances of her husband's death intensified the ordeal for Rose Pike.

Andrews was lost in his own grief, calling to mind cherished memories of a man who had died a cruel death beneath the very locomotive he was driving. The worst of it was that he was now being hounded beyond the grave, made to bear responsibility for something he did not do. Andrews's grief was mingled with a seething fury. He yearned to clear his friend's name and defy Pike's detractors. When they reached the house, he was still deep in thought.

Madeleine led the way in, removing her black hat with its thick veil and hanging it on a peg. She reached out to take her father's hat from him. Andrews grabbed her hand.

'When will you see Inspector Colbeck again, Maddy?'

'I don't know, father,' she said.

'Tell him to catch the monster who caused that crash,' he said with sudden urgency. 'Until that's done, poor Frank will never be able to rest in peace.'

The security arrangements were still in place when Colbeck returned to Thornhill's estate but at least he did not have to identify himself again. Broken arm back in its sling, the politician was seated at the table in his library, reading some correspondence. He looked up as Colbeck entered the room.

'Do you have anything to report?' he asked.

'I feel that I made some progress,' said Colbeck, 'especially after my talk with the Reverend Follis.'

'Don't listen to that meddling fool.'

'I found him anything but foolish, sir.'

'He should stick to what he's supposed to do,' said Thornhill, 'and not interfere in political matters about which he knows absolutely nothing. I only have to open my mouth and the Rector of St Dunstan's is writing to the newspapers.'

'Yes,' said Colbeck, 'I've seen one of his letters.'

'His comments are quite uncalled for, Inspector.'

'I don't see why – he's one of your constituents.'

Thornhill's laugh was hollow. 'If I had to rely on the votes of men like Ezra Follis,' he said, 'my Parliamentary career would have been woefully short. Fortunately, I have a number of like-minded supporters in Brighton. That's why it's such a pleasure to represent the town.'

'But you don't actually represent them,' argued Colbeck. 'Only a small percentage of the population is registered to vote. The only thing you represent is a minority.'

'That's because most people in the town lack the necessary property qualification. Brighton is besieged by newcomers and by foreign riffraff. They don't deserve the vote. Anyway,' he went on, testily, 'why are we talking about Ezra Follis?'

'He was able to give me some pertinent information.'

'Whatever it is, I don't want to hear it.'

'As you wish, Mr Thornhill,' said Colbeck, easily. 'What I really came back to ask is if you had changed your mind about the speaking engagement tomorrow evening.'

'It would be sheer madness to attend.'

'I disagree.'

'You have not been shot at, Inspector.'

'As a matter of fact, I have sir – and on more than one occasion. To be frank, it's an occupational hazard for which I don't much care.' He stepped closer. 'Supposing that you were *not* in any danger? Would you consider fulfilling your commitment then?'

'That question is purely hypothetical.'

'I'd nevertheless be interested in your answer.'

'Then I'd answer in the affirmative,' said Thornhill, stoutly. 'A broken arm would not stop me from expressing my views on a public platform. People look to me to shape their opinions.'

'In that case, you mustn't disappoint them.'

'I don't follow.'

'Instruct your secretary to have your name reinstated at once in the advertisements,' advised Colbeck. 'At the moment, someone else is stepping into the breach to speak on the same subject. It might aid your decision if I tell you that your replacement is the Reverend Follis.'

Thornhill was stung. 'I won't stand for that!'

'Someone has to address that meeting.'

'What are you trying to do, Inspector – get me killed?'

'No, sir,' replied Colbeck, 'I'm trying to ensure the arrest of the man who fired that shot at you. If you do as I say, you won't even have to leave the house tomorrow evening – until it's safe to do so, that is.'

After his long, tiring vigil on the previous day, Victor Leeming did not look forward to repeating the experience but there were extenuating aspects of his present assignment. He could expect no violence from Matthew Shanklin and there was no possibility of being lured into an alleyway so that he could be clubbed to the ground. The street in which he was standing consisted of matching rows of terraced houses. It was a district in which he did not look out of place in his normal apparel. Instead of staying in the same place, he patrolled up and down the street, one eye kept on the Shanklin residence at all times.

By mid-afternoon, his wait was over. A cab came round the corner and rolled past him before stopping a short distance away. Matthew Shanklin got out, paid the driver and turned to go towards his house. Leeming moved smartly. After ordering the driver to wait, he intercepted Shanklin.

'Excuse me, sir,' he said, 'I'd like a word with you.'

'I'm afraid that I don't have time to talk now, Sergeant,' said Shanklin, walking away until Leeming grabbed his arm. 'Take your hands off me!'

'When I called at your office this morning, they told me that you were ill for the second day running.'

'That's quite true. I've just been to see my doctor.'

'What's his name, sir?'

'Where does he live?'

'Why do you ask that?'

'I think you know, sir,' said Leeming. 'There's no illness and
no doctor. When I spoke to Mrs Shanklin this morning, she
seemed totally unaware that you were supposed to be unwell.'

'I told you before,' protested Shanklin, a hand to his brow,
'that I'm a martyr to migraine attacks.'

'Then you'll have another one very shortly, sir.'

'What are you talking about?'

'I have a warrant for your arrest,' said Leeming, taking the
paper from his pocket to show him. 'You must come with me.'

Shanklin was rocked. 'On what charge am I being arrested?'

'We have reason to believe that you are party to a
conspiracy to cause a train crash on the Brighton line.'
Shanklin's eyes darted to his house. 'No, sir, I'm afraid that I
can't let you go in there first. You'll have to accompany me to
Scotland Yard.'

'But I've done nothing wrong,' bleated the other.

'You can tell that to Superintendent Tallis.'

Accepting that there was no escape, Shanklin gave in. He
gulped in air and looked around guiltily. Leeming saw no need
to put handcuffs on him. Easing him back into the cab, he
stepped in after him. The driver, who had watched the arrest
with fascination, did not need instructions.

'Scotland Yard, is it, guv'nor?' he said, snapping the reins to
set the horse in motion. 'I thought there was something funny
about him when I picked him up at the railway station.'

Leeming spent the journey trying to find out where Shanklin had been all day but the man refused to tell him. On the orders of the superintendent, Leeming said nothing about the handwriting on the letter and the funeral card. It was a revelation Tallis wanted to keep for himself. On arrival at their destination, Leeming paid the driver and hustled his prisoner into the building. They went straight to the superintendent's office.

Edward Tallis was so pleased with the arrest that he permitted Leeming to stay while he questioned the suspect. His technique differed radically from that favoured by Colbeck. While the inspector was effortlessly polite, drawing out information slowly by the most subtle means, Tallis chose a more direct and intimidating approach. After the preliminaries, he made Shanklin sit down so that he could loom over him.

'Did you send Mr Bardwell a funeral card?' he demanded.

'No,' replied Shanklin, caught off-balance.

'Did you send a note to your office this morning, explaining that you were to unwell to go to work?'

'Yes, Superintendent – I had a migraine.'

'It did not prevent you writing this letter,' said Tallis, snatching it off his desk to wave in front of him. 'Do you recognise this as yours?'

'Yes, I do. Where did you get it from?'

'We wanted an example of your handwriting, sir, so that we could compare it with this.'

Picking up the funeral card in the other hand, Tallis held it beside the letter and watched the suspect's reaction. After swallowing hard, Shanklin tried to talk his way out of the situation.

'The writing is similar, I grant you,' he said, 'but not the same.'

Tallis grinned wolfishly. 'I can explain the slight discrepancy,' he said, shaking the letter. '*This* one was written when you were troubled by a migraine. Your hand trembled. The only thing that afflicted you when you scribbled the message on the card was cold malevolence.'

'Fortunately,' said Leeming, 'Mr Bardwell never saw the card.'

'Leave this to me, Sergeant,' warned Tallis.

'I felt that he ought to be told.'

'I can handle this interview.'

Leeming backed away. 'Of course, sir.'

'Well, Mr Shanklin,' said the superintendent, 'are you going to persist in your denial? We know that you had motive, means and opportunity to send this card. When you were first interviewed by Sergeant Leeming, you made no bones about your hatred of Mr Bardwell. You revelled in his pain.'

- 'I had good cause to do so,' argued Shanklin.

'Then you did send that taunt to Mr Bardwell?'

Shanklin chewed his lip. Confronted with the evidence, there was no hope of evading the truth. 'Yes, I did,' he confessed.

'Nothing can excuse the wording on that card. However, that's a minor matter compared with the crime for which you're charged.' Tallis's index finger was accusatory. 'Did you or did you not conspire to derail the Brighton Express?'

'I swear that I did not, Superintendent.'

'The evidence indicates otherwise.'

'What evidence?' wailed Shanklin. 'If everyone who has a grudge against Horace Bardwell is suspected, this room would be filled to capacity. He's a loathsome human being. I admit freely that I'd derive immense satisfaction from reading his obituary – even though it would conceal the ugly truth and praise him to the skies. But I did not,' he emphasised, 'take any steps to cause a train crash that might have killed him.'

'We believe you engaged someone else to do it,' said Leeming.

'Thank you, Sergeant,' cautioned Tallis. 'Don't interrupt.'

'Tell him, sir.'

'All in good time,' said the other.

He put the card and the letter aside then perched on the edge of the desk. He waited patiently. The superintendent might be relaxed but Shanklin was squirming in his seat. Tallis locked his eyes on the suspect and spoke with deliberate calm.

'Do you understand the seriousness of the crime, sir?'

'I did not commit it,' retorted Shanklin.

'That's not what I asked you. Please answer my question.'

'Yes, of course I understand how serious it is.'

'Twelve people were killed and dozens were badly injured, Mr Bardwell among them. Would you agree that a man who connived at such a disaster is nothing short of a fiend?'

'I could not agree more, Superintendent.'

'Then why did you do it?' snapped Tallis, moving to stand over him like a vulture over a carcass. 'Why did you and your confederate commit that crime? Why did you kill and maim innocent people in the reckless pursuit of a private feud? You and Dick Chiffney will hang for what you did. The pair of you deserve no mercy.'

'No!' howled Shanklin in despair. 'I'd never sink to anything like that. It's downright evil. What sort of a man do you take me for? You must believe me, superintendent. I had nothing whatsoever to do with the crash. As for Dick,' he said, 'I haven't seen him for months.'

'Then you *do* know the man.'

'Yes, I do.'

'That's not what you told me,' said Leeming.

'We have a connection at last,' said Tallis. 'It needed one person to plan the crime and another to execute it, one person to spy out the right place with his telescope and another to act on his orders. I suggest that you, Matthew Shanklin, were in league with Chiffney.'

'I'd never trust a man like Dick,' said Shanklin.

'Why not?'

'He's far too unreliable.'

'Then you suborned someone else to help you.'

'My only crime was to send that malicious card.'

'Tell us how you know Chiffney,' said Leeming, 'and explain why you denied it earlier.'

Shanklin shook his head wearily. 'I was too ashamed to admit it, Sergeant,' he said. 'Dick is a distant relative of mine. I keep as far away from the rogue as possible. He prevailed upon me to get him a job with the LB&SCR then he lost it by knocking out the foreman's teeth. That was typical of him. Dick Chiffney is a menace.'

Chiffney was frustrated. Having been unable to carry out his orders in Brighton, he returned by train to London that evening and went into a tavern near the station to have a few drinks before he felt able to face Josie Murlow's cross-examination. Instead of taking good news back to her, he had to admit failure. When he got back to the house, he went up the stairs and saw her waiting at the top, hands on her hips.

She looked even more bellicose than usual.

'Where've you been?' she snarled.

'You know that, my darling. I had to go to Brighton.'

'You've been away all day, Dick.'

'I'm sorry about that,' he said, taking her by the arm to lead her back into their bedroom. 'Let me explain.'

She was roused. 'You've been drinking – I can smell it on you.'

'I only had one pint.'

'And what did *she* have?' Josie challenged. 'What did your fancy woman drink? That's where you've been, Dick Chiffney, isn't it – strolling along the promenade in Brighton with someone else on your arm! While I've been shut away here like a prisoner, you've been dipping your wick at the seaside.'

'That's a lie!' he shouted. '*You're* the only woman I want, Josie. You should know that by now. Nobody compares with you, my love. In any case,' he said, pointing to his face with a harsh laugh, 'this ugly mug of mine frightens women away. Only you had the kindness to take me on. Do you think I'd forget that?'

'There's nobody else, then?'

'I give you my word.'

She was pacified. 'So tell me what happened.'

'I waited and watched in vain.'

'What were you supposed to do?'

'That doesn't matter. The point is that I wasn't able to do it.'

'Were you there to kill someone, Dick?'

'No, no,' he said, evasively.

'Then why did you take that gun with you?'

'It was for my protection, Josie. There's lots of thieves about. You can't be too careful.'

'Don't try to pull the wool over my eyes,' she said. 'Any thief would have more sense than to take on a man like you. That gun was given you for a purpose – and so was that rifle. Now stop feeding me lies or I'll walk out of here now.'

'You mustn't do that, Josie – you could be *seen*.'

'The police are after you, not me.'

'Just let me do the job,' he pleaded, 'then the pair of us can get out of London altogether. I know you're upset because all your things are back at the house but they can be fetched. As soon as it gets dark, I'll sneak back and get whatever you want.'

'The only thing I want is the truth,' she declared, giving him an ultimatum. 'If I don't hear it in the next few minutes, then you can find someone else to lie to because I'll be on my way home.'

Chiffney was in an awkward predicament. If he told her the full truth, he would be breaking his word to the man who was employing him. He would also risk losing Josie altogether. When she realised the enormity of what he had already done, she would be horrified and might well want nothing to do with him. While she would happily flout the law when it served her purpose, she would never condone the crime in which Chiffney had become involved. On the other hand, to withhold everything from her would provoke Josie into walking out and he was desperate to prevent that. After careful consideration, he decided on a partial confession.

'I met this man some weeks ago,' he began.

'What's his name?'

'Now that's something I can't tell you, my love, because I don't know it myself. He made sure of that. What I can tell you is that he lives in Brighton and he's not short of money.'

'Why did he get in touch with you?'

'He wanted someone who could do a job for him without asking any questions. My name was mentioned to him and he got in touch.' He smirked. 'It was the best bit of luck I've had since I met you.'

'What sort of job is it?'

'A dangerous one,' he admitted.

'I knew it,' she said, wide-eyed with alarm. 'He's paying you to murder someone, isn't he?'

'Let's just say that he wants a certain man hurt bad. I hurt him once already and that's why I got that money. But there's more to come if I hurt him again.' She was patently worried. 'It will be over in seconds, Josie,' he went on, slipping an arm around her. 'This man means nothing to us – why should we care what happens to him?'

'Who is he?'

'He lives in Brighton, that's all I can tell you.'

'Why does the other man want him hurt?'

'Revenge,' said Chiffney. 'I don't know what he did to the man who's paying me but it must have been something terrible. In other words, he *deserves* what's coming to him.' He pulled her close. 'So now you know the truth, Josie. I've been living off you too long and it made me feel bad. When I had a chance like this, I couldn't turn it down. I'm being paid more than I could earn on the railway in ten years. Think what we could do with the money.' Releasing her, he stood aside and indicated the door. 'If you're too scared to be my woman any more, you can walk out right now. Is that what you want to do, Josie? Make up your mind.'

It took her an instant to do so. She started to undress.

'Let's go to bed,' she decided.

CHAPTER THIRTEEN

Expecting to report to the superintendent the moment he returned from Brighton that evening, Robert Colbeck discovered that Tallis was in a meeting with the Commissioner, defending his officers against the jibes made about them in the newspaper and trying to justify the time and money allotted to the investigation. Colbeck instead invited Victor Leeming into his office to tell him what he had learnt in the course of his trip to the south coast. Before the inspector could speak, however, Leeming blurted out his own news.

'I arrested Matthew Shanklin,' he said, proudly.

'Did the handwriting match?'

'Yes, Inspector – he admitted sending that funeral card.'

'Is he still in custody?'

'No – he's been released on bail.'

Colbeck was staggered. 'For a crime of this magnitude?'

'Mr Shanklin had nothing to do with the train crash, sir.'

'Are you sure of that, Victor? I was beginning to feel certain that he and Chiffney were working in partnership.'

Leeming told him the full story, pointing out that he would

much sooner face questioning by Colbeck than submit to the kind of badgering interrogation perfected by Tallis. In sending the funeral card, Shanklin was guilty of malicious behaviour designed to inflict pain on a man he despised. Beyond that, no other charges could be brought against him.

It was a setback for Colbeck. Disappointed that Shanklin was innocent of any part in the crime on the Brighton line, he was at least glad that he had been flushed out into the open. One name could now be eliminated from the major inquiry. The problem was that it left them with only a single suspect.

'Did Mr Shanklin tell you where he'd been today?' said Colbeck.

'He claimed that he'd taken the day off to visit friends.'

'That was an arrant lie.'

'I know that he went somewhere by train because the cab driver remembered picking him up at a railway station.'

'He'd been to Brighton. Far from visiting friends, he was there to call on his sworn enemy, Horace Bardwell.'

'How do you know?' asked Leeming.

'I looked in at the hospital before I left,' said Colbeck. 'I wanted to see how Mr Bardwell and some of the other survivors were faring. Shanklin, apparently, came into the ward in order to gloat over Mr Bardwell. From what I could gather, there was quite a scene. Mr Bardwell was so upset that he had to be sedated for a while.'

'That ought to be mentioned when Shanklin comes to court.'

'It will be, Victor. I'll make sure of it.'

'What else did you find out in Brighton?'

'A great deal – it's difficult to know where to start.'

Colbeck told him about meeting Giles Thornhill, spending

time with Sidney Weaver and taking tea with Ezra Follis. He also talked about the visit to the gunsmith. Leeming was puzzled.

'Why did you advise Mr Thornhill to speak tomorrow?' he said.

'It's the only way to bring our assassin out of hiding. As long as the man is at liberty, Mr Thornhill's life is in constant danger.'

'But you're putting him in even more danger by urging him to speak in a public meeting, sir. He could be shot dead on the platform.'

'I think that highly unlikely, Victor,' said Colbeck.

'Why is that, sir?'

'Put yourself in the position of the man with the rifle.'

'Could his name be Dick Chiffney?'

'In all probability, it is. Imagine that you were stalking Mr Thornhill. When you see an advertisement for a public meeting addressed by him, what would you do?'

'Sit at the back of the hall and wait for the right moment.'

Colbeck grinned. 'You'd never make an assassin, I'm afraid.'

'Wouldn't I?'

'No, Victor – the first thing you need to do is to conceal your identity. How can you do that if you appear in public? You'll be seen by people who can give an accurate description of you. Also, of course, there's the small matter of making an escape from the hall. You could well be chased by some public-spirited citizen.'

'All right,' said Leeming, deflated, 'tell me what you'd do.'

'I wouldn't let Mr Thornhill get anywhere near the hall.'

'Then where would you kill him?'

'Near the house,' said Colbeck. 'It's more private and would save me the trouble of shooting over other people's heads in the hall. The man we're after has been inside the grounds before, remember. He knows how to find his way around.'

'But you told me the estate was well guarded.'

'It is at the moment. Very few men will be on duty tomorrow.'

'Has Mr Thornhill agreed to make that speech?'

'He's giving it serious thought, Victor.'

'If he refuses to go,' said Leeming, 'then your plan will have no chance at all of success.'

'Oh, I don't think he'll refuse somehow.'

'Why is that, Inspector?'

'Pride is at stake,' explained Colbeck. 'If Giles Thornhill is not available tomorrow, he'll have to yield the platform to a man he dislikes intensely and I can't see him doing that.'

'Who is the man?'

'The Rector of St Dunstan's.'

Ezra Follis rose at his habitual early hour and shaved with care in order to avoid the scratches on his cheeks. Tiring of the bandaging around his head, he ignored the doctor's advice and unwound it to reveal some gashes on his forehead. There were wounds in his scalp as well but he could not see them in the mirror and they had ceased to remind him of their presence. Now that he had discarded the bandaging, he felt much better. After dressing in his bedroom, he took a smoking cap from the wardrobe and put it on. Follis did not, in fact, smoke but the cap had been a gift from the female parishioner who had made it for him and he did not have the heart to refuse it.

When he came down for breakfast, Mrs Ashmore was

already busy in the kitchen. They exchanged greetings, commented on the weather then discussed the day's commitments. It was only when the housekeeper finally turned round that she saw what he had done.

'You've taken it off,' she scolded.

'It was like having my head in a vice.'

'Doctor Lentle will be very cross with you.'

'Only if he finds out what I've done,' said Follis, 'and I know I can count on you not to tell him. Besides, I've finally found a use for this cap that Mrs Gregory made for me. How does it look?'

'Very becoming,' said the housekeeper.

'Do you think I should take up smoking?'

She was stern. 'No, Mr Follis, it will make a stink. My husband used to smoke and the smell was terrible. I think that pipe of his was one of the things that took him away before his time. He had this awful hacking cough.'

'Yet it didn't stop him smoking.'

'He just wouldn't listen.'

'A common fault of the male gender, I fear,' he conceded. 'We're always deaf to sound advice about our health.' He became serious. 'The truth of it is that I felt something of a fraud with all that bandaging on. Those lying in hospital were the real victims. Some have lost limbs in the crash and Mr Bardwell has been blinded. I'm embarrassed when people offer sympathy to *me*. I don't deserve it.'

'You deserved every ounce of it,' she said, softly. 'I saw what other people didn't see. I watched you struggling as you went up those stairs. I heard you groaning in pain during the night. You put on a brave face for your parishioners but I know the truth.'

'Thank you, Mrs Ashmore,' he said, touching her gently on the shoulder. 'I have no secrets from you.' He adjusted the cap slightly. 'I wonder if I should wear this when I go to that meeting.'

'I think your own hat would be more suitable.'

'It's not an ecclesiastical function. I'll be speaking to the good citizens of Brighton about the future of their fair town. It will be a talk and not a sermon.'

'You can hold an audience wherever you speak.'

'I'm not sure how some of them will cope with the shock. They're expecting to hear Giles Thornhill and they get the Rector of St Dunstan's instead. We're as different as chalk and cheese.'

'I've always preferred cheese,' she said with a half-smile. 'Now, off you go into the dining room and I'll serve breakfast.'

He looked at the clock on the wall. 'I've got the verger coming at eight-thirty and the dean at nine. Then the ladies of the sewing circle will be descending on us. I must remember the smoking cap for that because Mrs Gregory is certain to be among them. No sooner do they go than I have to discuss the implications of holy matrimony with those delightful young people whose banns will be read for the first time next Sunday.' He smiled apologetically. 'We'll needs lots of cups of tea, I'm afraid.'

'That's what I'm here for, Mr Follis.'

'And how grateful I am to have you!' he said. Follis breathed in deeply then exhaled with a broad smile. 'You know, I really do feel so much better. I can even face the dean with equanimity in spite of the criticism I'm certain to incur from him. He always has some rebuke for me. If my recovery continues,' he went on, chirpily, 'I might even change my mind about Thursday.'

'You mean that you'll stay overnight in London?'

'I mean exactly that, Mrs Ashmore.'

'Very good, sir,' she said, obediently.

'Do you have any objection to that?'

'It's not my place to object, Mr Follis. You must do whatever you wish. You'll never hear a word of complaint from me.'

She turned away so that he could not see her disappointment.

The day began early at Scotland Yard. Summoned to the superintendent's office, Colbeck saw the morning newspapers strewn across his desk. Tallis was embittered.

'Is there any profession more abhorrent and untrustworthy than that of journalism?' he asked, scowling. 'They pour their poison into the unsuspecting minds of the British public and warp their judgement. Our press is nothing but an instrument of torture.'

'I think that's a gross exaggeration, sir,' said Colbeck.

'Then you've not read the morning editions.'

'I've not had time, superintendent.'

'This one,' continued Tallis, slapping a newspaper, 'suggests that we're causing widespread distress among both survivors of the crash and relatives of the victims by daring to suggest that foul play was an element in the disaster. This author of this vicious article claims that *we* are the ones guilty of foul play by persisting with an investigation that is wrong-headed and redundant. What do you say to that?'

'We'll have to make the gentleman eat his words, sir.'

'Gentleman!' bellowed the other. 'I see nothing gentlemanly in this brutal prose. We are being soundly cudgelled, Inspector. You are traduced by name and I by implication. In trying to uphold the law, we are mocked unmercifully.'

'I always ignore such censure,' said Colbeck.

'Well, I don't, I can tell you. Newspaper editors should have statutory restraints imposed upon them. They should not be allowed to trade freely in sly innuendo and outright abuse. They should be prevented from holding up the Metropolitan Police Force to mockery.'

'With respect, sir, it's our job to do that.'

'What do you mean?'

'By appearing to make mistakes,' said Colbeck, 'we lay ourselves open to ridicule. The only way to stop that happening in this case is to solve the crime at the heart of it.'

'According to the newspapers, there *is* no crime.'

'Then I'll enjoy reading them when we make an arrest and prove that Captain Ridgeon's assessment of the crash was both hasty and misguided. Nobody is entitled to unstinting praise,' he went on, reasonably. 'We have to earn it. It's annoying to be pilloried in the press but we can rectify that.'

'I want an abject apology from every editor,' demanded Tallis.

'That may be too much to ask, Superintendent.'

'Confound it, man – it's their duty to help us!'

'They'd argue that it's their duty to report events in as honest and unbiased a way as they can. Sadly, that's not always the case but it's no use fulminating against them. Unless they print something defamatory, there's little we can do.'

'I can write strong letters of denial.'

'That would be pointless at this stage, sir,' said Colbeck. 'In a war of words, the press always has more ink. Besides, in order to defend what we're doing, you'd have to reveal some of the evidence we've gathered and that would be imprudent. Those responsible for that train crash have already been warned that we are after them. If they realise how close we are, they may bolt altogether.'

Tallis stood up. 'How close are we, Inspector?'

'I anticipate significant progress by the end of the day.'

'You thought we'd achieve that my matching Mr Shanklin's handwriting with that on a funeral card.'

'I was too optimistic,' admitted Colbeck.

'And are you being too optimistic today?'

'No, sir – I'm being much more cautious.'

Tallis opened a box on the desk and took out a cigar, cutting the end off it before thrusting it into his mouth and lighting it. He puffed vigorously until the cigar began to glow and acrid smoke curled up to the ceiling.

'We *need* that significant progress, Inspector,' he said. 'It's the only way to stop these jackals from snapping at our heels.'

'Never be upset by press criticism,' advised Colbeck. 'There's a very simple way to avoid it.'

'Is there?'

'Yes, Superintendent – cancel the newspapers.'

Before Tallis could muster a reply, Colbeck bade him farewell and left the office. Victor Leeming was waiting for him in the corridor. Having read one of the morning newspapers, he knew how violently the superintendent would react and was grateful that he had not had to confront him. He was surprised how unruffled Colbeck was.

'What sort of mood was he in?' asked Leeming.

Colbeck grinned. 'Mr Tallis wants us to bring him the head of every journalist who has attacked us,' he said. 'I think he'd like to stick them on poles and throw paper darts at them.'

'I'd throw more than paper darts, Inspector.'

'The most effective missile would be an arrest, Victor.'

Colbeck took the sergeant into his office so that they could talk without interruption. He gave Leeming an abbreviated account of his conversation with Tallis then turned his attention to the day ahead.

'We'll have to catch the Brighton Express,' he said.

'I'm not looking forward to that, sir,' confessed Leeming. 'I'll keep thinking about what happened last Friday.'

'The line has been repaired and the debris removed.'

'You can't remove my memories so easily.'

'No,' said Colbeck, sadly. 'The disaster will be printed indelibly on the minds of many people. Those passengers set out on what should have been a routine journey and ended up in a catastrophe.'

'Thanks to Dick Chiffney.'

'We have to prove that. What's the situation with Josie Murlow?'

'She's vanished, sir,' said Leeming. 'I had a man watching her house but she never returned to it. She and Chiffney have obviously gone into hiding elsewhere.'

'Have you circulated a description of her?'

'Yes, Inspector – every policeman in the area is looking for her. Josie Murlow is a difficult person to mistake, as you saw for yourself. If she does break cover, someone will spot her.'

'Chiffney is the person we really want,' said Colbeck, 'and we lack precise details about his appearance. All we know is that he's very unprepossessing and has a bad squint.'

'I know something else about him, sir,' recalled Leeming, rubbing the back of his head. 'Chiffney hits hard.'

'We must strike back even harder.'

'He won't be able to sneak up on me next time. It's the thing about this investigation that really fires me up – the chance to meet up again with Dick Chiffney.'

'That chance may come sooner than you expect, Victor.'

'I hope so.'

'Who knows?' said Colbeck. 'By the end of the day, you might well have had the satisfaction of snapping the handcuffs on the elusive Mr Chiffney.'

A night in his arms had reconciled Josie Murlow to the fact that Chiffney had been ordered to kill someone. It was not the first time he had been hired by anonymous gentlemen. She knew that he had been paid to assault people in the past and had accepted that without a qualm. Chiffney liked fighting. He might as well make some money with his fists. Murder, however, was another matter and she had been frightened when she first realised what he had been engaged to do. Now that she had grown used to the idea, however, it did not seem quite so unnerving. Indeed, it gave her a perverse thrill.

What still troubled her was her own position. Knowing of his intentions without reporting them to the police meant that she was condoning Chiffney's actions. In law, therefore, she would be seen as an accessory. Josie shuddered to think what would happen if they were ever caught but she consoled herself with the belief that it was almost impossible. Chiffney had convinced her that there was little risk attached to the enterprise. He simply had to strike decisively then withdraw from the scene. Payment would then follow.

Lying in bed, Josie wallowed in the comfortable certainty
that they would not be caught. All that she had to do was to
trust her man. He had, after all, bought her the necklace out
of his first earnings and other gifts would soon come.
Abandoning her house did not worry her. She had long ago
grown weary of its lack of space and its endless deficiencies.
Everything she valued had been taken from the place in a
series of midnight visits. As well as bringing all of her clothing
and her trinkets, Chiffney had even collected her favourite
sticks of furniture. Henceforth, they would share a far better
lodging.

As she gazed up at him, Chiffney was reaching for his jacket
before slipping it on. On impulse, Josie heaved herself out of
bed.

'Let me come with you, Dick,' she said.

'You stay here, my darling.'

'But I'm your woman. I want to be at your side.'

'The police could be out looking for you.'

'They won't be looking for me in Brighton,' she argued. 'If
you hail a cab outside the house, nobody will see me going to
the station. Now we've got money,' she went on, getting
carried away, 'we can travel first class. I've never done that
before.'

'This is something I have to do on my own, Josie,' he said.

'I know that, Dick, and I won't get in your way. When the
time comes, you simply leave me and go about your business.
Afterwards, I could be a help to you.'

'How do you mean?'

'I'm like a disguise,' she explained, grinning away. 'A man
and a woman together look respectable. Nobody would give
us a second glance. When you're on your own – even in that

new suit you bought – people will notice that face of yours and those big, rough hands. You don't look quite so respectable then, Dick.'

He was tempted. 'That's a good point, Josie.'

'Can I come with you, then?'

'He won't like it. He told me to come on my own. If he realises you know more than you ought to, the gentleman might call the whole thing off. No,' he concluded, 'it's too risky.'

'There's no need for him to see me.'

'I'm sorry, my love. You'll have to stay here.'

'I won't be cooped up again,' she said, gazing around with a flash of anger. 'Look at the place – there's hardly room to move since you brought all my things here.'

'You can go downstairs and sit in the kitchen.'

'I want to be with you, Dick.'

He sniffed. 'I can't take that chance.'

'Why not?'

'Because you'd be a distraction,' he said. 'Instead of keeping my mind on what I had to do, I'd be worrying about you. It's no good, Josie. I have to go alone.'

'All right,' she suggested, bargaining with him, 'why don't we both travel to Brighton separately and only meet up afterwards?' he shook his head. 'What's wrong with that?'

Chiffney was blunt. 'It's not going to happen.'

'But I *want* it to happen, Dick,' she said, stamping a foot. 'We're in this together. I won't be left out all the time.'

'Stop it!' he shouted, temper fraying.

'Don't you yell at me, you noisy bugger!'

'Shut your gob and listen. There's one very good reason why I don't want you anywhere near Brighton today. I have to be alone. I've got a job to do, Josie. I failed yesterday and the gentleman was very annoyed with me. If I let him down again, he may find someone else and I could end up without a single penny. Is that what you want?'

'No,' she said.

'Then that's the end of it.'

Josie sulked in silence. She watched him as he reached under the bed for the rifle then wrapped it in a piece of sacking. He also stuck the pistol in his belt and stuffed ammunition for both weapons in his pockets. Getting back down on his knees, he groped under the bed once more. This time, he brought out a large telescope and hid that in the sacking with the rifle. In spite of bubbling anger she felt towards him, Josie was curious.

'Who gave you that?'

'He did,' said Chiffney. 'I need to spy out the lie of the land.'

As the train set off from London Bridge station, Victor Leeming braced himself for an uncomfortable journey. Its only virtue was that it would be a relatively short one. The previous investigation had entailed a long train journey to Crewe and back. An even earlier one had forced him to travel to France, undergoing the sustained terror of crossing the Channel by boat before committing himself to the rattling uncertainty of the French railways. All things considered, the Brighton Express was the lesser of many evils. At least he was in the hands of his fellow-countrymen.

'Don't look so anxious,' said Colbeck, seated opposite him in an otherwise empty carriage. 'There's no danger. Lightning doesn't strike twice in one place.'

'Then the accident could happen at another spot on the line.'

'There'll *be* no accident, Victor.'

'Then why do I feel so unsafe?'

'You simply haven't adjusted to rail travel as yet.'

'I never will, Inspector,' said Leeming, watching the fields scud past. 'I can never understand why you like trains so much.'

'They're passports to the future. Railways are redefining the way that we live and I find that very exciting. The concept of steam power is so wonderfully simple yet so incredibly effective.'

'You should have been an engine driver, sir.'

'No,' said Colbeck, wistfully. 'I know my limitations. I'd love to work on the footplate but I lack the skill needed. I make my own small contribution to the smooth running of the railway system by trying to keep it free of criminals. However, let's not harp on about a subject that tends to unsettle you,' he went on. 'How are preparations for your wife's birthday?'

'They're not going very well, sir.'

'I'm sorry to hear that.'

'Mr Tallis will expect me on duty next Sunday unless we can bring this investigation to a close. And, no matter how much I fret about it, I still can't decide what to buy Estelle.'

'Do you have any ideas at all?'

'I thought about artificial flowers in a glass case.'

'Women always love flowers, Victor – though I think your wife might prefer real ones on her birthday. You could get them at the market.'

'They wouldn't last, sir, that's the trouble. Anyway, that's only one present and I have to buy *two* – one from me and one from the children. I've been racking my brain for days.' He became tentative. 'I wonder if I might ask you something personal.'

'Ask whatever you wish.'

'What did you buy for Miss Andrews when it was her birthday?'

'If you must know,' said Colbeck, laughing, 'I bought her a new easel and some artist's materials. Not very feminine, I know, but that was what Madeleine wanted me to get her. Mind you, there were a few other gifts as well by way of a surprise.'

'Such as?'

'The item that really pleased her was a new bonnet.'

'Now that's just what Estelle needs,' said Leeming in delight.

'There you are – one of the birthday presents is decided.'

'If I let the children give her the bonnet, I could give her a new shawl. It won't be long before autumn is here and she'll need one. Thank you, Inspector. You've taken a load off my mind.'

'If you want more suggestions,' said Colbeck as a memory surfaced, 'you might get them from the Reverend Follis.'

Leeming was baffled. 'What does *he* know about buying gifts for a wife, sir? You told me that Mr Follis was a bachelor.'

'He is, Victor, but I have a strong feeling that he's a man of vision where women are concerned.'

While he waited, Ezra Follis looked at the books on the shelf. He had given them to Amy Walcott in a particular order so that her reading was carefully controlled. Most were anthologies of poetry and he knew how diligently she had studied them. Amy was an apt pupil. She was happy to let him make all the decisions about her education. He selected a volume and leafed through the pages, an action that was much easier to perform now that both hands had been freed from their bandages. His eye settled on a particular page. After making a note of it, he closed the book again.

He was in Amy's house but he moved around it with easy familiarity. Leaving the drawing room, he went along the corridor and ascended the stairs to the first landing. Follis walked across to the main bedroom and tapped gently on the door.

'May I come in yet, Amy?' he asked.

'I'm not ready,' she said from the other side of the door.

'I've been waiting some time.'

'I know that, Mr Follis.'

'The servants will be back before too long.' There was a lengthy pause. 'Perhaps you've changed your mind,' he said, tolerantly. 'That's your privilege. I didn't mean to trouble you, Amy. I'll let myself out and we'll forget all about this, shall we?'

'No, no,' she said in desperation. 'I want you to come in.'

'Are you happy about that?'

'I'm very happy.'

'You have to be certain about this.'

'I am, Mr Follis. I'm ready for you now.'

Turning the knob, he opened the door and stepped into the room. Amy Walcott was standing nervously in the middle of the carpet. Her feet were bare and she was wearing a long dressing gown. Pathetically eager to please, she managed a fraught smile.

'There's no need to be frightened,' he said, moving away so

that they were yards apart. 'No harm will come to you, Amy. I wouldn't hurt you for the world – you know that.'

'Yes, Mr Follis, I do.'

'I'll sit here.' He lowered himself on to the ottoman near the window then made a gesture. 'If you feel embarrassed, you can keep the dressing gown on.'

'I don't want to let you down.'

'There's no way that you could do that. The very fact that we're alone here together is a joy to me, Amy. You mustn't feel constrained to do anything that you don't want to do.' He smiled encouragingly. 'You look beautiful enough, as it is.'

'Nobody ever thought I was beautiful before.'

'That's because they don't see you through my eyes. I know the full truth about you. You're a good woman, Amy Walcott, beautiful on the inside and lovely on the outside.'

The compliment made her blush. 'Thank you, Mr Follis.'

'Will you read something to me?'

'In a moment,' she said, finding some confidence at last. 'I want to please you first. I've never done this before so you must excuse me if I don't do it properly.' She screwed up her courage. 'I'm going to take it off for you now.'

Undoing the belt, she opened her dressing gown and let it fall to the floor. She stood there sheepishly in a white nightdress with bows at the neck and sleeves. After feasting his eyes on her, Follis gave her a warm smile of appreciation. Her confidence began to rise.

'What have you chosen for me this time?' she said.

'Keats,' he replied, holding out the book. 'Page sixty-six. It's a beautiful poem for a very beautiful woman to read to me.'

Amy Walcott was suffused with a radiant glow. He loved her.

* * *

Josie Murlow was jaded. It was scarcely an hour since Chiffney had gone and she was already chafing with boredom. There was nothing to do and nobody with whom she could talk. Walter, the old man who owned the house, was willing to give them temporary shelter but they were confined to the bedroom and the kitchen. The remainder of the property was reserved for his family. Had she been allowed to go into the garden, Josie might have been less restless. As it was, she was pacing up and down like a tiger in a cage, picking her way through the relics of her old life that had been rescued from her hovel.

During the long reaches of the night, when she and Chiffney were entwined in carnal lust, everything had seemed perfect. They would have enough money to flee London and set up a home in another city where they were unknown. It would be a new departure for both of them, an affirmation of their commitment to each other. The fact that it would be bought with blood money, and that a man had to be murdered first, was never discussed.

In daylight, alone and feeling sorely neglected, Josie began to see it all differently. She would be sharing her life with a killer, a man who was on the run. If the police ever caught Chiffney, they would catch her, too, and she would suffer the same fate as him. There was also a new fear. She had never been afraid of Chiffney before, knowing how to handle him and bend him to her will. What would happen if they fell out? A man who had killed once would not hesitate to do so again. Josie had traded blows with him in the past but the fights had always ended in a drunken reconciliation. Chiffney might end the next one in a more final way.

But it was too late now. She had to trust him. The police were searching for her as well as Chiffney. It never even crossed her mind to inform against him. Her whole life had been spent in skirting the law. Josie could simply not side with the police for any reason. What she really wanted was to be with Dick Chiffney, to enjoy a day in Brighton where she could walk freely by the seaside. She also wanted to know exactly what he was doing there. Who was paying him to kill another man and what crime had Chiffney already committed in order to get the money to pay for her necklace and his new suit?

Spending another day in self-imposed solitary confinement was anathema to her. Josie Murlow was a gregarious woman. She thrived on company. Without it, she was lost. Chiffney had left her money to send out for drink and she also had her own not inconsiderable savings, retrieved from a hiding place in her house. Reaching into her purse, she took out a handful of sovereigns and let them fall through her fingers on to the bed. It was ironic. With all that cash at her disposal, she was nevertheless unable to buy the human company she craved. It was insufferable.

She looked around the room with something akin to despair. Then she noticed something draped over a chair beside the wardrobe. Josie's manner changed in an instant. Perhaps there *was* a way to get what she wanted without putting herself and Chiffney in danger. Perhaps she had a means of fulfilling her desire to go to Brighton, after all. She had the money, the urge and the perfect disguise. Josie doubted if Chiffney himself would recognise her. All it required from her was the courage to implement the plan. The prospect of escape was too tempting to resist. She made the decision in a second and let out a whoop of joy.

Josie Murlow began to tear off her clothes as fast as she could.

Victor Leeming was so over-awed by the opulence of the mansion that he was tongue-tied. The marble-floored hall of Giles Thornhill's house was larger than the whole area of the sergeant's modest dwelling. He had never seen so many sculptures before and the wide, curved staircase seemed to sweep up to eternity. Valise in one hand, he stood there and marvelled. When he and Colbeck eventually went into the library, Leeming was still open-mouthed.

Thornhill was seated at the table with a decanter of sherry and a half-filled glass in front of him. He did not bother to get up as they came in. When Colbeck introduced his companion, Leeming was given only a cursory glance.

'I'm pleased to see that you took my advice, sir,' said Colbeck.

'Against my better judgement,' remarked Thornhill.

'Apart from the man at the gate, there were no other guards and I caught no glimpse of the mastiff either. He'd frighten anybody away.'

'That was the intention, Inspector.'

'We drove past the town hall,' Leeming put in. 'We saw your name on the poster outside.'

'I'll not be displaced by the Rector of St Dunstan's.'

'Why is that, sir?'

'The man is a thorough nuisance, Sergeant,' said Thornhill, nastily. 'He's caused no end of trouble to me and to many others in the town. If there's anything I loathe, it's a turbulent priest.'

'The Reverend Follis looked harmless enough to me.'

'I believe that Mr Thornhill was referring to Thomas a Becket,' said Colbeck, stepping in. 'As well as being Archbishop of Canterbury, he was Chancellor, the equivalent of today's Prime Minister. Becket then fell out with Henry II and was duly exiled. When he returned to England, the people welcomed him but the king did not. "Who will rid me of this turbulent priest?" the king is supposed to have cried. Four knights responded by murdering Becket in Canterbury Cathedral.' He turned to Thornhill. 'Am I misinterpreting you, sir?'

'Not at all,' said Thornhill. 'Becket's story showed the idiocy of combining Church and State. It's a fatal compound. Politics and religion should be kept separate. Unfortunately, nobody seems to have told that to Ezra Follis.'

'Even if they did,' said Colbeck, 'he'd probably ignore them.'

'The fellow is a law unto himself. He's a renegade priest.'

'Wait a moment, sir,' said Leeming, entering the debate. 'I thought that you wanted to close all the shops and public houses on a Sunday.'

'I have been involved in drafting an early version of the Sunday Trading Bill,' admitted Thornhill. 'That's quite true, Sergeant.'

'You just told us that politics and religion should be separate.'

'I stand by that.'

'Then why do politicians want to interfere with Sunday?'

'We're not interfering with it – we want to protect it. We believe that the Lord's Day should be properly observed.'

'But that's religion, sir,' Leeming contended.

'It's a political decision.'

'Yet you want to take it for religious reasons.'

'It's a valid point, Victor,' said Colbeck, cutting the argument short, 'but this is perhaps not the ideal time to discuss the matter. We have more immediate concerns.' He indicated the valise. 'The sergeant has brought a change of clothing with him, Mr Thornhill. Is there somewhere for him to put it on?'

Thornhill got up and crossed to the bell rope. Shortly after it had been pulled, a servant appeared. In response to his orders, he led Victor Leeming out of the library.

'Your sergeant is unduly argumentative,' said Thornhill. 'To be candid, I really don't know why either of you is here. I still have the strongest reservations about this whole business.'

'We're here to save your life, sir.'

'When there are only *two* of you? How can you possibly do that?'

'Watch us,' said Colbeck.

Having checked to see how many people were on guard at the gate, he walked around the perimeter of the estate to find the point of access he had used before. After climbing a fence, he was confronted by a high, thick hedge and had to go along it before he found the gap. Once through it, he moved stealthily in the direction of the house, stopping from time to time to look round and listen. He saw nobody patrolling the grounds and sensed that he was in luck. Emboldened, he crept on through the undergrowth with the rifle slung across his back. He felt certain of success this time.

The secret lay in meticulous preparation. Hiding the rifle behind a yew tree, he went on unencumbered until the house finally came into view. Approaching it from the rear, he used his telescope to view the terrace where Giles Thornhill had been sitting before the first attempt on his life. The window shattered by the bullet had now been boarded up and the myriad glass fragments swept away. Whichever exit Thornhill chose from the house, it would not be that one.

He worked his way around to the front of the house in a wide circle. There was good cover among the trees and bushes. It allowed him to get within seventy yards of the front entrance. He peered through the telescope again. Outside the portico with its matching fluted columns, he had expected at least one armed guard but the house seemed unprotected. The only person he could see was a gardener, ambling across the forecourt with a wooden wheelbarrow. The man vanished behind some shrubs. Buttered by the sun, Giles Thornhill's mansion looked serene and majestic.

If he left by the front door, as was most likely, Thornhill would be taken by his private carriage to the hall where he would be speaking. The stable block was off to the right. When the vehicle drew up outside the portico, Thornhill would be obscured as he came out of the door. It was when he stepped up into the open carriage that he would present a target. That moment was crucial. The man simply had to fire with deadly accuracy and the job was done.

He moved from place to place before he settled on the exact spot from which he would shoot. Shielded by thick bushes, he had an excellent view of the forecourt. There were hours to go yet. He was able to retrieve his rifle, take it to his chosen position and settle down. Since there would be a long wait, he had brought bread and cheese to eat. In case his nerve faltered, he had a small flask of brandy but he did not think it would be required.

It was early evening before there was any sign of movement. The doors of the stable block were opened and a horse was led out. It had already been harnessed. Two men pulled out a landau from the stable and fitted the shafts into the harness. One of the men disappeared for a minute then emerged again in a frock coat and top hat. He climbed up onto the driving seat and picked up the reins, flicking them and calling out a command to the horse. The landau headed towards the house. The gardener, now weeding a flowerbed, waved to the driver.

Watching it all from his vantage point, the man held his weapon ready. His heart was pumping and sweat was starting to break out on his forehead. As his hands trembled a little, he felt that he needed the brandy, after all, and gulped it swiftly down. It gave him courage and stiffened his resolve. His moment had finally come. Raising the weapon, he put the butt into his shoulder, crooked his finger around the trigger and took aim. After rumbling across the gravel, the landau pulled up outside the house.

There was a momentary wait then the front door opened and a tall figure stepped out, one arm in a sling. He opened the door of the carriage and took a firm grip so that he could pull himself up with his other hand. In that instant, with Giles Thornhill completely exposed, the man tried to control the tremble that had come back into his hands and pulled the trigger. His victim collapsed in a heap.

CHAPTER FOURTEEN

It was only a single shot but its effects were remarkable. A man collapsed in the landau, birds took to the air in fright and the horse reared and pulled with such force between the shafts that the driver had difficulty in controlling it. Perhaps the most remarkable thing was that the gardener leapt over his wheelbarrow and sprinted towards the bushes in the distance as if he had been waiting for a signal to do so. The assassin had already taken to his heels. Convinced that his mission had been successful, he gathered up his telescope and weapon before running off into the undergrowth.

The sharp crack of the rifle shot seemed to resonate for an age, rising above the squawking of the birds and the frantic neighing of the horse. Happy and exhilarated, the assassin ran on until the noises began to fade behind him. They were replaced by another sound and it made his blood congeal. He could hear a body crashing through the bushes behind him. Somebody was chasing hard and seemed to be gaining on him. He tried to quicken his pace but he was hampered by the heavy rifle and troubled by cramp from having stood in the same position for so many hours.

He was still hundreds of yards from the edge of the estate. There was no way he could outrun the pursuit. When he came to a clearing, therefore, he stopped and waited. Breathing hard and gripped by panic, he turned round. He tossed the telescope to the ground. Since he had no time to reload the rifle, he grabbed it by the barrel to use as a club. He could hear running feet getting closer all the time, swishing their way rhythmically through the grass. Whoever was following him had to be stopped or even killed.

He began to shiver with fear. Shooting a man from a distance had been easy. Confronting and overpowering someone prepared for action was a very different matter. There would be a fight. If his pursuer were armed, he would have the advantage. The assassin was no longer in control and that was frightening. Holding the rifle, he stood ready to strike. He then got a first glimpse of the man, coming through the trees at a steady pace. The next second, the gardener burst into the clearing and saw him.

It was no time to hesitate. Palms sweating, the man swung the rifle with vicious intent, hoping to knock out his adversary with a single blow. But the gardener was agile as well as fast. He ducked beneath the makeshift club and got in a solid punch to the other man's stomach that made him gasp in pain. Dropping the rifle, the winded man tried to run away. Flight was in vain. The gardener was quicker and stronger than him. Overhauling him within seconds, he dived on the assassin's back and forced him to the ground, sitting astride him while delivering a relay of punches to his head and body that took all resistance out of him.

Having subdued his man, he pulled a pair of handcuffs

from his pocket and clipped them on to the man's wrist so that he was pinioned from behind. The gardener could afford to relax. His quarry had been caught, pacified and restrained. It was time to roll him over.

'Well,' said Victor Leeming with a grin, 'I was hoping that you and I would meet again, Mr Chiffney. You attacked me from behind the last time. We met on equal terms today.'

Leeming's grin froze immediately. The person on the ground was not a cross-eyed ruffian with an ugly face but a fair-haired young man who was gibbering with terror. It was not Chiffney.

When he stepped back into the hall of the house, Robert Colbeck took off the sling he had been wearing to support his arm and handed it to a servant. Giles Thornhill looked on in admiration.

'That was a very daring thing to do, Inspector,' he said. 'It was daring and extremely rash. I watched it all through the window. I thought you'd been hit.'

'I only pretended to be, sir. I wanted him to think I'd been killed so that he'd run off. Sergeant Leeming will catch up with him.'

'Why take such a risk?'

'I didn't think I could persuade you to do so, Mr Thornhill.'

'It would have been suicide.'

'No,' said Colbeck. 'He fired at you from fifty yards before and missed. He'd have been farther away this time. I was trading on the fact that he's not a marksman and might therefore be nervous with a weapon in his hands. If he'd been a ruthless killer, you wouldn't still be alive. I had to offer him a second chance to shoot you.'

'Then I'm deeply grateful,' said Thornhill, 'and I'll be writing to your superiors to tell them so.'

'Be sure to mention Sergeant Leeming, sir. He not only tended your garden for several hours, he was in the right place to give chase when the shot was fired. We knew it would come from those trees and they must be seventy yards away. From that distance,' said Colbeck, 'I had the feeling that I could pass for a Member of Parliament.'

'Do you think the sergeant will have affected an arrest?'

'I'm sure that he has, Mr Thornhill.'

'What I want to know is who exactly that devil is.'

Colbeck indicated the door. 'Let's go and meet him.'

Victor Leeming did not waste any time trying to question his captive. Hauling him to his feet, he shoved him against a tree to take a close look at him. Pale-skinned and square-jawed, the prisoner was tall, well-favoured and in his early twenties. He wore old clothing that blended with the surroundings. Leeming retrieved the rifle and slung it over his shoulder. Holding the telescope in one hand, he used the other to take the man by the scruff of the neck and propel him along.

As they walked back towards the house, nothing was said. Glad to have captured him, the sergeant was disappointed that he had not caught Dick Chiffney. That would have been a real triumph. Though the man made one desperate attempt to break free, Leeming was too quick for him. He stuck out a foot and tripped him up. Pitching forward on to the ground, the captive bruised his forehead and dirtied his face. He got no sympathy from the sergeant. Pulling him to his feet again, Leeming took a firmer hold on his collar and hustled him along. Having tried to shoot a distinguished politician, the young man had also done his best to kill a Scotland Yard detective. After the long walk back to the house, he would, in time, take a shorter one to the gallows.

Colbeck and Thornhill waited side by side on the forecourt. The horse had now calmed down, the birds were singing once again and peace had been restored. Leeming came out of the trees with his prisoner ahead of him. When the young man saw that Giles Thornhill was alive and unharmed, he let out a cry of dismay. All his efforts had come to nothing. The thrill he had felt as the body dropped down in the carriage was replaced by a sense of dread. He would now have to face trial without the satisfaction of knowing that he had killed his intended victim.

Letting go of his collar, Leeming prodded him over the last thirty yards with the telescope. Head down and shamefaced, the man could not even bring himself to look at the person he had tried to shoot. Colbeck took over.

'I'm pleased to meet you at last,' he said, suavely. 'My name is Detective-Inspector Colbeck and I was the man at whom you mistakenly fired the shot. I'm very grateful to you for missing me. You were arrested by my colleague, Detective-Sergeant Leeming, who was posing as a gardener. I can see that the two of you have become closely acquainted.'

'He tried to take my head off, sir,' said Leeming.

'That makes two attempted murders in one day.' Colbeck gestured at his companion. 'I don't think there's any need to introduce Mr Thornhill, is there?' he said. 'Well, now that you know *our* names, perhaps you'd be good enough to tell us yours.'

The young man raised his head. 'My name is Heinrich

Freytag,' he said, defiantly, 'and I have no regrets for what I try to do.' His English was good but his accent guttural. 'Mr Thornhill, he does not deserve to live for what he did.'

'And what *did* I do?' asked Thornhill, bemused.

'You kill my father.'

'That's absolute nonsense. I've never even heard of him.'

'You didn't need to know him,' said Freytag, angrily. 'He was a foreigner and that was enough to make you hate him.'

'When did you come to Brighton?' asked Colbeck.

'Six years ago. We were living in Berlin when riots broke out. Our house was burnt to the ground so my father decided to bring us here. He said that England was a civilised country and we would be safe.' He shot Thornhill a look of disgust. 'That was before he heard about men like this one.'

'I'm entitled to my opinions about immigrants,' said Thornhill, 'and I won't be dissuaded from expressing them.'

'I know,' said Colbeck. 'I studied reports of your speeches when I was at the offices of the *Brighton Gazette*. Your views on foreigners cropped up time and again.'

'I don't want them here, Inspector.'

'What right have you to keep us out?' demanded Freytag. 'What harm have we done to you? We fled Germany to start a new life here. Do you think we *wanted* to leave our own country?'

'That's no concern of mine,' said Thornhill.

'It sounds as if it might be, sir,' observed Leeming.

'All I did was to address a few public meetings.'

'Oh, no,' said Freytag with feeling, 'you did a lot more than that. You made people angry. You made them think that we do not deserve to live in Brighton. One night, after you speak at a meeting, a drunken mob came looking for foreigners.

They saw the name of Freytag over our shop and they
smashed all the windows. My father came out to protest and
was hit by a stone. A week later, he died in hospital from a
heart attack.'

'I take no responsibility for that,' said Thornhill.

'You *sent* those men to the shop.'

'I deny that.'

'You build up their hate and let them loose on my father,'
said Freytag, pulsing with resentment. 'He died because of
cruel words you say against all foreigners. You should pay
with your life.'

'Did you bring this to the attention of the police?' said
Colbeck.

'They would not listen. They say my father died of a heart
attack because he was getting old, not because he was hit by
the stone. They tell me that Mr Thornhill is an important man
in Brighton and that I am wrong to say bad things about him.'

'I've heard enough of this balderdash,' announced
Thornhill. 'This man is a potential killer. Take him away and
charge him, Inspector. You're welcome to have use of the
landau for the purpose. I'll ride into town.'

'Thank you, sir.'

Colbeck nodded to Leeming who pushed the prisoner
towards the carriage then helped him unceremoniously into it.
Freytag looked back sourly at Thornhill. The politician was
unrepentant.

'I shall enjoy giving evidence at his trial,' he said.

'Do you still intend to speak to that meeting?' asked
Colbeck.

'Of course, I do. Now that the danger has been removed, I
can fulfil the engagement without fear of attack.'

'Nothing that Herr Freytag said has changed your mind, then?'

'Why should it?'

'You heard him, sir. Indirectly, you may have played a part in his father's death. That's why he sought revenge.'

'His father died of heart failure.'

'It could have been brought on by the attack on him.'

'I had no part in that.'

'If the young man is correct, the people responsible heard you speak that night.'

'Whose side are you on, Inspector?' said Thornhill, hotly. 'I won't be put in the dock. I'm the victim here. That rogue tried to shoot me. He's the criminal.'

'I agree, sir,' said Colbeck, 'and he'll pay for his crime. Nothing can excuse what he did. I just think that you might consider the motive that impelled him. In your position, I'd feel sobered.'

'But you're not in my position, are you?' retorted Thornhill. 'There's no room for sentiment in politics, Inspector. It's a hard world. A politician must have the courage of his convictions. I don't repudiate anything I've said. Please don't ask me to mourn Freytag's father,' he went on, glancing towards the landau. 'He shouldn't have been here in the first place. One less foreigner in Brighton is a cause for celebration in my eyes.'

He turned away and marched off to the house. Colbeck could imagine all too easily how Thornhill's rhetoric could incite the wilder element in his audience to violence. It made him decide to attend the meeting that evening. His first priority, however, was to deal with Heinrich Freytag. He strolled across to the carriage.

'Leave him to me, Victor,' he said. 'You'd better go back into the house to change or Mr Thornhill will think I've abducted his gardener.'

'Watch him carefully, sir,' advised Leeming, getting out of the landau. 'After I'd caught him, he tried to make a run for it.'

Handing him the rifle and the telescope, the sergeant headed for the door. Colbeck examined the weapon and saw the name on a metal plaque. It had been made in Berlin. Climbing into the carriage, he sat opposite Freytag and patted the rifle.

'This is a very old,' he noted. 'Did it belong to your father?'

'Yes,' replied the German.

'You were not used to firing it, were you?'

'No, Inspector. That's why I miss. Mr Thornhill is an evil man. I'll never forgive myself for not killing him.'

'How many times did you try?'

'Twice – and both times I miss.'

'So you didn't try to kill him another way?' said Colbeck. 'You didn't want him to die in a train crash, for instance?'

'No,' said Freytag, his face a mask of hatred. 'I want to kill him myself and watch him die. When I hear that he is injured in that crash, I am angry that he might have been snatched away from me. Mr Thornhill took my father's life so I need to take his. I despise you and the sergeant for stopping me.'

Colbeck sighed. Their success was tinged with failure. They had saved a politician's life by capturing his would-be assassin but they were no nearer finding the person who had caused the disaster on the Brighton line. He was still at large.

* * *

Sturdy, upright and of medium height, the man was impeccably well-dressed. His full beard of black, curling hair was salted with grey. His deep voice had the rasp of authority.

'How much longer do you need?' he demanded.

'I haven't caught him in the right place yet, sir,' said Chiffney. 'Whenever I've seen him, he's been with other people.'

'That was your excuse yesterday as well.'

'I don't want to shoot the wrong person.'

'The way things are going, I doubt if you'll be shooting anyone. What's holding you back, man? You swore to me that you'd do anything for money yet you keep letting me down.'

'I didn't let you down when I arranged that crash,' said Chiffney, groping for approval. 'If I'd been caught levering that rail away, I'd be in prison right now, waiting for the noose. I took a big risk for you.'

'And you got your due reward.'

'It wasn't my fault he didn't die when the trains collided.'

'Perhaps not,' said the man, 'but it's your fault that he's still alive now. I gave you the weapons, I taught you how to fire them and I showed you exactly where he lived. Yet you've spent the best part of two days in Brighton, lying in wait but too cowardly to pull the trigger when you see him.'

Chiffney was insulted. 'I'm not a coward, sir.'

'Then why haven't you obeyed your orders?'

'A coward wouldn't have brought the express off the track the way I did. A coward wouldn't have taken this job on in the first place. I got my faults, sir – God knows I have – but there's nobody as can call Dick Chiffney a coward.' He banged his chest. 'I've never walked away from a fight in my life.'

'You're not involved in a brawl now,' said the man. 'This is far more serious than giving someone a bloody nose. It takes nerve. I'm beginning to think you don't have that nerve.'

'That's a rotten lie!'

'Then do what I'm paying you for.'

They were in a quiet street where they had arranged to meet. Dick Chiffney was still carrying the rifle and telescope in the sacking. Having driven there in a trap, his companion remained in the vehicle. The problem for Chiffney was that the accusation against him contained more than a grain of truth. His courage had indeed faltered. In the course of two days, he had had a number of opportunities to shoot his victim but his finger had always hesitated on the trigger.

Something had stopped him firing. In setting up the train crash, he knew that several people would be killed and many more would be badly injured. Yet their individual fates did not trouble him in the least because he was not there at the time of the disaster. Shooting someone in cold blood and watching him die was not quite so easy. To his embarrassment, Chiffney had discovered the glimmering of a conscience that had never existed before. With the victim in his sights, he had been fettered by guilt.

His employer was not prepared to tolerate any more delays.

'Time is running out, Chiffney,' he warned. 'If he's still alive at the end of the day, our contract is null and void.'

'But I need that money, sir,' pleaded Chiffney.

'Then *earn* it.'

'I can't get near him if he stays indoors.'

'He won't do that this evening,' said the man. 'I've done your job for you and discovered that he'll be going to the town hall within the hour. Somewhere along the way, you must kill him.'

'Yes, sir – I swear that I will.'

'You won't need the rifle. I want you to get close enough to make sure. Shoot him with the pistol.' He held out a hand. 'I'll take the rifle.'

'What about the telescope, sir?'

'You might need that.'

Chiffney reached into the sacking to remove the telescope then handed over the rifle. The man laid the sacking down in the trap. Chiffney was worried. His hand was being forced and that unsettled him. He would have preferred to shoot from a distance so that he could escape more easily after the event. Getting close to his victim presented problems yet they had to be overcome. He had given his word to Josie Murlow and could not go back on it. She was expecting him to return with enough money to transform their lives. Thinking about Josie helped to make his misgivings disappear.

'I'll do it, sir,' he vowed. 'I'll blow the bastard's head off.'

Josie Murlow was having second thoughts about her decision to come to Brighton that day. In responding to an overpowering urge, she had not bothered to consider its consequences. What she believed would be a perfect disguise was also a profound hindrance. Josie was dressed in widow's weeds. Black from head to foot, she had gained respect and sympathy from everyone she met but she was not able to do any of the things she had planned. It would look unseemly for a grieving widow to stroll merrily along the promenade, still less to go on the beach or walk on the pier over a thousand feet out to the sea.

There was another handicap she had not foreseen. Since she had not worn the dress for some years, it was now too tight on her, straining at her increased dimensions like a small fishing net trying to hold a large whale. The hot weather only added to her discomfort. Behind the black veil, perspiration trickled down her face. Her armpits were dripping pools, her crotch was sodden and a constant rivulet ran down her spine with meandering malevolence.

All that she could do was to walk, watch, rest and take occasional refreshment. Josie saw the Royal Pavilion, the town hall, the assembly rooms, the baths, the theatre and some of the finest hotels in the kingdom. She waddled through the Lanes, the oldest quarter of the town, a rabbit warren of narrow, twisting, brick paved passages lined with fisherman's cottages. She was also astounded by the number of schools, almshouses, infirmaries and other charities. Brighton was a fine town in which to live. It was not, however, the ideal place to visit in tight clothing on a summer's day.

Whenever she stopped to take tea at a small restaurant or sat down from exhaustion on a bench, a compassionate citizen would offer his or her condolences and oblige her to invent either a dead husband whom she had never had, a mother whom she did not, in fact, remember or – by way of variation – a daughter who had been knocked down in London by a runaway horse. While she got some cruel amusement out of deceiving people so plausibly, it did not atone for the pain and boredom from which she was suffering.

She struggled back to the railway station three times in a row, intending to abandon her scheme and return to London. What held her back on each occasion was the thought that her efforts would have come to nought. Josie had gone to Brighton to be there when Chiffney committed murder and created a happy life for them. She had fantasies about intercepting him at the station, or even travelling on the same train as him without revealing her identity until they reached London. Even now, as the early evening brought no relief from the heat, she somehow felt that she had to stay until he came.

Dick Chiffney was her man. They belonged together.

Heinrich Freytag caused no trouble. Though he continued to rail against Giles Thornhill, he made no attempt to escape. Accepting that his plan had failed, he was resigned to his fate. After charging him, Colbeck and Leeming were driven into Brighton so that their prisoner could be placed in custody at the police station. The landau then returned to Thornhill's estate, leaving the detectives still in the town. Leeming could not understand Colbeck's desire to attend the meeting.

'It's the last thing *I'd* wish to do, sir,' he said. 'I don't want to hear Mr Thornhill talking down his beaky nose at me.'

'Yes, he has cultivated a patrician air, hasn't he?'

'If you stay for the meeting, you'll have to catch a later train.'

'I'm in no hurry to get back to Scotland Yard,' Colbeck confided. 'The superintendent is relying on good news from Brighton.'

'We arrested a man for attempted murder.'

'But he had nothing to do with the train crash.'

'Mr Tallis should be impressed by what we did, Inspector.'

'Not when we're under siege from the press. The only thing that would impress him is the capture of Dick Chiffney. That will get us favourable headlines in the newspapers and force Captain Ridgeon to eat some humble pie. We'll have to begin a new search for Chiffney tomorrow. Meanwhile,' Colbeck went on, 'there's no need for you to stay here, Victor. I'm sure you'd much rather get home to your family.'

'I would, sir – thank you.'

'We'll share a cab and it can drop you off at the railway station.'

Leeming was able for once to look forward to a train journey. It would take him back to his wife and children without the intervening torment of delivering a report to Edward Tallis. They hailed a cab and climbed into it. The horse set off at a steady trot in the direction of the station, its hooves clip-clopping on the hard surface. Colbeck was preoccupied. It was the sergeant who eventually spoke.

'I'm sorry that we gained nothing at all from our visit,' he said.

'But we did,' said Colbeck with amusement. 'If nothing else, we discovered an alternative career for you. Mr Thornhill will always readily employ you as a gardener.'

'No, he won't – pulling out those weeds made my back ache.'

'I was only joking. You're too good a detective to lose.'

'I don't feel that I've been at my best in this investigation, sir.'

'That's largely *my* fault, Victor.'

'I don't agree with that,' said Leeming. 'You put us on the right track from the very start.'

'Your loyalty is gratifying,' said Colbeck, 'but the truth is that I made mistakes. A moment ago, I was just thinking about a painting that Madeleine is working on at present. The subject is the Round House. I fancy it might have relevance to our present situation.'

'Well, I can't see the slightest connection.'

'Inside the Round House is a turntable. Locomotives go in one way and come out the other. We failed to do that, Victor. Once we decided to go one particular way, we pressed on regardless in the same direction. What we really needed,' he said, thoughtfully, 'was a sort of mental turntable – something that rotated our minds so that we viewed this crime in a different way.'

'I wish I knew what you meant, Inspector,' said Leeming.

'We were too blinkered,' admitted Colbeck. 'Once we concluded that the train crash was a vengeful act against a single individual, we set about looking for possible targets. Horace Bardwell was an obvious possibility.'

'And so was Giles Thornhill.'

'Yet in both cases we were misled. It's time to get on a turntable and swing round so that we can look at the situation from another angle. It's something for you to think about on the train.'

'I would if I had a clue what you were talking about, sir.' The cab drew up outside the station. Leeming was on the point of getting out when he saw someone and stiffened. 'It *can't* be her,' he said, staring at a figure walking towards the entrance. 'And yet it looks so much like her.' He pointed a finger. 'Do you see that woman, Inspector?

'What about her?'

'I think it's Josie Murlow.'

'No,' said Colbeck, studying her. 'She might have the same shape but what would Josie Murlow be doing in mourning?'

'I've no idea, sir, but that's definitely her. I'd put money on it.'

I can't be that certain, Victor.'

'That's because you didn't walk behind her for as long as I

did,' said Leeming. 'I'd know that rolling gait of hers anywhere.'

At that moment, the woman turned around and lifted her black veil so that she could dab at her forehead with a handkerchief. It was all the confirmation the two detectives needed.

'You're right,' said Colbeck, excitedly. 'It *is* Josie Murlow.'

'Why has she come to Brighton?'

'I don't know but I suspect that Chiffney won't be too far away. We must have a change of plan. Instead of going home, I think you should stay and watch her. I hope you don't mind, Victor.'

'I'd insist on it, sir,' said Leeming with enthusiasm. 'If it's a choice between watching her and sitting on a train trying to put my brain on a turntable, I know which one I'd prefer.'

'Make sure you're not caught unawares this time.'

'Chiffney won't be allowed to creep up on me twice. Anyway, he doesn't know what I look like. I was in disguise when he hit me.'

'Josie Murlow might recognise you.'

'How well can she see through that black veil?'

'Take no chances.'

'I promise you that she won't lay eyes on me,' said Leeming, confidently, 'until I have to arrest her, that is.'

Ezra Follis had had a burdensome day but he only allowed himself a nap late in the afternoon. As soon as he woke up, he prepared to go out. Mrs Ashmore came into the drawing room of the rectory as he was putting on his hat in front of the mirror.

'You're never going to that meeting at the town hall, are you?' she said with disapproval.

'That's exactly where I'm going, Mrs Ashmore.'

'But I thought they didn't need you any more.'

'They *always* need me – especially if Giles Thornhill is speaking. The good people of Brighton need someone to talk common sense. They'll certainly get none from the platform.'

'You'd be far better off resting, Mr Follis.'

'I can't rest while that man is preaching his vile gospel,' said Follis, resolutely. 'I'll heckle him every inch of the way.'

She was concerned. 'I don't want you to get into trouble again.'

'Don't fret about me, Mrs Ashmore,'

'I'm bound to fret,' she said. 'Mr Thornhill has too many friends in high places. He can turn them against you. I haven't forgotten the last time you went to a meeting of his.'

Follis cackled. 'Neither have I,' he said, gleefully. 'I challenged almost every statement he made that evening and got loud applause for doing so.'

'But look what happened afterwards. Mr Thornhill made sure that nasty things were written about you in the newspapers and he reported you to the bishop. You were warned.'

'I've lost count of the number of times the bishop has warned me and I daresay that he's done so as well. There are times when the Church of England must speak out, Mrs Ashmore. We shouldn't stand by when an elected Member of Parliament is using his position to incite hatred and distort people's minds. We must fight against bigots like Thornhill.' He took her by the hand and squeezed it. 'I'm sorry,' he said, gently. 'I shouldn't bore you with my opinions. You know them well enough by now.'

'I know them and I respect them,' said the housekeeper, 'but they do worry me sometimes.'

Ellen Ashmore was disturbed. While she admired the rector for his outspokenness, she feared its consequences. He was always being given severe reprimands from the bishop and urged to amend his behaviour. Only that morning, the dean had come to remonstrate with him yet again. Hearing the two men argue, the housekeeper could not resist putting her ear to the door of the drawing room. Though she could not pick up every word, she heard enough to alarm her. The dean was chastising Follis over an article he had written about what he perceived as the shortcomings of the Church. If he did not recant, the Rector of St Dunstan's was threatened with the loss of his living.

'I'd hate to leave here,' she confessed.

'There's no reason why you should,' he assured her.

She gave a pained smile. 'When my husband died,' she recalled, 'I thought that I'd never be happy again. But you rescued me, Mr Follis. You taught me that I had to go on. It was almost as if I was dead and you brought me back to life. I'll never forget that.'

'I've been amply rewarded by your service to me.'

'I'd do *anything* for you, sir. You must know that.'

'You've been a rock, Mrs Ashmore,' he said. 'You're much more than a housekeeper to me. You're a friend, a companion, a nurse and I don't know what else. When the world turns against me – or when the bishop admonishes me – I always have you to offer love and support. That means a great deal to me.'

She was deeply moved. 'Thank you,' she said.

'Your devotion has been heartening.'

'I don't ever want to leave this place.'

'We shall both have to leave one day,' he said, cheerily,

'when old age prevents me from climbing up into that pulpit. This rectory has been a source of continuing joy to me but that will not go on forever. In the fullness of time, I shall *have* to retire.'

'Where will you go, sir?' she asked, apprehensively. 'I know that you have a house in London and that you own property here as well. Will you stay in Brighton?'

Follis was struck by the combination of tenderness and hope in her eyes. Within her limitations, she had been a godsend to him. When he had lost his previous housekeeper, Follis did not think he would ever find anyone as compatible and understanding. In Ellen Ashmore, he had done just that. Removing his hat, he laid it on the table then he took her by the shoulders to pull her close.

'Wherever I go,' he promised, 'you'll come with me.'

'Do you mean that?' she cried with delight.

'Of course, I do. We've been through so much together that I'll never part with you now. You're *mine*, Ellen – you always will be.'

Then he kissed her full on the lips.

Dick Chiffney was determined not to fail this time. There was far too much at stake. All that he had to do was to fire one shot and make his escape. That would not be difficult. The town hall was close to the Lanes, the labyrinth of passageways built way back in the seventeenth century. Chiffney had familiarised himself with the quarter. There would be lots of people outside the town hall but, in the confusion caused by the gunshot, he felt confident of getting away through the Lanes. His employer would be there to watch the murder take place. Once he saw that the victim was dead, he would meet

Chiffney at the railway station and pay him the agreed amount. The two men would never see each other again.

A single criminal act could secure Chiffney's future. While the crowd was still clustered around the dead man outside the town hall, he would be running for an express train. Back in London, he would shower Josie Murlow with money. She had finally accepted that what he was doing was for the benefit of both of them. Any scruples she had about the way his payment was obtained had now vanished. Chiffney and she were accomplices, drawn together by lust and united by someone else's death. They were well-matched.

People had already started to arrive for the meeting. Outside the town hall, a magnificent edifice with a classical façade, was a poster bearing the name of Giles Thornhill. Dozens of citizens wanted to know his opinion about the future of Brighton. Since the advent of the railways, it had become a much larger and more boisterous place than hitherto, invaded by holidaymakers in the warmer months. There were many residents who disliked this regular influx of what they saw as the lower orders and they wondered if their Member of Parliament could do something about it.

Chiffney knew nothing of politics. Since he would never have a vote, he took no interest in who actually ran the country. He had never even heard of Thornhill but was impressed by the size of the audience that the man was drawing. That pleased Chiffney. The bigger the crowd in the street, the greater would be the commotion. When the pistol went off, everyone would be too busy trying to take cover to notice him haring off to the Lanes. Shoot, run, collect his money – it was as simple and straightforward as that. All fear had left him now. He was supremely ready.

Knowing the direction from which his target would arrive, he positioned himself in a doorway and used the telescope to scrutinise each cab that approached and each group of people coming on foot. The man he wanted was nowhere to be seen. Time was slowly running out. It would not be long before the meeting started. Chiffney began to worry that his victim might not turn up. It was absurd. He had seen the man half-a-dozen times during the day yet had been unable to shoot. Now that he was eager to pull the trigger, he had no target.

Cold fear seized him. He might not, after all, have the chance to earn his reward. At the last moment, Chiffney had been thwarted. He had been misinformed. The man was not coming. He had cheated death. Just as he was about to give up all hope, he saw another cab turn into the road. Even with the telescope, he could not identify its occupant but he somehow knew that his target had come. Stuffing the telescope into his pocket, he unbuttoned his coat so that he could put his hand around the pistol. It was already loaded. Murder was only seconds away.

The cab drew up outside the town hall and a man got out. He reached up to pay the driver. Chiffney darted across to him with the pistol drawn. He got within yards of the dapper figure.

'Ezra Follis?' he shouted.

'Yes,' said Follis, turning. 'Who wants me?'

'I do!'

Chiffney fired the gun and saw him recoil as the bullet struck him. Before the rector had even hit the ground, his attacker was running away as fast as his legs would carry him.

*   *   *

Robert Colbeck was inside the town hall when he heard the gunshot and the screams that followed it. Rushing out into the road, he saw people sheltering in doorways or crouched down on their knees. Right in from of him was a small group of men, bending over a body on the pavement. Colbeck went over to them and saw Ezra Follis, his face contorted with agony as he clutched the wound in his shoulder. Colbeck took charge at once.

'Someone fetch a doctor!' he ordered. As a man hurried off, Colbeck took out a handkerchief, put it over the wound. 'Press down on this to stem the bleeding,' he told one of the bystanders before speaking to Follis. 'Can you hear me, sir?'

'Yes, Inspector,' murmured Follis.

'What happened?'

'Thornhill stopped me going to the meeting.'

'I'll tell you what happened,' said one of the men. 'The Reverend Follis got out a cab when someone jumped forward and shot him.'

'Is that correct?' asked Colbeck.

'Yes,' replied Follis. 'It was over in an instant.'

'Can you describe the man?'

'He was as ugly as sin, Inspector. He had the face of Satan.'

'Dick Chiffney!' said Colbeck to himself.

Victor Leeming had kept her under observation from behind the newspaper he had bought at the railway station. Josie Murlow was seated on a bench from which she could see the main entrance. Every so often, she glanced up at the clock. When a train came in, she got up as if about to catch it. At the last moment, however, she changed her mind and went back to the bench. Leeming could not see her face but he could sense her irritation. The train pulled out and she watched it go. Seeing her distracted, the sergeant drifted closer to the entrance so that he would be in a better position to intercept Chiffney.

In the event, it was not Dick Chiffney who came but Colbeck. A cab came towards the station with the horse at a gallop. When the animal was reined in by the driver, the cab came to an abrupt halt and out leapt Colbeck. After handing some coins to the driver, he strode briskly over to Leeming.

'Has he come yet, Victor?' he asked. 'Is Chiffney here?'

'No, sir.'

'Then he will be any minute. He's just shot the Reverend Follis.'

'Never!'

'Chiffney escaped on foot, apparently, so I'll have overtaken him in the cab. Besides, he won't run all the way here for fear of arousing suspicion.'

'How do we know he's coming to the station?'

'Josie Murlow is waiting for him. I'll wager that's why she's in Brighton today.' He glanced around. 'Let's separate so that he has to pass between us.'

'Yes, Inspector,' said Leeming, pleased at the prospect of action.

'Don't move until I give the signal. With luck, he might even make contact with his paymaster. We can arrest both of them.'

'Mr Tallis may yet have good news from Brighton.'

'Take up your position, Victor, and be very careful.'

'Why is that?'

'Chiffney is armed.'

They parted company and moved to either side of the entrance. Both had their backs to Josie so there was no danger of their being recognised. People were streaming into the station and going to their respective platforms. None of them realised what was about to happen. The detectives did not have long to wait. As more people converged on the terminus, Colbeck and Leeming both noticed the strapping man with a hunted look. The pronounced squint and the hideous face left them in no doubt. It was Dick Chiffney.

They let him walk past them into the station. He was tense and agitated, looking around with great anxiety as if expecting to see someone. What the detectives could not understand was why he ignored Josie Murlow and why she made no attempt to speak to him. Chiffney's interest was in someone else but that person was nowhere to be seen. He became desperate, breaking into a trot as he searched every corner of the station, bumping into people in his haste. As he looped back towards the entrance, Colbeck and Leeming could see the sweat glistening on his face.

Josie Murlow was on her feet now, watching him as intently as the detectives yet hesitating to approach him. Seeing the anguished state he was in, she held back. When she heard another train clanking towards the station, she looked over her shoulder. Chiffney also registered it, torn between wanting to find someone and needing to escape from Brighton. Colbeck had waited long enough. Whoever Chiffney had expected was obviously not there. It was time to strike.

Colbeck gave the signal and both detectives started to move towards Chiffney. Their determination was so evident and their walk so purposeful that they gave themselves away. An innate sense of survival made Chiffney look up at them. He was a killer on the run and he knew he must not be taken. As they got within ten yards, he pulled out the pistol and brandished it.

'Keep back,' he said, 'or I'll shoot.'

'You can't kill both of us with one bullet,' said Colbeck, calmly. 'In any case, you can't shoot straight, Mr Chiffney. You only managed to hit the Reverend Follis in the shoulder.'

Chiffney was in a panic. They not only knew his name, they were aware of his crime. Worst of all, he had not killed his target. That explained why the man who had retained him was not there. He would never pay Chiffney for a bungled murder.

Colbeck extended a palm. 'Hand the gun over, sir,' he said.

'If you come any closer,' warned Chiffney, 'I'll kill you.'

'I doubt very much if you've had time to reload in the rush to get here. Now, are you going to hand it over or shall we take it from you?'

Chiffney looked helplessly down at the weapon, confirming that it was not loaded. When he saw Leeming edging forward, he flung the pistol at him and caught him in the chest. The sergeant reeled back in pain. Colbeck stayed long enough to make sure that Leeming was not seriously injured. He then looked up to see Chiffney running away. Discarding his top hat, Colbeck gave chase. He was not simply after a man who had shot Ezra Follis. He was pursuing a callous villain who had deliberately caused a train crash that led to many deaths. It put extra speed into Colbeck's legs.

The crowd parted as the two men hurtled across the station. Realising that he might soon be caught, and wearied from his earlier run through the Lanes, Chiffney tried to elude Colbeck by jumping down on to the track. He was oblivious to the fact that the oncoming train was now steaming towards the platform. Josie Murlow saw the danger only too clearly. Throwing back her veil, she yelled at the top of her voice.

'Look out, Dick – the train is coming!'

Intended to save his life, the warning actually condemned him to death. Chiffney was so astonished to hear her voice that he stood still and turned around. When he saw her dressed in black, he was utterly bewildered. He had no idea what Josie was doing there in such unlikely attire. By the time he tried to move, it was too late. Tripping over the rail in his urgency, he fell directly across the path of the locomotive. Its large, merciless, revolving, cast-iron wheels sliced through him and rolled on uncaringly past the blood-covered remains.

Josie's Murlow's howl of despair reverberated around the whole station. Unwittingly, she had worn the appropriate dress, after all.

CHAPTER FIFTEEN

Coming off duty that evening, Caleb Andrews went straight home for once. Ordinarily, he would have joined his fireman for a drink in the tavern near Euston station but he chose to avoid the jocular company of other railwaymen. Since they knew of his friendship with Robert Colbeck, some of them were bound to tease him about the Railway Detective's apparent failure and Andrews did not wish to give them that opportunity. He still had faith that Colbeck would prove that a crime had taken place and clear Frank Pike's name in the process.

Even though natural light was fading, Madeleine was still at her easel when he got back. She broke off to give him a welcoming kiss.

'Are you still working this late, Maddy?'

'I enjoy it,' she replied.

'There's not another woman in the whole country who'd look twice at the Round House,' he said, inspecting the painting. He let out a whistle of admiration. 'It's good,' he went on, 'it's very good. Your mother would've been so proud to know our little girl would grow up to be an artist.'

'I'm not a *real* artist, Father.'

'Yes, you are. You're as good as any of them that hang their paintings in art galleries. This is one of your best,' he went on, still gazing it. 'I've driven that locomotive more than once and I can see that you've got every single detail right.'

'That's why I've taken so much time over it.'

'I wouldn't mind putting it on the wall in here.'

'There's no chance of that, Father,' she said. 'This is a present for Robert – even though he doesn't know it yet. It was Robert who really made me believe that I had some talent.'

'I was the one who suggested taking you to the Round House,' he reminded her. 'By rights, that painting is mine.'

'If you're so fond of it, I'll do a copy when I've finished this one.'

'Why don't you do a copy for Inspector Colbeck?'

'He deserves the original.'

'So do I, Maddy.'

It was only a token protest. Andrews pulled the newspaper from his pocket and unfolded it. He turned to the relevant page. By way of warning, he rolled his eyes.

'I glanced at this before I left the station,' he said, offering it to her. 'There's a cartoon about Inspector Colbeck.'

It was not a flattering one. Taking the newspaper, Madeleine looked at it with annoyance and concern. The cartoon depicted Colbeck, groping around a railway line in the gloom with a magnifying glass. There was a look of desperation on his face as he said "There must be a crime around here *somewhere*!" The caption was unkind – The Railway Detective Is Still In The Dark. Madeleine closed the paper angrily and thrust it back at her father.

'It's so spiteful,' she complained. 'This was the newspaper that called him the Railway Detective in the first place. They were full of praise for him then. Have they forgotten all the cases he's solved?'

'Don't get so upset, Maddy.'

'I feel like writing a letter to the editor.'

'He probably wouldn't print it.'

'Someone needs to stand up for Robert.'

'Oh,' said Andrews with a grin, 'I think that Inspector Colbeck can do that for himself. He doesn't need your help, Maddy. The press have thrown stones at him before and they never seem to hurt him.'

'They hurt *me*,' she said, 'and I don't like it.'

'What I don't like is the slur they're casting on Frank Pike's name. Unless that official report is shown up for the nonsense that it is, Frank will be blamed for the crash. I want the truth to come out.'

Madeleine was positive. 'It will, Father,' she said, 'I'm sure. Robert won't let us down. No matter how long it takes and no matter how much criticism he gets, Robert will carry on with the investigation until everything is brought to light.'

In the circumstances, Victor Leeming was happy to accompany Colbeck back to Scotland Yard. They had substantial progress to report and that would gladden even the flint heart of Edward Tallis. If there was approbation on offer, Leeming wanted his share of it. When the detectives entered the superintendent's office, they were not met by the pungent odour of his cigars. The air in the room seemed fresh for a change. Tallis was standing at the window. He swung round to face them.

'Don't you dare tell me that you've drawn another blank,' he said with quiet menace. 'Bring some cheer into my life.'

'I think we can contrive to do that, sir,' said Colbeck, smoothly.

'Yes,' agreed Leeming. 'We had an interesting day in Brighton.'

'But did you make any *arrests*?' asked Tallis.

'We have two people in custody.'

'Who are they?'

'Inspector Colbeck will explain.'

'I wish that somebody would. I need to hear good tidings.'

'If you'd care to sit down,' said Colbeck, 'I'll do my best to give them to you.'

After all three of them had taken a seat, Colbeck delivered his report with characteristic aplomb. The superintendent's face was a block of ice that slowly melted into something recognisably human. A fleeting smile actually appeared beneath his moustache.

'You captured the man who tried to shoot Mr Thornhill?'

'Yes,' replied Colbeck. 'Strictly speaking, I was the person that Herr Freytag tried to kill and Victor was the arresting officer. He showed great bravery in tackling an armed man.'

'Well done, Sergeant,' said Tallis.

'Thank you, sir,' said Leeming, savouring the moment.

'As for that rogue, Dick Chiffney, death under the wheels of a locomotive was poetic justice. Now he *knows* what it's like to be killed in a railway accident.' His gaze shifted to Colbeck. 'I take it that you got full details of the crime from this harlot of his.'

'Not yet,' said Colbeck. 'Josie Murlow was in such a state of hysteria when we arrested her that we could get nothing coherent out of the woman. The only thing she admitted was that she was expecting Chiffney to make a lot of money in Brighton that day.'

'Yes – by shooting the Reverend Follis.'

'Why would anyone want to kill a clergyman?' asked Leeming.

'We'll discover that when we catch Chiffney's paymaster,' said Colbeck. 'As I told you, Victor, we were looking in the wrong direction. We thought that Mr Bardwell or Mr Thornhill had been the target on that express. Instead of looking at business and politics, we should have used a turntable and swung round to examine religion.'

Tallis was perplexed. 'What's this about a turntable?'

'Don't ask me, sir,' said Leeming, helplessly.

'It's just a metaphor,' explained Colbeck. 'The thing we don't yet have, of course, is the name of the man behind it all. It may be that Chiffney himself didn't know it and neither does Josie Murlow. She swore that she had no idea who employed Chiffney.'

'What about the Reverend Follis himself?' asked Tallis. 'Surely, he knows who his enemies are.'

'He was unable to help us, Superintendent. By the time we'd finished at Brighton station, Mr Follis was in hospital, having the bullet taken out of his shoulder. Because he was in such pain,' said Colbeck, 'they'd used chloroform. I'll speak to him tomorrow though it's not certain that he'll give us the name we want. In his own way, the Rector of St Dunstan's has upset as many people as Mr Bardwell and Mr Thornhill put together. With so many people wishing him ill, he may have great difficulty identifying the right one.'

'In short,' said Tallis, glowering, 'you have absolutely no clue as to who this man might be.'

'That's not true, sir. We have this.' Colbeck opened the leather satchel he was carrying and took out a telescope. 'Chiffney also had a weapon in his possession but it was crushed beneath the train. This, however,' he continued, 'was not damaged. As you can see, it's a fine instrument and hardly the thing that Chiffney would own himself. It must have been loaned to him by his paymaster.' He passed it over to Tallis, who extended it to its full length then inspected it. 'That's the best clue we have, Superintendent.'

'It may be the only one we need,' said Tallis, excitedly. 'It's got his name engraved on the side here – he's a Mr Grampus.'

'With respect, sir,' said Colbeck, taking the telescope back from him, 'Grampus is not the name of a man. It's the name of a ship. Our suspect was in the navy.'

Word of the attempt on Ezra Follis's life spread like wildfire around Brighton. Before he had even recovered from the effects of the chloroform, friends and well-wishers were calling at the county hospital. Sidney Weaver was the first there. Having been at the town hall for the meeting, he felt that he had a more dramatic event to report in the road outside. Ellen Ashmore and Amy Walcott were only two of the women who rushed to the hospital. Other female parishioners also wanted the latest news of their beloved rector. They joined the churchwardens, the verger and many others who tried to get to the victim's bedside. A hospital already filled with survivors of the train crash was now even more overcrowded.

A senior doctor told them that the patient's condition was now stable and that, in spite of a loss of blood, he was in no imminent danger. However, he insisted, Ezra Follis would not be strong enough to see anyone until the morning. Reluctantly, people slowly drifted away. The only person who lingered was the editor of the *Brighton Gazette*, wanting more detail about the seriousness of the injury so that he could include it in his newspaper report.

Giles Thornhill arrived later in the evening. Because of his status and because he had donated generously to the hospital coffers, his request to see the patient was treated with more respect. When told of his visitor, Follis, though still drowsy, nevertheless agreed to see him. Thornhill came into the ward and felt a pang of sympathy when he observed the clergyman's condition. Heavily bandaged, Follis lay in bed with his face as white as the sheets covering him. He looked impossibly small and fragile. His voice was a mere croak.

'I'm sorry I missed your talk,' he said.

'Half of the audience did so as well,' said Thornhill, resignedly. 'When they heard that someone was firing a gun outside, they got up and fled.' There was the hint of a smile. 'Was it a deliberate trick on your part to interrupt the meeting?'

'Even I wouldn't go to that extreme, Mr Thornhill.'

'How are you?'

'I'm still in pain and feeling very sleepy.'

'Then I won't hold you up,' said Thornhill. 'I just wanted to say how sorry I am that this happened. It's ironic that we have something in common at last.'

'Yes,' said Follis, 'someone tried to kill you as well.'

'The young man is now in custody. Inspector Colbeck set a trap for him and he fell into it. But yours is a very different case,' he went on. 'I was shot at from a distance. From what I gather, you were only yards away from the man who fired at you.'

'Luckily, he was a bad shot. He was aiming at my head but the bullet hit my shoulder.' Follis quivered at the memory. 'It was like a red hot poker going into my flesh.'

'I hope you make a complete recovery.'

'Thank you, Mr Thornhill.'

'Did you recognise the man?'

'I've never seen him before in my life.'

'What possible reason could he have to attack you?'

'I don't know,' said Follis with weary humour. 'My sermons are not *that* objectionable. It must have been someone with a grudge against religion, I suppose.'

'The man who shot at me was driven by a grudge. It had become an obsession. He could think of nothing else. At least, I know that he's safely under lock and key and has no accomplice. Unfortunately, that's not the situation with you.'

'I don't follow you, Mr Thornhill.'

Well,' said the other, 'if your attacker escaped, he might come back to try again. Or he might have a confederate, sworn to the same foul purpose. Grudges never disappear – they get stronger with the passage of time. Acquire a bodyguard quickly,' he urged. 'You could be in serious danger.'

Follis felt as if the bullet had hit him all over again.

It was not the first time that Josie Murlow had spent the night in a police cell. On previous occasions, however, she had been hauled before a magistrate, fined then released. Legal process would take a very different route this time. Until her trial, she would remain behind bars. She had spent a miserable night, alternately bemoaning her fate and raging against the men who had, in her opinion, driven Dick Chiffney to his grotesque death. Her temper was fiery. When she was given food, she hurled it back at the policeman who had brought it.

Hearing of her conduct from the custody sergeant, Tallis decided to interview her where she was. He and Colbeck were shown to Josie's cell. The superintendent had no time to introduce himself. As soon as she saw Colbeck, she flung herself at the bars and reached a hand through in a vain attempt to grab him.

'You killed Dick Chiffney!' she screeched.

'That's not true,' said Colbeck.

'You're nothing but a murderer!'

'Control yourself, woman!' ordered Tallis in a voice that compelled obedience. 'Do you want to be restrained?' he asked. 'Do you want to spend the rest of your time here in chains? Do you want my officers to hold you down and feed you through a tube? Is that what you want?' Cowering in her cell, Josie shook her head. 'Then let's have no more of this unacceptable behaviour.' He stood to attention. 'My name is Superintendent Tallis and this, as you well know, is Inspector Colbeck.'

'Good morning,' said Colbeck. 'When we brought you back to London on the train, you were in no mood for conversation. That was understandable. Today, however, we must establish certain facts.' He met her withering glare. 'Do you know where Mr Chiffney had been before he came to Brighton station?'

She was surly. 'Dick said he had a job to do.'

'Did he tell you what that job entailed?'

'No – he wouldn't tell me anything.'

'Then let me enlighten you,' Colbeck continued. 'Mr Chiffney was lurking outside the town hall so that he could shoot a clergyman named Mr Follis. He fired a pistol at him from close quarters.'

She was jolted. 'Dick would never do a thing like that.'

'There were several witnesses, Miss Murlow. I was close to the scene myself. That's why I hailed a cab and hurried to the station. We'd seen you waiting there and knew that Mr Chiffney would come.'

'You're wrong,' she said, waving an arm. 'Dick didn't even know that I was in Brighton. He told me to keep away.'

'Why did he do that?' asked Tallis.

'He thought I'd distract him from...what he had to do.'

'And what was that?'

Josie shrugged. 'I don't know, sir.'

'I fancy that you do. You're an accessory to attempted murder.'

'I'm not, sir, I swear it!'

'Who was Mr Chiffney working for?' asked Colbeck.

'He never told me the man's name.'

'But you did know he was being paid by someone?'

'Oh, yes,' she said, 'Dick showed me the money he got for the first job he did though he wouldn't tell me what it was. As for that man's name, I don't think Dick knew it himself.'

'So you're not aware what that "first job" actually was?'

'No – Dick vanished and I thought he'd run out on me. When he came back, he had lots of money. He said there'd be even more when he did something else in Brighton.'

'It's time you learnt what Chiffney did first of all,' said Tallis, 'then you might not hold his memory so dear. Did you know that there was a train crash on the Brighton line last week?'

'Of course – everyone was talking about it.'

'The man who engineered that crash was Chiffney.'

'No!' she exclaimed, refusing to believe it. 'Dick would never cause a train crash. I know him. He liked working on the railway. Why should he want to do something as terrible as that?'

'You've already given us the answer,' said Colbeck. 'He did it for money. He did it because he was out of work. He did it because he was dismissed by the company and wanted to get his own back.' Josie staggered back in horror. 'There seem to be lots of things that Mr Chiffney forgot to tell you, don't there?'

Josie's mind was racing. They had no reason to lie to her. The man she had been mourning had set off to commit murder for their mutual benefit. The thought that he had already caused the deaths of several other people turned him into a complete monster and she quailed as she recalled the intimacies they had shared in the wake of the train disaster. Josie had coupled with the Devil himself. She felt ashamed and corrupted. The sight of Chiffney, carved to pieces on a railway line, no longer enraged her. In the light of his crime, it was a fitting end. She elected to forget Chiffney altogether. He belonged to her past. All she worried about now was saving her own skin.

'It's not very much,' she said, ingratiatingly, 'but I'll tell you all I know.'

Victor Leeming was in good spirits. Now that the investigation was nearing its end, his chances of being at home for his wife's birthday had improved. Despatched to the Navy Office by Colbeck, he had gathered the information they needed and could now return. Before he did so, however, there were still gifts to be bought for Sunday and he might never have such a good opportunity again. It would not take long. If he were caught attending to family business while still on duty, Leeming knew that Superintendent Tallis would suspend him instantly. Colbeck would take a more tolerant view. He realised how much the sergeant loved his wife.

Leeming consulted a list he drew from his pocket. It had been compiled from records at the Navy Office. Somewhere on the list, he believed, was the name of the man who had hired Dick Chiffney to orchestrate a train crash. The consequences had been horrendous. The sergeant had visited the scene with Colbeck. Both men had been shocked by the scale of the disaster. Leeming remembered the sight of the wreckage, the smell from the bonfires and the groans of agony from the remaining victims. Suddenly, the purchase of his wife's birthday presents no longer seemed important. It was put aside until after the arrest of the man who had conceived the tragedy. His capture was paramount.

Leeming hurried away. The investigation took precedence. He and Colbeck had to return to Brighton. Besides, the town did not merely harbour a wanted man. It had shops.

Until he woke up the next morning, Ezra Follis had not realised he had so many friends. Cards, flowers and gifts of all kinds had flooded in from the most unlikely sources and there was an endless queue of people waiting to see him. Since he was still weak, he only agreed to see selected visitors and limited their time at the bedside. The bishop, the dean and the churchwardens were the first to be allowed in. Of the others, only Ellen Ashmore, Amy Walcott and a handful of close friends were permitted a few minutes each.

By late morning, Robert Colbeck arrived and he was conducted straight to the patient. Follis was pleased to see him.

'There's a rumour that you caught the man who shot me,' he said, hopefully. 'Is that true, Inspector?'

'In a manner of speaking,' replied Colbeck. 'Sergeant Leeming and I accosted him at the railway station but he tried to run away. In doing so, he managed to get himself run over by an incoming train.'

Follis shuddered. 'What a gruesome death!'

'I shouldn't waste too much sympathy on him, sir. He was the person responsible for the train crash. He levered a section of line away so that the Brighton Express would be derailed. That's why this hospital is filled to capacity.'

'Who was the villain, Inspector?'

'His name was Dick Chiffney.'

'I've never heard of him,' said Follis, mystified. 'Why should he want to harm so many people in that crash then try to shoot me?'

'The two events are complementary,' explained Colbeck. 'They were both intended to bring about your death. When the first failed to do so, a more direct approach was taken.'

'This is all about *me*?' gasped Follis, shaken to the core. 'Was it because of me that people were killed and maimed in that disaster? I find that horrifying. In effect, all that suffering was my fault.'

'No, sir – you were a victim of the crash.'

'But it might never have taken place had I not been aboard that train. Are you *certain* about this, Inspector?' Colbeck nodded. 'Then I'll have it on my conscience for the rest of my life. I'm beginning to wish that I'd never survived that crash.'

'It's only because you did,' said Colbeck, 'that we're able to get to the truth. Had you perished, we'd never have connected you with the people who committed the crime. The Brighton Express was not chosen lightly, Mr Follis. In the mind of the man who was behind the disaster, it had a great significance. That's what made us believe that an individual passenger was the target.'

Colbeck told him about the evidence that led them to think that Horace Bardwell or Giles Thornhill might be that individual passenger, recounting how both Matthew Shanklin and Heinrich Freytag had been subsequently arrested. Follis was only half-listening. He was still trying to grapple with the fact that he had indirectly brought about so many deaths and injuries. He was eaten up with guilt.

'We need your help, sir,' said Colbeck.

'Haven't I done enough damage already?' moaned Follis.

'Chiffney was hired to kill you. Now that he's dead, we must find his paymaster. That's where you can be of assistance.'

'I fail to see how, Inspector.'

'Do you know of anyone – anyone at all – who had made threats against you or is nursing a deep hatred of you?'

'Yes,' said Follis, 'I could give you several names. The first one is my bishop. He's threatened many times to have me ousted from the rectory and must loathe the very sight of me.'

'I'm being serious, sir.'

'Then the simple answer is that I've offended a lot of people in the course of my ministry but I don't think that any of them would go to such lengths to wreak their revenge.'

'We have one important clue,' said Colbeck. 'We're fairly

certain that the man in question has a naval background. Can you think of any sailor who might hold a grudge against you?'

'No,' said Follis, eyelids flickering rapidly, 'I can't.'

Colbeck knew that he was lying.

Ellen Ashmore had been crying. Though she had wiped away the tears and done her best to appear composed, Victor Leeming could tell that the housekeeper had been weeping. When he had introduced himself, she let him into the rectory and they went into the drawing room.

'Mr Follis won't be out of hospital for days,' she said. 'I saw him earlier and he's very poorly.'

'It's you that I came to see, Mrs Ashmore.'

'Oh?'

'I want to ask you a few questions,' said Leeming. 'Shall we sit down?' When they had settled down opposite each other, he tried to reassure her. 'There's no need to look so anxious. You're not in any kind of trouble.'

'I'm not worried about myself, Sergeant,' she said. 'The only person I'm thinking about at the moment is the rector.'

'That's only right, Mrs Ashmore. You've been his housekeeper for some time now, I hear.'

'I've been here for years.'

'And is Mr Follis a good employer?'

'It's a pleasure to work for him,' she said, brightening for an instant. 'Mr Follis is a wonderful man.'

'Not everyone shares your high opinion, I'm afraid,' observed Leeming. 'Someone was hired to kill him. As it happens, that person later lost his life. But the man who hired him is still at liberty and still poses a threat to the rector.'

She blanched. 'Do you mean that someone else will try to

kill him?' she cried. 'Please – you must stop them!'

'Inspector Colbeck is at the hospital now. One of his main concerns will be Mr Follis's safety. He'll organise protection for him. But what I want to ask you is this,' he went on. 'Someone was waiting to ambush the rector outside the town hall. How many people knew that Mr Follis would be going to that meeting?'

'Lots of them,' she said. 'At one point, he was due to replace Mr Thornhill as the speaker. People would have seen his name on the posters. When he was told that he wasn't needed, he insisted on going even though I felt that he should rest. He usually goes to any meeting that Mr Thornhill addresses. Mr Follis can't resist an argument.'

'So people who know the rector would expect him to be there.'

'Yes, they would.'

'Let me ask another question – did you see anything recently that aroused your suspicion?'

'Well, I did see something odd yesterday,' she recalled, 'but I thought nothing of it at the time. There was a man in the churchyard. People come in regularly to leave flowers by a grave or simply to pay their respects. Over the years, I've got to know them by sight. This man was a stranger,' she said. 'When he saw me looking, he bent down as if he was reading the inscription on a headstone.'

'Can you describe him in any way, Mrs Ashmore?'

'I only had a glimpse of him.'

'Was he big or little, old or young?'

'Oh,' she said, 'he was a big man and near your age, I suppose. And there was something else about him,' she added. 'I remember seeing his eyes. He had a squint.'

'It must have been Dick Chiffney,' said Leeming. 'He was the man who shot Mr Follis.'

She was scandalised. 'He was *here* in the churchyard?'

'So it appears.'

'I should have warned Mr Follis. He'll never forgive me.'

'You weren't to know who the man was or what he had in mind.'

'I feel dreadful.'

'There's no need for you to get upset, Mrs Ashmore,' he told her. 'Nobody could accuse you of putting the rector's life in jeopardy. Inspector Colbeck has told me how well you look after Mr Follis.'

'That's all I *want* to do,' she said.

'Then let's see if you can help to identify the man who hired Chiffney.' He took a piece of paper from his pocket. 'This is a list of names I'd like you to look at. The Inspector has a copy and will be showing it to Mr Follis. Since you've been here so long,' he continued, handing her the list, 'I'd like you to look at the names as well.'

'Who are these people, Sergeant?'

'They're officers from HMS *Grampus*. It docked in Portsmouth for repair recently so these men are on leave. We think that one of them may have a connection with St Dunstan's. Do you recognise any of those gentlemen?'

'Let me see.' She ran her eye down the list and stopped at the last name. 'This one,' she said, pointing to it. 'Alexander Jamieson.'

'And is Mr Jamieson a parishioner?'

'It's Captain Jamieson and he's away at sea a great deal. But his wife used to worship at St Dunstan's regularly.' She looked up. 'We haven't seen her for some time.'

* * *

Dorothea Jamieson could not believe what had happened to her. Ten days earlier, she had been living in a large house with servants at her beck and call. She was a handsome woman in her late thirties, noted for her elegance and widely respected in the community. All that now seemed like a dream. Instead of enjoying the comforts of her home, she was locked in a filthy, evil-smelling outhouse with only mice and spiders for company. An old mattress had been dragged in, a rickety chair had been provided and – the greatest humiliation of all – a wooden bucket stood in a corner for when she had to answer the calls of nature.

There was no hope of escape. The door was securely locked, and the narrow windows, set high in the wall, were barred. Even with the help of the various implements stored there, she could not force a way out. The only saving grace was that it had not rained during the time of her incarceration or the holes in the roof would have let in the water. As it was, she had had to endure stifling heat on most days. Nights alone in the dark had been terrifying.

Hearing footsteps approach in the courtyard, she stood up and waited tremulously. A key turned in the lock and the heavy door swung open. Dorothea shielded her eyes against the bright sunlight that poured in. Her husband stepped into the outhouse and shut the door behind him. He looked at her with disgust. The beautiful young woman he had married almost twenty years ago looked haggard and unappealing. Her hair was tousled, her skin blotched and her dress crumpled from having been slept in.

'How much longer is this going to go on, Alexander?' she asked.

'As long as I choose,' he replied.

'I'll do *anything* to win back your good favour.'

'You're doing it, Dorothea – by suffering.'

'You can't keep me here forever.'

'I can do whatever I like with you.'

'But I'm your *wife*,' she pleaded.

'Oh, you've remembered that, have you?' he said with sarcasm. 'You always do when I come ashore. It's a pity you don't remember it when I'm away at sea.'

'But I do – I'm proud that Captain Jamieson is my husband.'

'My name is simply a shield behind which you hide.'

She spread her arms. 'What am I supposed to have done?'

'You know quite well what you did and, until you confess it, you'll stay locked up here like an animal. I want to hear you tell me the truth, Dorothea. I want to *know* what happened.'

'Nothing happened!' she wailed.

'Don't lie to me!'

He raised his hand to strike her then held back at the last moment. Dorothea cringed in front of him. She looked wretched. Her time in the outhouse had robbed her of her good looks, her dignity and her confidence. Jamieson felt no compassion for her. As he stroked his beard and gazed down at her, his only emotion was a deep hatred. He would keep her locked up indefinitely.

'I prayed that you'd come home safely from your voyage,' she said, 'but, when you did, you flew into such a rage. I've been trapped in here for over a week now. It's *cruel*, Alexander. My only sustenance has been bread and water.'

'That's all you deserve.'

'Do you despise your wife so much?'

'What I despise,' he said, 'is the woman who's been posing as my wife while acting as someone else's mistress.'

Dorothea backed away. She knew that he had a temper but she had never been its victim before. She still had the bruises on her arms where he had grabbed her before pulling her across the courtyard to the outhouse. Confronted with his accusations, she had thought it best to say nothing for fear of stoking his rage. Dorothea had hoped that her husband might calm down as the days passed and even allow her back into the house. If anything, his fury had intensified.

'I suspected something the last time I was home,' he said, 'but I was unable to prove anything. Before I sailed, I engaged a private detective to keep an eye on you.'

'That was an appalling thing to do,' she said with as much indignation as she could gather. 'What sort of husband stoops to spying on his wife?'

'One who fears that he's being cuckolded, Dorothea. It was, alas, no groundless fear. When I saw the report about you, I refused to accept it at first. Then I read the damning evidence.'

'What evidence, Alexander? Am I not entitled to defend myself against it? Will you really accept someone else's word against mine?'

'The evidence concerned Thursday of every week.'

'I went up to London to see some friends,' she explained.

Jamieson sneered. 'One particular friend,' he said.

'I always came back late in the evening – ask the servants.'

'I did ask them but they were ready to lie on your behalf. That's why I dismissed them and why there's nobody in the house to hear your cries for help. They said that you always came back home,' he continued, 'but the man following you is certain that you spent the night at a certain address on a number of occasions.'

'I missed the train, that's all.'

'A woman like you never misses a train, Dorothea.'

'I remember now,' she said, lunging at the first excuse that came to mind. 'The weather was inclement. I was forced to stay over.'

'On every single occasion?'

'Yes, Alexander.'

'And always in the same house?'

'My friend, Sophie, pressed me to stay. Why not ask her?'

'Because I'm sure that she'd lie on your behalf as readily as the servants,' he said. 'Besides, she doesn't live in that house. It's owned by the Reverend Ezra Follis.'

'That's right,' she said, changing her tack. 'He offered me shelter on those nights when the weather turned nasty. Yes, that's what really happened. Why not speak to Mr Follis himself?'

'I never want to exchange another word with that philanderer. The man is a disgrace to the cloth,' he said, contemptuously. 'I'm sure that he made you feel that you were special to him but the hideous truth is that you were just the next in line, Dorothea. You shared a bed that had already been tainted by other women.'

'I didn't share a bed with anybody.'

'Then you must be the only one of his victims who didn't. The detective I hired was very thorough. He gave me all their names. He even tracked down Marion Inigo.'

She was stunned. 'Mrs Inigo, who used to be his housekeeper?'

'Yes, Dorothea,' he replied, 'except that she was never actually married. Marion Inigo used to spend Thursday night at that very same house with the Rector of St Dunstan's. She lives in London now, bringing up their child in the cottage he bought her.'

'I don't believe this,' she said, abandoning all pretence of innocence. 'Ezra would never look at a woman like Marion Inigo. He got rid of her because she was becoming too familiar.' She wrinkled her nose. 'She was nothing but a *servant*.'

'That servant is the mother of his son.'

'It's impossible.'

'I have incontrovertible proof.'

She was distraught. 'Can this be true?'

Jamieson relished her pain. 'Would you like the names of his other conquests?' he taunted.

Dorothea reeled as if from a blow. Her romance with Ezra Follis had rescued her from long, lonely months when she was on her own. She had taken immense pains to be discreet. Yet not only had her infidelity been exposed, she now discovered that the man who claimed to love her had seduced a string of women before her. It was crippling.

'Goodbye, Dorothea,' said her husband, opening the door. 'I'm going to London myself today so you'll have to manage without any food until tomorrow. If,' he added, 'I decide to bring you any, that is.'

'Where are you going, Alexander?'

'I intend to look at his house for myself. I want to see where my marriage was ruined and make sure that no other trusting husband is cuckolded there.'

She grabbed his arm. 'You won't *hurt* Ezra, will you?'

'I'll do exactly that,' he said, flinging her aside. 'When I've destroyed his house, I'll destroy him.'

Jamieson went out, slammed the door and locked it. Dorothea lay on the ground where she had fallen and wept. Her situation was hopeless. All that she could think of doing was to pray for forgiveness.

Seated in the hansom cab, Colbeck and Leeming were driven towards the house owned by Captain Alexander Jamieson. They felt that they at last had the evidence they required.

'When I read out the names on that list,' said Colbeck, 'Mr Follis denied having heard of any of them. He even stuck to his denial when I showed him the telescope. Then you turned up at the hospital with a positive identification from Mrs Ashmore and that forced him to tell the truth. He *did* know Captain Jamieson.'

'Why did he lie so stubbornly to you, Inspector?'

'The rector had something to hide.'

'If this Captain Jamieson is a suspect,' said Leeming, 'you'd have thought that Mr Follis would volunteer his name at the start.'

'I'm sure he had good reason to deceive us,' said Colbeck. 'I'll be interested to discover exactly what it is.'

The cab pulled up outside a big, white, detached Regency house standing on an acre of land. After ordering the driver to wait, Colbeck got out. Leeming followed him up the steps to the front door. They rang the bell several times but to no effect. Telling the sergeant to stay at the front of the property, Colbeck went around to the side. He peered over the fence into the garden.

'Is anyone there?' he shouted, cupping his hands. 'We're looking for Captain Jamieson. Is he at home?'

There was no response from the house itself but he heard a

cry from the outhouse on the other side of the courtyard. The voice was too indistinct for him to hear the exact words but he could tell that a woman was in distress. He called Leeming and the sergeant bent down so that Colbeck could step on to his back and jump over the fence. Running to the outhouse, he tried the door and found it locked.

'Who's that inside?' he asked.

'I'm Mrs Dorothea Jamieson,' she answered.

'My name is Detective Inspector Colbeck and I was hoping to speak to your husband. Is he here?'

'No, Inspector – can you get me out?' she begged.

'Stand back from the door.'

After trying to kick it open, he put his shoulder to the timber but it still would not budge. Colbeck looked around and saw a plank of wood nearby. Picking it up, he used it like a battering ram to pound away at the door. After resisting for a short while, the lock suddenly snapped and the door was flung back on its hinges.

Crouching in the corner by the mattress was the pathetic figure of Dorothea Jamieson. She looked up with a fear that was tempered with relief. Someone had rescued her at last. Bursting into tears, she got up and hurled herself into Colbeck's arms.

He caught the first available train to London even though it stopped at various stations on the way. Finding an empty carriage near the front, Captain Jamieson sat down and opened the newspaper he had just bought. It was not merely something to divert him on the journey. It would act as kindling when he burnt down Ezra Follis's house and destroyed the scene of his wife's betrayal. Once that was done, he could seal the clergyman's fate by hiring a more reliable killer. Only when his wife wept over the Follis's dead body would his vengeful feelings be appeased.

The signal was given, the locomotive started up and the train moved slowly along in a series of jangling harmonies. Jamieson was happy to be on his way to exact retribution. What he did not realise was that two men had just run along the platform beside the moving train and leapt into the last carriage.

'That was dangerous,' said Victor Leeming, breathlessly, as he sat down. 'If I'm forced to travel by train, I at least expect it to be standing still when I get on it.'

'We had to catch this one,' said Colbeck, 'whatever the risk.'

'How can you be sure that he's on it?'

'You heard what his wife told us. Captain Jamieson left only minutes before we arrived. He'd have got to the station not long ahead of us. Since I've been travelling up and down to Brighton so much, I learnt the timetable by heart. This was the first possible train he could have caught.'

'I bet he didn't wait until it was moving,' said Leeming.

The carriage was largely empty. Their only companion was an elderly man trying to read a book through his monocle. He ignored them studiously. Leeming leant in close to whisper to Colbeck.

'Why do you think he locked his wife up, sir?'

'I don't know, Victor,' replied the other, 'but I wouldn't advise you to do it to Estelle by way of a birthday present. It could never compete with a pretty new bonnet and shawl.'

The train chugged on until Hassocks Gate station came into

sight. It gradually slowed down and ran beside the platform until stopping with a jerk. Colbeck got out alone, leaving the sergeant at the rear of the train to cut off any escape attempt by their quarry. Walking along the platform, Colbeck glanced into each carriage, searching for the bearded man whose description he now had. Since additional passengers had just joined it, the train was half-full. There were lots of faces to check. Colbeck saw a couple of men with beards but they were the wrong age and the wrong shape to be Alexander Jamieson.

It was a long train at a short stop. Before the inspector had checked every carriage, it began to move again. He trotted alongside it, peering into the few remaining carriages. When he spotted the man with the black beard, he knew that he had found his suspect. Pulling open the door, Colbeck dived in and closed it behind him.

'Captain Jamieson?' he asked.

'Who the devil are you?' demanded the other.

'My name is Inspector Colbeck and I've come to arrest you.'

Jamieson's reaction was immediate. He threw a punch that caught Colbeck on the chin and dazed him for a moment. Trying to get away, Jamieson opened the door to jump down on to the line, only to find that another train was coming towards them. In desperation, he instead climbed upwards on to the roof of the carriage, hoping to work his way back along the train so that he could leap off at the next station while Colbeck was still in the carriage near the front.

Having spent most of his life at sea, Jamieson had a sailor's nimbleness and sense of balance. He felt secure on the roof of a moving train and safe from any pursuit. He had not taken

account of the detective's resolve and agility. Removing his
hat, Colbeck followed him through the door and got a firm
grip before pulling himself up on to the roof. Jamieson was
already two carriages away from him but his movement was
hampered by the luggage that had been stored on top of the
train. Colbeck, too, had to clamber over trunks, valises and
hatboxes while maintaining his balance on the swaying roof.
Jamieson was amazed to see that he was being followed.

'Give yourself up, Captain Jamieson,' advised Colbeck,
getting closer all the time. 'There's no escape. I have another
man on the train to help me. You can't elude the both of us.'

'We'll see about that,' snarled the other.

'We're trained detectives, sir, well used to arresting violent
suspects. We're not a defenceless woman like your wife whom
you can lock up in your outhouse.'

Jamieson was startled. 'How do you know about that?'

'We know everything about you. We know what you paid
Dick Chiffney to do and why you hate the Reverend Follis.
You can either surrender while it's safe to do so,' said
Colbeck, 'or risk being thrown off onto the rails. Which is it
to be?'

'Neither,' said Jamieson, walking towards him and
snatching up a leather trunk. 'Goodbye, Inspector.'

He hurled the trunk with all his strength. Had it struck him,
Colbeck would have been knocked off the train altogether. As
it was, he ducked beneath the missile and let it go past his
head. Before Jamieson could pick up another piece of luggage,
Colbeck leapt on to the next carriage and tackled him around
the legs. As he fell backwards, Jamieson's head struck the edge
of another trunk and he was momentarily stunned. Colbeck
seized his advantage, getting on top of him and pummelling

away with both fists. The black beard was soon stained with blood.

Jamieson fought back, writhing and bucking until he managed to dislodge Colbeck. The two of them were now perilously close to the edge of the roof, grappling wildly as they tried to get the upper hand. Jamieson was strong, doing all he could to force Colbeck off the train and send him to certain death. For his part, the detective wanted to capture his man alive. He had already lost Chiffney under the wheels of a locomotive. He was determined that a train would not rob him of another arrest.

As they wrestled among the items of luggage, some of them were knocked off the roof and bounced on the adjacent track. Colbeck did not wish to join them. Jamieson went for his neck, using both thumbs to press down hard in an effort to strangle him. Colbeck responded at once, getting a hand under the other man's chin and pushing it up with all his energy until Jamieson's head was forced so far back that he had to release his grip on Colbeck's neck.

Before he could get another hold on his adversary, Jamieson was thrown sideways by Colbeck then swiftly mounted. Though he punched him time and again in the face, Colbeck could not subdue him completely. He chose another way to bring the encounter to a decisive end. Rising to his feet, he grabbed a trunk and lifted it high with both hands. When Jamieson tried to get up, Colbeck brought the heavy object crashing down on his head. It knocked him senseless. Jamieson did not feel the handcuffs as they were put on his wrists.

The fight had taken place during the short journey to Burgess Hill station. When the train lurched to a halt,

Leeming got out and came running along the platform. He was astounded to see Colbeck standing on the roof of the train with Jamieson lying beside him.

'Ah, there you are, Victor,' said Colbeck, gratefully. 'I'm glad you came. I need a hand with this luggage.'

Captain Harvey Ridgeon accepted that he had made a serious error. As soon as he heard the news, he took a cab to Scotland Yard. Colbeck and Leeming were in the superintendent's office to hear the Inspector General of Railways offer a gracious apology. It was accepted by Tallis without even a tinge of bitterness.

'We have one consolation, Captain Ridgeon,' he said. 'The villain served in Her Majesty's navy – at least he was not an army man!'

'Soldiers can also make terrible mistakes,' admitted Ridgeon. 'I happen to be one of them. Unlike Captain Jamieson, however, I'm able to learn from it.' He turned to Colbeck. 'I think I can guarantee that I'll never again question the judgement of the Railway Detective.'

'Thank you, sir,' said Colbeck.

'I shall be writing to Mrs Pike to make it clear that her husband was in no way responsible for that crash.'

'I think she'll appreciate that, sir.'

'Yes,' said Tallis, 'but I doubt if she'll be pleased to learn that the real cause of that disaster lay in the sexual peccadilloes of the Rector of St Dunstan's. He seems to have led endless women astray.'

'Captain Jamieson's wife was one of them,' noted Colbeck. 'The lady spent the night with him in London then returned on the Brighton Express the following day. It's the reason why that particular train occupied Jamieson's mind. He knew that Mr Follis travelled on it every Friday, returning from his latest adventure in London. Since the express had come to symbolise his wife's infidelity, Jamieson wanted to destroy both the train and one of its passengers.'

'With no thought for all the others on that train,' said Leeming.

'Captain Jamieson will have an appointment with the hangman,' decreed Tallis. 'If it were left to me, a certain clergyman should dangle beside him. The rector should not go unpunished.'

'Oh,' said Colbeck, 'I think you'll find that he's been adequately punished, sir. His ministry is over and he'll leave Brighton with his reputation in tatters.'

'Don't forget that he was shot as well,' Leeming reminded them. 'His shoulder will never be the same again.'

'That's only a physical wound, Victor. The mental scars will never heal. Mr Follis was stricken with guilt when he realised the pain and misery his actions had indirectly caused. Imagine how he must feel about the way that Mrs Jamieson was treated by her husband,' Colbeck went on. 'That was Mr Follis's doing and he's accepted the full blame.' ,

'How ever did he attract so many women?' wondered Leeming.

'Let's have no crude speculation, Sergeant,' warned Tallis. 'This case is revolting enough without adding salacious details.' He sat back in his chair and eyed his cigar box 'Now that Captain Ridgeon has tendered his apology, I should like to talk to him alone. You and the inspector are free to go.'

Sensing that the two men were about to trade reminiscences

of army life, Colbeck opened the door and left the room. Leeming was on his heels. 'There's one good thing to come out of this,' he said, happily. 'Now that we've solved the case, I'll be able to spend Sunday at home, after all.'

'Not necessarily, Victor.'

'Surely you don't expect me to work on Estelle's birthday, sir?'

No,' said Colbeck, 'but I suggest that you might not wish to stay at home.' He took something from his pocket. 'The railway company was so delighted with our efforts that they gave me these – four first class return tickets for the Brighton Express on Sunday. Overcome your dislike of rail travel,' he urged, handing the tickets to Leeming. 'Give your dear wife an additional birthday present and take the whole family to the seaside for the day.'

Knowing that he would call that evening, Madeleine Andrews had taken the trouble to put on her best dress. There was no danger that her father would interrupt them. Now that the Railway Detective had been vindicated, Andrews could go for a drink after work and lord it over those who had dared to criticise his friend. He would not be back for hours. Madeleine listened for the sound of a cab but it never came. Instead, she heard, in due course, an authoritative knock on the front door. When she opened it, Colbeck was beaming at her.

'I thought you'd come by cab,' she said, ushering him in.

'I did,' he replied, taking her in his arms to kiss her. 'It dropped me off at the Round House. I wanted to take a look inside it before I came on here. I walked the rest of the way.'

'Then you've come from one Round House to another. I

finished my painting of it earlier today so you'll be able to compare it with the real one.'

Colbeck crossed to the easel. One arm around her waist, he gazed intently at her work, admiring its colour and its completeness. A locomotive was in the process of being turned in the way he had just seen happen in real life. Madeleine's painting had the accuracy of a photograph combined with an artistic vitality that was striking.

'It's remarkable,' he said, seriously, 'quite remarkable.'

'Do you really mean that?'

'You must have been inspired.'

'I was, Robert,' she replied. 'I drew inspiration from the fact that it's going to a very good home.'

'Why – have you sold it already?'

'It's a gift to one of my patrons. I hope you enjoy looking at it.'

Colbeck gaped. 'It's for *me*?' he said, laughing in delight. 'Thank you so much, Madeleine. I'll cherish the gift. It's a pity that I didn't have this turntable with me in Brighton. It might have prompted me to solve the case much sooner.'

'I don't see how.'

'There's no need why you should. All you need to know is that I'm thrilled with the painting. I've had so much pleasure looking at the picture of the *Lord of the Isles* you gave me. I see it every day.' He gestured at her latest work. 'This is another wonderful example of what you can do when you pick up a paint brush.'

'There is one condition, Robert,' she warned.

'What sort of condition?'

'You can have your turntable in the Round House if I can have an explanation of why you weren't surprised that the

Reverend Follis asked me to read a particular passage from the Bible.' She crossed to the bookshelf. 'Shall I find it for you?'

'There's no need Madeleine,' he said. 'Leave your Bible where it is. I know that chapter from Corinthians very well. *"And now abideth faith, hope, charity, these three; but the greatest of these is charity."* Did I get it right?'

'You quoted it word for word.'

'That depends on the translation you use because one of those words is the key to the entire chapter. The word is "charity". Change it to its true meaning of "love" and you'll perhaps understand why Mr Follis wanted it read to him by a beautiful young woman.'

Madeleine was uneasy. 'I'm not certain that I like that.'

'Don't worry,' he said, 'I'm sure that he had no impure thoughts inside his church. He reserved those for elsewhere. Instead of treating the word in its widest sense, embracing all forms of love, the rector saw only its more physical aspects. When I confronted him about his transgressions, he told me that they were crimes of passion.'

'I'm surprised that you left me alone with the man.'

'You were in no danger, Madeleine,' he said, 'especially when you were on consecrated ground. And at that point, of course, I was unaware of how unholy his private life actually was. I took you to Brighton to confirm my suspicion that Ezra Follis was far more interested in women than someone in his position ought to be.'

'I wish you'd told me that beforehand, Robert.'

'It was better if you had no preconceptions. That's why I was so interested to see what your reaction to him was.'

'Well,' she said, 'it's taught me one lesson. I'll be a lot more careful when somebody asks me to read from the Bible again.'

He smiled broadly. 'Does that include me?'

'You're the exception, Robert,' she said, kissing him softly. 'I'll read anything you ask me.'

'I was hoping you'd say that,' he told her, taking a gold-edged card from his inside pocket. 'I'd like you to read this.'

She was amazed. 'It's an invitation to the opening of an exhibition at the National Gallery,' she said, reading the card and gasping with joy. 'I'll be able to meet some famous artists.'

'I'll have the most accomplished one of all on my arm,' said Colbeck, proudly. He lifted the painting off the easel. 'How many of them could bring a steam locomotive to life like this? Precious few, I daresay.' He regarded the painting with a fond smile. 'Perhaps we should take it along with us to show them how it's done.'